TOMORROW
ALWAYS
LIES

Also by Doug Solter

Spies Like Me

Skid

Rivals

Legends

Champions

TOMORROW ALWAYS LIES

BOOK 2 OF THE GEMS SPY SERIES

Doug Solter

Tomorrow Always Lies. Copyright © 2018 Doug Solter.

First Trade Paperback Edition

ISBN-13: 978-0-9981466-2-1

Cover Art Design by Travis Miles

Website: www.probookcovers.com

To my dad, for his endless support.

TOMORROW ALWAYS LIES

CHAPTER 1

Across the frozen lake, an eight-dog sled team pushed ahead at a relentless pace, their soft fur wet from the blowing snow, which pricked Nadia's exposed skin and blinded her view ahead. Her hands tightened on the reins. The arm clinging around her torso also tightened, a reminder that she wasn't alone. Emma clung to her because it was ten degrees below zero and because her friend was scared, just like she was.

Nadia glanced over her shoulder. The icy wind had freed Emma's long hair from under the hood of her parka. It flew around like a giant blond flag.

Nadia craned her neck. The snowmobile was still chasing them. The driver revved his engine, desperate to overtake the sled. The second man behind the driver held something in his left hand. As he aimed it, the pistol gleamed in the Alaskan sunlight.

Nadia and Emma ducked as a bullet pinged against the side of the sled. She pulled the reins and made the dogs veer to the right. That way the left-handed shooter would have a more difficult time trying to aim while still behind his friend.

"How far out is Olivia?" Nadia asked.

Emma squeezed closer while taking a deep breath to calm herself. She took out the portable radio and squeezed the button.

"Hello? Olivia? This is Emma. Where are you? We need—"

Another gunshot bounced off the sled, causing both girls to jump.

"We need help! How far out are you?" Emma asked.

The radio crackled to life. "During a mission, we use our code names, you twit!" the girl's voice said in a sharp British accent. "Emerald is ten minutes inbound. What's your situation, Black Opal?"

"Our situation? Um—not good. Super-stressed right now. Being chased and shot at." Emma peeked over Nadia's shoulder. "And our poor dogs are getting tired."

"Roger. Any contact with Ruby? Over." Olivia asked.

"Nope. We haven't seen her for, like, an hour. I hope she's okay."

"Roger. Keep your heads down. I'm coming as soon as I can. Emerald out."

Emma touched Nadia's shoulder. "What do you think?"

"We can't keep up this pace for ten minutes," Nadia said.

Emma pointed at the dogs. "They look so tired. I wish we could stop and let them rest."

"I know. But if we stop, I'm afraid we'll die."

"Please don't say die."

"Do you have any cosmetics left?" Nadia had left her purse behind.

"Why, do you need some lip balm? My lips are cracking too."

Nadia forgot that Emma was still new to this. She waited for her friend to catch up.

"Oh. You mean *those* cosmetics. Yes, I have some *Red-hot* lipstick. *Raise the Roof* rouge. *Forest Fire* mascara."

"That's good. If they catch up, we might have to use them."

"What's that over there?" Emma pointed to where the frozen lake met the shore. Two big snow tractors plowed through the snow at full speed. Each tractor was filled with more men, who didn't look too friendly. The tractors drove onto the ice.

"Those snowmobile goons have friends," Emma said.

Nadia pulled at the reins and guided the tired dogs away from the tractors.

Now the snowmobile and the tractors were closing in.

Nadia whistled and snapped the reins to encourage the dogs to go faster.

"Don't push them so hard," Emma said.

"I'm sorry, but do we have a choice?"

The dogs ran hard, their tongues hanging out as they huffed and puffed. There wasn't much more they could do.

Until they came across a giant hole in the ice.

Nadia pulled back on the reins. "Whoa! Whoa!"

Luckily for Nadia, the dogs saw it first, kicking their legs as they tried to stop themselves on the ice. But the sled's momentum still pushed them all forward towards the giant hole.

Nadia grabbed the handle and pulled the sled's brakes, which dug into the ice. Metal scraped against ice, creating a spine-tingling squeal before the sled came to a stop.

"Great. What do we do now?" Emma asked.

The opening was at least one hundred meters across. Nadia reasoned that running around the edge of the hole would give the tractors enough time to catch them.

"Should we try to swim across?" Nadia asked.

"No way. We'd freeze to death."

Emma was right. There was no choice.

"Do we surrender?" Nadia asked.

Judging by her face, Emma didn't like that idea either.

The girls turned to watch the two tractors closing in on them. When they reached within forty meters of the girls, the tractors stopped, allowing four goons from each tractor to climb out. The hard-looking men smiled at each other with a strange, wicked glee. They knew they had these girls trapped. The two on the snowmobile also arrived on the scene.

All ten men closed on the two girls.

"I don't like this at all," Emma said. "Will they let us surrender?"

"Maybe we should hope they kill us," Nadia said.

Emma gave Nadia a haunted look, realizing her point. Ten grown men. Two young girls. A remote part of Alaska.

No one would hear them scream.

Nadia's thoughts were interrupted by a snowmobile revving its engine as it burst from the trees at full speed. A girl with long black hair was at the controls. She streaked across the ice and cut in front of the men. The girl dropped a small object on the ground.

As the snowmobile cleared the men, the object flashed and went off with a loud bang. The sound punched the ice, causing it to shatter under the men's feet, dropping them all into the icy water.

The snowmobile headed for the dogsled and slid to a stop.

"Who wants a ride?" the girl with long black hair asked. Her light skin with cool pink undertones appeared much paler thanks to the weather. But Miyuki's shiny personality still shone through.

"So happy to see you." Nadia hopped out of the sled and climbed on the back of the snowmobile.

But Emma didn't move. "We can't leave these dogs behind."

The tired animals waited for the girls to tell them what to do next.

"There's no room," Nadia said.

"We admire your compassion," Miyuki added. "But that may be difficult."

The men were dragging themselves out of the water. The shock of the cold still made their bodies sluggish. But they were recovering.

Emma didn't move.

"The dogs should be fine," Nadia said. "They're used to this type of weather."

"Time is short," Miyuki said. "We should get the hell out of Dodge City before those bad hombres come back."

Emma glanced at the men as they shook off the chill and attempted to stand back up. Then she looked at the dogs, who waited obediently for the girls. Eight clouds of breath coming from eight snouts. Emma lowered her head and pushed herself to the snowmobile. She sat behind Nadia and Miyuki.

The men were picking up their guns. Would they work after being underwater?

Miyuki didn't wait to find out. She pulled out another piece of "special" cosmetics, popped the bottle top, and tossed it to the side. The bottle hissed as thick smoke poured out. The wind carried the smoke across the frozen lake, obscuring the men's vision. Miyuki gunned the engine and raced the snowmobile around the edge of the one-hundred-meter hole.

Nadia looked over her shoulder as the smoke now surrounded the men, causing confusion as to where they could safely go without falling back into the lake. Miyuki kept the snowmobile at full throttle, allowing the three girls to leave the men far behind.

Soon a helicopter appeared overhead. Emma's radio came to life.

"Black Opal, this is Emerald. Is that Ruby driving the snowmobile? Over." the girl with the British accent asked.

"Yes," Emma replied. "She saved our bacon back there."

"Roger. Stand by. I'm coming into land."

The helicopter found a nice patch of flat snow and settled down. The girl at the controls had curly ribbons of golden-brown hair squashed by a radio headset. Her brown face was accented with bronze undertones.

The three girls abandoned their snowmobile and climbed aboard the aircraft. When everyone was safely inside, the girl pilot, Olivia, pushed the throttle up, and the helicopter rose from the ground as it once again became airborne.

Emma tried to say something, but the girls couldn't hear over the helicopter's engine noise. Olivia pointed at the headphones hanging near her seat. All three girls put on a pair.

"I'm so glad I found you," Olivia said over the headset.

"We're glad both of you found us," Nadia added.

"No problem. We buddies." Miyuki put her arms around Nadia and Emma.

But Emma didn't look happy. "We have to go back."

"Go back? Why?" Olivia asked.

"Those dogs. We can't leave them out there in the cold."

"I told you. They'll survive," Nadia said. "Those dogs are bred for the cold. Most likely they'll stick together and hunt to survive."

"They have a sled chained to them, remember? They'll die out there," Emma said. "We have an obligation to save them."

Nadia had forgotten about that. The dogs couldn't go anywhere. They were stuck. Perhaps those men who chased them would do the humane thing and shoot the poor animals rather than leave them out in the cold to die. Or maybe they would take the dogs with them. But those were evil men. Men who would leave poor animals outside to freeze to death.

"You two almost got shot back there," Olivia said as she pulled back on her stick, commanding the helicopter to clear the top of a ridge. "I'm not going back there to give those blokes another chance for target practice."

Emma was right and Nadia knew it. They were acting selfish.

Miyuki read the faces of her friends. She nodded. "Emma's right, we should go back."

"Those dogs did save our lives," Nadia added.

"You never leave a furry comrade behind," Emma said proudly.

Olivia peeked over her shoulder. All three girls now smiled at her. Olivia pressed her foot on the left rudder and brought the helicopter around to a new course. "Stupid flipping dogs."

It took the helicopter ten minutes to reach the frozen lake. As Olivia circled, Nadia could see the two big snow tractors still parked, and black trails of smoke escaped their exhausts. But she couldn't see any of the men.

"Where is everyone?" Miyuki asked.

"I think they're warming up inside the tractors," Nadia said.

"Not all of them," Olivia said. "Look, near the dogsled."

She was right. The two men from the snowmobile were looking through their stuff, hoping to find that missing thumb drive, the one now safely tucked away in Nadia's inside pocket.

"I'm calling this off," Olivia said. "It's too dangerous."

"It's three against two," Miyuki said. "We can take them down quick if we jump."

"Jump?" Emma asked. "From the helicopter?"

Nadia's stomach tightened. Like most of Miyuki's ideas, this was extremely reckless, but then Nadia thought of the dogs and how they could have been wounded or killed during their sled chase. They should at least try to save them.

"I'll go with you," Nadia said.

"How about you, Emma?" Miyuki asked.

"I can't…I just can't," Emma said.

Nadia couldn't blame her.

"But once we land, I'll grab the dogs and back you up if you need me," she said.

"The goons are exiting their tractors. We do it now or never." Olivia watched for a response.

Miyuki nodded to Nadia. She was ready.

"Hold on to your tights." Olivia dived the helicopter towards the ground.

The two men near the sled looked up in astonishment as Olivia brought the helicopter within meters of the ground before flaring the aircraft. The rotor blades created a blast of cold wind that made both men cover their faces and hold on to the sled for dear life. The poor dogs were getting a blast too.

Nadia swallowed as she popped open her door and leaped from the helicopter. Her boots slid on the ice, but she recovered enough to use her forward momentum to close in on the sled. Miyuki stormed in from the other side, attacking the smaller of the two goons with a kick to his stomach.

The larger goon saw Nadia coming. He blocked her kick and palm strike. The goon tried to punch her, but Nadia avoided it.

She tried another kick, but the man shifted and followed up with a punch that landed on Nadia's shoulder blade. The sharp pain made her yelp. Nadia doubted she could take this guy alone.

A boot hit the goon's cheek, throwing him off balance as he stumbled back. The boot belonged to Emma. She had skipped the dogs and came to back Nadia up. Emma got off another kick into the goon's midsection, causing him to collapse to his knees while holding his stomach. Nadia rushed up beside Emma and launched another kick to the man's face. This knocked him out cold, and he dropped a pistol, which skidded across the ice. Thank goodness they hadn't given him a chance to use it.

"Good job!" Miyuki yelled as she began to untie the dogs from her side of the sled.

Nadia and Emma did the same on their side. The dogs jumped and yelped with excitement.

A light flashed across the girls' faces. It was a spotlight from the waiting helicopter. Nadia wondered what Olivia was doing. She then understood when she saw one of the big tractors closing in on their position. The other tractor was still parked, but the men outside it were holding…

A bullet whistled past Nadia's ear.

Miyuki led her four dogs toward the helicopter and jumped up inside. The animals hesitated, but Miyuki's excessive encouragement persuaded them to jump up anyway as she stuffed them in the back.

Another bullet ricocheted off the ice.

Nadia pulled two dogs by their collars as Miyuki encouraged them to jump. The dogs already inside barked, almost as if telling their friends it was okay. Nadia's two dogs jumped and squeezed inside the helicopter. Miyuki shifted the dogs around to make as much room as possible.

Nadia lifted dog number seven up into the helicopter.

"Hurry up!" Olivia yelled from the pilot seat.

The moving tractor now slid to a stop, and four goons were jumping out.

Nadia searched for Emma and found her near the sled with the last dog. She ran over to them.

"We have to go."

"This one isn't too happy." Emma moved towards the husky and it growled.

"Then we must leave him."

"Do you have any dog treats?"

"Dog treats? We must go now, Emma."

"Stand in front of him."

"Emma, we don't have—"

"Do it."

Nadia didn't care for her tone, but she stood in front of the dog, which growled again.

As the dog focused on Nadia, Emma came around from behind and grabbed his collar. The dog shook and barked. He must have been scared to death, but Emma kept her cool as she hugged the dog and whispered in his ear. The dog sat down and relaxed. Emma kissed the dog's forehead and its tail wagged. Emma then jumped up. "C'mon, boy! Let's go!"

To Nadia's amazement, the mean dog was gone and replaced by a happy dog, which ran to the helicopter with Emma. Nadia chased after them and helped lift the last dog into the helicopter. Miyuki then helped both girls cram into the cabin as she slid the door closed. The helicopter was packed.

As Olivia lifted off, Nadia could hear her cursing. The helicopter was wobbling as Olivia fought with the controls.

Nadia closed her eyes and said a small prayer in Arabic.

The helicopter moved forward, hugging the ground as it went faster and faster.

Nadia put on one of the cabin headsets. "Is everything alright?"

Olivia's agitated voice came on. "We're overloaded. I can barely keep her in the air."

"Do we need to land?"

"She's heavy, but we'll make it, I think."

Nadia observed the cabin. Three girls and seven full-grown Siberian huskies made it a tight fit. The dogs didn't complain as they lay on top of each other and enjoyed the warm cabin. Dog number eight, the one Emma had helped, sat in the copilot seat next to Olivia. He sniffed at Olivia's curly golden-brown hair.

"Are these dogs vicious?" Olivia asked over the radio.

"That one's a sweetheart. Just rub under his mouth," Emma said over the headset.

Olivia hesitated, but she stroked under the dog's mouth. The Huskie showed its gratitude by licking Olivia's face all the way back to Fairbanks.

CHAPTER 2

Emma yawned as their crowded passenger jet taxied into the gate at San Francisco International. Since the Gems had flown coach this time, they had to wait for the passengers ahead of them to exit the plane before it was their turn to take out their carry-on luggage from the overhead bins. But soon they rolled their luggage down the air bridge and into the main terminal.

The new smells and sounds of the terminal were just enough to keep Emma awake. Once her head touched any soft pillow, that would be it. Emma would sleep for a few weeks at least. The other girls felt about the same. Even Miyuki, who always had the energy of a power station, didn't bother to hold her head up, causing her long black hair to droop towards the floor.

A bald man with a chest the size of a refrigerator greeted the girls with a warm and friendly smile in the arrivals area. His codename was Aardvark, and Emma was glad to see him.

Aardvark scooped up all four pieces of luggage and hauled them outside the terminal, where the morning sun brushed the clouds orange. The birds chirped as they jumped back and forth across the curved metal light posts in the parking lot. Aardvark opened the doors of a waiting black SUV. The girls climbed inside while the man loaded the luggage in back, then climbed behind the wheel.

As the man drove away from the terminal, Emma could already feel herself sinking into the soft leather seat of the SUV as sleep seduced her like a piece of rich chocolate cake. Emma turned on her side and allowed the comfy seat to hold her like a baby. Soon Emma drifted off to sleep as her mind dreamed of better times...

Like her dad laughing at something Emma had said.

Like the pride her dad showed when Emma was all dressed up

for the mayor's ball.

He felt so close now. So real.

Emma reached out to touch him. But her father only faded away like a figure of smoke.

"Why are we at school?" Miyuki asked.

The girl's voice pierced her dream and caused Emma to open her sleepy eyes.

"What's going on?" Emma looked out her window. Their high school's familiar chalky white building sat there like a concrete monument to monotony. Aardvark parked the SUV near the drop-off area and left the driver's seat. The man popped open the hatch of the vehicle and took out their school backpacks. This caused other students of West Berkeley High to stare and point at the large man that didn't belong on campus.

Aardvark held their four backpacks and waited with a polite smile.

"Looks like we're going to school," Miyuki said with sadness.

"We just finished a weekend mission," Emma said. "We get to call in sick on Monday."

"We didn't have any chance to sleep on the plane, love," Olivia said. "Not with that baby crying the entire flight."

"No chance at all," Miyuki added.

"Surely we're not well enough to attend school," Nadia said.

Aardvark frowned, his sympathetic eyes softened to their plight. But he shrugged and waited for them. These were the moments when Emma wished Aardvark could talk. But that deep scar running vertically down his throat was a dark reminder why the poor man couldn't. Besides, Aardvark would only tell them he was under orders.

Emma was going to fight this. "I'm calling my grandmother. This is stupid."

Olivia and Nadia glanced at each other. They got out of the car and surrendered by taking their backpacks from Aardvark.

"C'mon, girls. Let's get this day over with," Olivia said.

Miyuki frowned and checked with Aardvark one more time.

The large man shrugged again.

Miyuki took her backpack. "Emma?"

Emma slipped out of the car with her phone glued to her ear. Grandma's phone was ringing.

She answered.

"Hey, Grandma Laura is making us go to school this morning, can you believe that? Seriously, we just got off the plane. I mean, we haven't had any sleep. Can we call in sick today? I mean, sleep deprivation is a legitimate reason to be sick. So can you come pick us up?"

"You can't skip school, young one," Grandma said on the phone. "You'll have to tough it out."

"But, Grandma—"

"You're the one who wanted to be like your mom."

"I know I did, but just this once—"

"You must face the consequences of your decision. Good and bad."

"But—"

"I will not tolerate any more buts. Go to school."

"Then I do this under protest," Emma said.

"Protest noted, young one." Grandma then hung up.

Seriously? Emma threw her phone in her purse.

Miyuki offered Emma her backpack, which she jerked from her friend's grasp. The girls then began their walk to West Berkeley High's main entrance.

Emma's first hour classroom had big windows that faced the morning sun. That was why the edges of the drawn plastic blinds were always glowing. Before class started, Emma had refused to buy anything to help her stay awake, mostly out of protest instead of being practical. Now Emma regretted that decision as she drifted in and out of consciousness. Mr. Gatlin's stirring lecture about prohibition in 1920s Chicago wasn't helping either.

Emma placed her elbows on the desk and locked them as she cradled her chin under her hands. Emma hoped this would make it look like she was listening while she sneaked in a short nap. The words of history faded into the background as Emma drifted away.

How wonderful it felt.

How peaceful.

How perfect.

"Emma?"

A voice sneaked into her bliss. What did it want?

"Emma?"

It called out to her, wanting her.

Emma wasn't sure that she wanted it.

"Emma, are you with us, young lady?" the voice asked.

Emma wasn't sure where she was.

And that was okay.

A loud whistle snapped Emma straight in her seat. *What happened? What's going on? Where am I?* The questions blasted Emma's brain while she shook off her sleepiness. She then noted a string of gooey saliva running down from her lower lip to the top of her history book. She wiped it off.

Everyone in class began laughing.

Emma slipped her hand over her eyes and hoped that the world would just go away.

Mr. Gatlin moved over to the white dry-erase board. "Emma, can you tell me what a speakeasy is?"

Emma slapped her sleepy brain awake. "Um…was that gangster slang for being quiet?"

More kids chuckled and laughed.

Mr. Gatlin shook his head. "If you had been paying attention and not sleeping, you would have answered, 'a speakeasy was a secret establishment that served illegal liquor during the 1920s.'" He paused. "Come see me after class."

Thirty-five minutes later the classroom emptied as Emma pulled on her backpack and waited for Mr. Gatlin to finish speaking to another teacher. Mr. Gatlin then closed the door and sat behind his desk.

"Is everything alright at home?" he asked.

"Oh yes. Everything is great," Emma said.

"Are your parents divorced, or are they still together?"

Both questions pressed so hard against Emma's chest that she couldn't breathe. Emma wished that people would stop asking.

"My mother and father are dead."

"I'm sorry. Wow." Mr. Gatlin sat up in his chair, glanced down at his desk, and pretended to straighten something up. The man knew he'd hit a nerve. "Who do you live with now?"

"My grandmother."

"Do you get enough sleep at home?"

"Normally yeah, but last night—there were special circumstances. It won't happen again. I promise."

Mr. Gatlin crossed his arms. "This isn't the first time you've been tired on Mondays. I realize this is first hour, but everyone else in class seems ready for the week. What's going on during the weekends that's causing you to be so tired, Emma?"

Let's see. Flying off to other countries. Assuming fake identities. Running down stairs chasing bad people. Having bad people chasing her down stairs. Freezing on a dogsled while bad guys were shooting at her. For Emma, it had been a typical weekend.

"I promise to get more sleep and not be so out of it during class, Mr. Gatlin. Can I make it up to you somehow? Do extra credit or something like that?"

"Is home a safe place for you? Does your grandmother drink?"

"She has some wine once in a while."

"Does she have a drinking problem?"

"My grandmother? No way."

"Does she take drugs?" Mr. Gatlin asked.

"Take drugs? Nope."

Emma knew her grandmother did smoke some marijuana. But one didn't swallow that, so Emma knew she was still being honest.

Mr. Gatlin looked around his desk again, as if building up to his next question. Emma just wanted it to be over with soon.

"Are you taking any drugs?"

Emma stopped herself from rolling her eyes. Why were adults obsessed with this topic?

"Me? No way," she answered.

Mr. Gatlin leaned forward. "Emma, if you have a substance-abuse problem, there are ways the school can help before it gets you expelled or thrown in jail."

"No, sir. I'm fine. I get crazy with the caffeine sometimes, but I'm not, like, addicted to it."

Mr. Gatlin leaned back in his seat. "Now if you don't feel comfortable talking about it with me, you can always talk to Mrs. Bracket. She's here for you too."

Emma held her tongue. Mr. Gatlin had no clue she was already seeing Mrs. Bracket on a regular basis thanks to her father's death.

"That's good to know," Emma said. "Thanks, Mr. Gatlin."

"Are you sure you don't want to talk about it?"

Emma was tired of this. If she didn't give him something soon, he wouldn't let her leave.

CHAPTER 3

On Tuesday, Emma drove her Mercedes through the rolling green hills of Napa Valley. The late afternoon sun made the rows of tender grapes shine on the vines as the car passed vineyard after vineyard.

"And believe it or not, Mr. Gatlin asked me if I was doing drugs," Emma said.

Miyuki giggled and covered her mouth.

"Did he really?" Nadia asked.

"What did you tell him?" Olivia asked, her eyes now off her phone.

"I finally admitted that I had a school project that was due, and I was up late working on it," Emma said. "So I decided to borrow some of my grandmother's sleeping pills."

"Ah. Good ad-lib," Miyuki said.

Emma stopped at a light. "He got on me about stealing medication, so I promised not to do it again because it obviously knocked me out during class."

Miyuki thought of something and giggled again. "We should do an intervention and save Emma from her nasty drug habit."

Emma laughed. "I'm not giving up my coffee. You'd have to kill me first."

The light turned green, and Emma moved the car forward.

"No one would believe you were on drugs," Olivia said. "You're too perfect."

Emma glanced at the rearview mirror. "What do you mean by that?"

"Only kidding, love. Why don't *you* relax?" Olivia put down her phone. "I'm only saying you couldn't sell yourself as a meth head."

"You have all your teeth." Miyuki smiled to show hers.

"And you have great hair," Nadia added.

Emma's hand was already combing the soft blond strands. She did have great hair. "Really? Do you think so?"

"Oy, watch the road before you turn us all into red pancakes," Olivia shouted.

Emma put the Mercedes back on the right side of the road. She turned the lane-deviation system back on before turning into a quaint little parking lot. A large welcome sign announced *The Burlington Winery, one of the world's finest producers of Cabernet Sauvignon.* Emma drove past the public wine-tasting building and the parking lot that the tourists used. She parked the Mercedes in front of a gate entrance hidden away at a far end of the winery grounds.

A long-haired hippie with round glasses came up to her car. He wiped his grape-stained fingers on his canvas smock. Just below that smock was a gun. The hippie took his time scrutinizing the face of each girl in the car. "Hey, sisters. Great day to be alive. Please look at the birdie and say cheese."

A small digital camera lowered from its hiding place and hovered in front of the windshield. All four of the girls smiled and said cheese. The camera beeped as it took a picture. It then lifted back to its hiding place, and the gated entrance opened.

"Enjoy your day," the hippie said.

Emma maneuvered the Mercedes through the gate and into a small stand-alone garage. The garage door closed behind them, and the concrete floor descended underground, revealing the Mercedes was on a vehicle elevator. Once the elevator reached the bottom, it stopped. The gate in front of the car lowered, and Emma rolled her car down a circular ramp that descended an additional five hundred feet below ground until the Mercedes reached an underground parking lot. Emma found a spot for her car and parked.

The girls approached the main security desk. Two guards with full-body armor watched everything while pointing their assault rifles towards the ground. A regular security officer compared the girls to their picture taken above ground before handing the girls their credentials.

Next the girls waited to go through a full security search, including a full body and retinal scan.

"Can we use the wine barrel next time?" Miyuki asked.

"That entrance is only to be used for emergencies or unless approved by a supervisor," Nadia said, regurgitating Mrs. B's words exactly.

Emma thought Nadia would make a great cop.

Clear to leave security, the girls walked into the sprawling, open-office area with two levels. The top level had glass walls separating most of the offices and meeting rooms. It was bright, using yellow, white, and light brown as the main colors. The bottom level was designed like a small jungle with fake trees.

Olivia led the girls into the "jungle" and climbed inside one of the numerous green pods scattered throughout the fake jungle. Inside were comfy chairs that formed a semicircle. The girls all made themselves comfortable.

Soon an older woman entered the pod, favoring a cane by her side. Mrs. B wore modern slacks with a certain amount of flare.

"Good afternoon, Gems." Mrs. B sat down with confidence and grace. She crossed her legs at the ankles. "How was school today?"

"It's alright," Olivia answered.

"We enjoy it," Miyuki said.

Emma couldn't help herself. "I could have used more sleep yesterday."

The other Gems threw a look at Emma.

"School is important, Black Opal," Mrs. B said. "We can't begin the habit of skipping classes after every mission. It would draw too much attention from your school."

"What about falling asleep in class? Does that draw too much attention?"

"From what I heard, you handled it well. Keep it up."

Emma wondered how Mrs. B could have known about that. Then she saw Olivia's guilty face.

Why did she tell that to Mrs. B? Emma thought that was not cool.

"Let's get started on our mission debrief, shall we?" Mrs. B removed a tablet from the wall of the pod. She tapped on a few menus, and the door to the pod closed and a low hum took over as cone of silence mode was activated. Basically this prevented any type of electronic surveillance from penetrating inside the pod.

For the next half hour, the Gems and Mrs. B discussed every detail of the mission. How well their cover identities worked. How good was the intelligence leading up to their mission. What they learned about their targets and if there were any possible threats from them in the future.

Finally Mrs. B nodded her head with satisfaction. "It appears that Operation Snow Tiger was a complete success. Excellent work, ladies. Oh, I should also mention that the Fairbanks ASPCA promises to find homes for those sled dogs you rescued."

"Yeah! That's a win-win," Emma said.

"They were so cute," Miyuki said.

Mrs. B relaxed her posture. "How is everything? Are you girls settling in alright?"

"Yes, ma'am," Olivia said.

"I love our new home!" Miyuki said.

Nadia hesitated. "I find the American public school system quite interesting."

"How so?" Mrs. B asked.

Olivia smiled at Nadia. "It's quite different from the Queen's Academy school in London. Isn't it, love?"

Nadia smiled. "Yes. Quite different."

"This is a good experience for the three of you. I'm quite certain you'll rise above the occasion," Mrs. B said. "How about Black Opal's grandmother? Is she treating you all well? Have you detected any...hostility from her at all?"

"What do you mean by hostility? My grandmother would never —"

"Black Opal, first off, my question was not directed at you. Second, I understand your grandmother's views about our organization, and I will respect them. But I only wish to know if she's been respecting mine."

"No hostility, ma'am. Actually she's been quite supportive of us," Olivia said.

"See?" Emma asked with a little attitude. "No problems."

Mrs. B ignored Emma and touched the pad. The hum disappeared and the door to the pod opened. Mrs. B took her cane and used it to stand. "That's all for today."

Standing outside the pod was a large Russian woman with blond hair, whom Emma recognized immediately. She was code-named Lioness. The woman bowed her head to Mrs. B.

"Black Opal is yours now," Mrs. B said.

"Hey, I'm still recovering from Operation Snow Tiger," Emma said. "Can we start back up tomorrow?"

"You're still too far behind in your training. We need to catch you up with the other girls," Mrs. B said.

"So that would be a no?"

Lioness stepped forward with confidence. "Come, Black Opal. Let's see what kind of mischief we can get you in today."

CHAPTER 4

Emma followed Lioness through the jungle and into the Labyrinth, a maze of dark blue walls, floors, and ceilings, where the Authority's deepest secrets lived underground. The only light source was a series of white strips running along the top and bottom of each wall. Lioness took Emma to the TR division, a massive area carved out like a giant cave. The full gym, indoor gun range, and the hand-to-hand combat area were all there, where Emma had started her training. Emma ducked into the women's locker area and changed into her training sweatpants, T-shirt, and running shoes, before she returned to face Lioness.

The large woman checked her tablet. "We'll continue working on your trade crafts. Let's see…your deception skills are at level four. Role-playing skills are at level five. Disguises are at level three." Lioness glanced up from her tablet. "Excellent marks at this stage of your training."

Emma felt proud. Lioness was not an easy lady to impress.

The woman returned her attention to the tablet. "However, your high-speed evasive driving is abysmal. We'll work on that. You're not ready for wet and dry demolitions yet. You still need personal firearms level one and—" Lioness stopped and her face lit up like the sun.

Emma knew that look. Whatever it was, it was never good.

"We haven't done skydiving level one yet, have we?" Lioness asked.

Emma wanted to run, but she was the lab rat in the middle of a real maze.

"Do we need to?"

Lioness laughed at Emma's silly question.

Emma's heart jumped every time the large cargo plane dropped a few hundred feet in altitude, like the aircraft was struggling to stay in the sky. The dim lights inside the fuselage showed an empty cargo area. The plane's thirty-year-old aluminum frame creaked and moaned. Emma shut her eyes and tried not to think of her father plunging to his death inside his private jet.

Her trainer's Russian accent cut through the mind-numbing noise of the propellers…

"First thing out of the aircraft. What do you do?" Lioness asked.

Emma opened her eyes. Lioness wore a chute pack and a helmet with a visor, the same thing Emma had on. Lioness looked stoked and ready to go.

"After you jump from the aircraft, what do you do?" Lioness repeated. This time using her radio which blared into Emma's earpiece.

"Die?" Emma replied.

The aircraft dropped like it fell into a hole, but then climbed out of it.

Lioness waited. She obviously hadn't heard Emma over the engines. Maybe that was a good thing.

The girl keyed her microphone. "I get into the arch position."

"Which is?"

"My head back. My hips forward. My knees at about shoulder width and slightly bent."

Lioness flipped a switch, and a light illuminated her face. "What should you be aware of?"

"My height awareness?" Emma asked.

"Correct," Lioness said. "You should practice general awareness. However, height awareness is critical and supersedes all other concerns besides pulling the chute." She pressed a button, and the rear floor of the aircraft lowered, creating a ramp. The air hissed around them as the rear of the aircraft became exposed to the night air.

Emma could see the lights of San Francisco in the distance. The sudden reality of what she was about to do slapped her across the face. Her stomach burned. Her legs quivered. She felt light-headed.

"Um, why can't we do this jump in the daytime?" Emma asked. "Wouldn't it be easier?" Her words came out shaky and hurried.

"Yes, but it wouldn't be as much fun," Lioness said.

The red light above them turned green. The signal to jump.

Lioness stepped towards the ramp.

Emma backed away.

"Come back here," Lioness said over the radio.

Emma clung to the door that led to the cockpit. It was locked, but she still clung to it as panic burned through her body. She activated her radio. "I'll do this in the daytime, okay? I promise. But I don't like this night-jump stuff."

"On a mission, Black Opal, you might not have that choice."

"Yeah, but this is training. Can't we wait?"

Lioness backed away from the ramp. "Of course we can wait."

Emma let go of the locked door. Her stomach settled down. A wash of relief coated her body. "Thank you. I'm serious. I'll so make this up to you. I promise. Hey, we should go shopping sometime. That'd be fun, right? I'll even buy us—"

In one quick motion, Lioness shoved Emma down the ramp and out of the aircraft. Emma found herself flailing in the air with nothing to hold on to as gravity pulled her into the darkness. She swallowed hard and tried to remember her ground training. Emma pulled her head back and pushed her hips out, forming the classic arch position.

A dark figure with a lit faceplate came into view as Lioness talked into Emma's earpiece.

"Good. Bend your knees a bit. Good. Keep your arms out. Good."

Emma checked her altitude on a watch that Lioness had made her wear. She was about 9,500 feet and descending. The city lights around San Francisco Bay now shimmered under her. They did look beautiful from way up here.

"When we deploy our chutes, we'll try a precision landing," Lioness said over the radio.

The two women sailed through the air for the next couple of minutes.

Emma's heart slowed. Her body relaxed. A feeling of peace swept over her as Emma realized something. She was falling out of the sky, literally plunging towards the ground and certain death. But she felt great, like a bird sailing through the sky.

Emma stopped questioning everything and just let gravity take full control of her body.

Time went by so fast. It didn't take long before she was at one thousand feet.

"Pull your chute," Lioness commanded over the radio.

Emma reached down and pulled the cord. She felt a quick jerk upward on her body as the parachute unfurled above. The chute held her firmly in its grasp, slowing Emma way down.

Lioness had pulled her chute and was now maneuvering herself behind Emma with precision.

"Activate your HUD display," Lioness said.

Emma turned on her microphone. "My what display?"

"It's on your sports watch menu. Select HUD."

Emma touched the digital watch, and sure enough, there was such a selection. So that was why Lioness had insisted on her wearing the watch. Emma touched HUD on the menu and her visor filled up with a crosshair and digital information.

"Oh, I have it now."

"Good. You should be seeing a blue dot—that will be the signal from our drop zone. It should be a private beach by the ocean," Lioness said over the radio. "Guide us in, Black Opal. Be as accurate as you can. If we miss the beach by a few meters, we'll land in the ocean and drown."

Great. No pressure there, thought Emma.

At first Emma was worried that she wasn't seeing the blue dot, but then it appeared on her visor. However, it was way off to the right.

"How do I make the chute go towards the target?" Emma asked.

"Use the handles above you. Pull on them to maneuver your chute. You might have to circle the target and bleed off altitude so we don't miss our drop zone," Lioness said. "You're doing fine so far."

Emma found the handles on the two straps that formed the parachute and put her fingers through them. She tried pulling the right handle, and the chute pulled right, swinging the blue dot closer to center than far left. Emma used the left handle to make a correction and got the blue dot to stay decently close to the crosshairs. Emma could barely make out the beach on her left. It helped that she was close enough to hear the ocean waves crashing against the beach. But she couldn't make out what was on the right side of the beach. Was it a fence?

No, they were trees.

Lioness came on the radio. "Keep us away from the trees. Landing in them is a good way to break one's leg."

Emma focused. She used the blue dot as a reference point as she started to circle around it to bleed off her altitude. Emma could now make out the beach as it touched the ocean. She then spotted a nice section of beach to land on. Emma pulled the right handle and came out of her spiral. The sand of the beach now raced up to meet her.

Emma pulled her head back just as she hit the sand and rolled her body into the fall as the momentum carried her a few feet along the beach before she came to a stop. Emma stood up and watched Lioness land on a tiny strip of more solid ground. The athletic woman landed at a run, which helped bleed off her momentum and made her look like a professional, unlike Emma who had just done a barrel roll like a kid.

Still, at least she didn't die.

Behind her, Emma noticed a man with a familiar face gathering up her parachute. Aardvark also helped Emma take off her equipment.

Lioness took off her helmet as she approached them. "Excellent jump. Did you enjoy it?"

Emma gave Aardvark her last piece of equipment "I have to admit that…yeah, that was kinda awesome."

"Good. Next time I won't have to push you out of the plane."

Emma combed back her long sweaty hair. She needed a shower. "Was that really level one? Because I've seen videos of new students actually strapped to their instructors when they jump for the first time. But you didn't do that with me."

"We needed to accelerate your training, so I decided to kill two birds with one stone. And you did it. Now you've officially passed level two skydiving. Well done."

Emma smiled to herself. Maybe she could be an awesome spy after all.

Aardvark finished packing up all the skydiving equipment inside the black SUV. He offered Emma a backpack, which she opened and found a set of clothes from home. Aardvark gestured towards the backseat, indicating she could change out of her smelly jumpsuit in the car before they left. The Authority thought of everything.

Lioness began to walk up the beach.

"Aren't you coming back with us?" Emma asked.

Lioness stopped. "Why would I do that?" She looked across the sand. "This is my private beach. I have a house just beyond the trees. Good night, Black Opal." The woman walked down the beach, then took a dirt path that disappeared into the trees.

A half hour later, Emma slipped into Grandma's house quietly, not wanting to wake anyone up. One of the lamps in the living room was on, casting a shadow on the polished wood floors. It wasn't until Emma crossed over the large Persian rug that she noticed her grandma reading on the couch. She wore an old '70s Fleetwood Mac concert T-shirt, but this time her white hair was plaited into one braid instead of two. Grandma closed the book she was reading.

"Were you waiting up for me?" Emma asked.

"It's late, young one," Grandma said.

"I know. Sorry, it's all that training that Mrs. B—I mean Grandma Laura is having me do."

Grandma folded her arms in her lap. "You look absolutely exhausted."

Emma let her backpack drop off her shoulder and fall to the ground. She sat next to Grandma on the couch and laid her head on the older woman's warm shoulder. "I didn't know there was this much training. With school during the day and the training at night…it's wearing me out."

"May I remind you that you chose to do this. I tried talking you out of it and I lost that argument, remember?"

"I know."

"Your father didn't want you to get involved with the Authority."

Emma closed her eyes. "Please, not now. It's late." She opened her eyes and kissed Grandma on the cheek. "Good night."

She went upstairs and passed by the other bedrooms. Miyuki's name was on the first door covered with bright flowers and a few slogans in Japanese. The next door had a small businesslike sign that read *Please knock first, thank you.* Emma peeked under the door, and there was no light on. Olivia and Nadia must be asleep too.

Emma went inside the last bedroom. Snoopy was on her bed. His head lifted and his tail wagged a million times. The Jack-Russell-terrier barked. She rushed over and gave the dog a shush while she petted him. "I know. I know. I love you too."

This made the little dog try hard to stand up, his weak back still supported by a brace from when Emma had accidentally hit him with her car.

Emma changed her clothes and slipped into bed, switching off her light. Snoopy waddled up right beside her and plopped himself down on the bed. The dog closed his eyes and, for the first time tonight, felt complete.

CHAPTER 5

Stirring her from sleep, Nadia's phone vibrated on the wooden nightstand. The bedroom was dark as Nadia picked up her phone and tried to focus on the lit screen. It was five-thirty in the morning.

Nadia slipped out of bed with care, making sure that Olivia was still asleep in the next bed over before she opened her drawer and took out her prayer mat. She unrolled it and placed it on the floor. Nadia knelt forward on it and bowed her head to the mat as she recited her daily prayers in whispers. She knew Allah would still listen. He had always listened to her before. After prayers, she rolled the mat carefully and placed it back into the drawer before going to the bathroom to prepare for the new day. Nadia was always the first girl awake, but she didn't mind.

After her shower, Nadia came back to the room to find Olivia up. Her large curly hair went in all directions, like the girl slept with her finger in an electric socket. However, Nadia observed that Olivia's hair was thick and gorgeous, while hers was long and lifeless.

Olivia gave Nadia a slight wave as she left the bedroom for her turn in the restroom. Olivia's mouth wouldn't start working for at least another half hour.

By the time Nadia and Olivia had dressed, Miyuki was out of her bedroom and wandered down the upstairs hallway like a zombie towards the bathroom. When Miyuki was done, that was when Emma usually showed her face.

But this morning she didn't.

Olivia sighed. "Guess we should wake her."

Nadia followed Olivia to Emma's bedroom door.

Olivia knocked hard. "Oy! Time to get up sunshine. Your

education is waiting."

Snoopy barked inside the room as the girl whined through the door…

"Go away," Emma said.

Miyuki rubbed her wet hair with a towel as she joined the wake-up party. Olivia tried the doorknob and it opened, so they stepped inside. Emma was still in bed, her eyes glued shut while her mouth moved. Nadia couldn't understand what the girl was mumbling about.

"Puppy!" Miyuki offered Snoopy a hug. The excited dog barked and scrambled to his feet as he crawled over the top of Emma to get to Miyuki. This caused Emma to roll over and moan. Miyuki cuddled the dog in her arms while Snoopy rewarded her with licks and kisses.

"Who's in my freaking bedroom?" Emma asked with a mumble.

"It's time to get up," Olivia said. "We're going down for breakfast if you'd care to join us."

Emma moved again, then craned her head forward to peek at the digital clock. "Oh God."

"We hope to see you in a few minutes," Miyuki said, carrying Snoopy out of the room.

Olivia followed, but Nadia hesitated at the door.

Emma propped herself up in bed and tilted her neck from side-to-side as it cracked. Her eyes then found Nadia.

"I'm up. I'm up," the girl almost screamed.

Nadia flashed a polite smile before closing the door behind her.

After breakfast with Emma's grandmother, the girls piled into Emma's Mercedes Coupe and put on their seat belts. Nadia found herself riding up front today. Behind the wheel, Emma shook her head and yawned before pushing the ignition button. The engine purred as Emma combed her long hair back and checked her tired eyes in the rearview mirror.

"Do you feel alright?" Nadia asked.

"What time did you come home last night?" Miyuki asked.

Emma sighed. "I don't remember. It was late." She put the car in drive, which would cause the Mercedes to take out part of the house.

Nadia tapped her finger on the gear lever as a friendly reminder.

Emma looked down and moved the lever to reverse instead. Emma gave Nadia a wink to indicate she was still fine.

Nadia wasn't so sure.

As they drove to school, Nadia noted Emma's eyes drooping as her face fought to stay awake. The girl yawned again as the Mercedes cruised towards a green light. It turned yellow. Emma didn't slow down. She wasn't reacting at all.

Nadia didn't want to embarrass her, but…

"Emma?" she asked.

The light turned red.

"Emma!" Nadia shouted.

Finally she hit the brakes, throwing the Gems against their seat belts as the car shuddered to a stop.

"Sorry about that," Emma said.

Nadia touched her arm. "Would you like me to drive?"

"Yes, let her drive," Olivia said from the back.

"No, I'll be fine," Emma said. "I just need to stop for coffee."

It took Emma twenty minutes to go through the Kaffee Cadre drive-thru, but she finally got her much-needed morning beverage, a jumbo iced coffee with chocolate and caramel drizzle on top of a white cone of whipped cream. At least Miyuki and Olivia each ordered sensible-sized lattes. Nadia didn't order anything. She enjoyed tea more than coffee and only preferred that in the afternoon.

Once Emma started drinking her iced beverage, Nadia could tell the sugar and the extra shots of espresso were having the desired effect.

"Oh my God," Emma said. "Jumping out of a plane was so terrifying at first. I was freaking out and I told Lioness that I didn't want to go but then she pushed me out of the plane and I was, like, holy crap she pushed me out of a plane! Then I was falling to the ground." Emma fired out the words like a machine gun. She had to pause in order to draw a breath and bite on to her straw to suck up more double-shot coffee into her bloodstream.

She continued. "But it was so cool because I was soaring through the air and I felt so free and I was, like, thinking to myself this isn't so bad. It's kind of fun."

"You feel like bird sailing across the sky," Miyuki said from the backseat.

"Yes!" Emma yelled. "It was exactly that. I loved it."

Another slurp of coffee and Emma was off again. "And then I deployed my chute and Lioness had me use the HUD thingy to guide us into a landing area on a beach and I did it and it was amazing because I've never done anything like that before and I was so stoked."

Emma sucked the straw so hard that her cheeks flexed inward. It reminded Nadia of the opium addicts she would see lurking in the dark alleys of Riyadh.

"How many shots of espresso are in that, love?" Olivia asked.

Emma whipped her head around. "Oh this?" She held up her precious drink. "Four. Five. I just showed him all my fingers on one hand, so that's five at least. I don't mind." Emma threw her eyes forward to the road. "I feel freaking great right now. I want to go skydiving again."

"Rock on. Me too," Miyuki said.

"I know, right? We'll have to do it together next time, or maybe Lioness will let you join me on my next—"

Emma's foot hit the brake pedal hard. Nadia braced once again as her seat belt tightened across her chest. The Mercedes quivered as it handled another panic stop quite well. The reason for the stop gazed through the windshield in surprise.

It was a boy about their age. He stood inches away from the Mercedes's front bumper.

Emma put down her window and stuck her head out. "What's the matter with you? Does this look like a crosswalk? There's a perfectly good intersection over there. Why don't you use it?"

The shocked boy in front of the car had a clean-cut way about him. He had an average build and an average face. However, his striking emerald-green eyes made up for all the rest.

"I'm very sorry," the boy said. He seemed sincere.

"Dude, you can't just walk across a busy street whenever you want. I could have killed you. I almost killed you. If I wasn't drinking this fantastic iced coffee beverage, I would have flattened you like a piece of bread. I once hit a poor dog with this car, but he was an innocent creature. You, on the other hand, should know better than to just walk across the street without looking."

The boy who had almost been hit by the car lowered his chin. His face was so sad. As if he were taking Emma's lecture seriously, like the girl were his mom. It was strange. The boy retreated to the sidewalk and continued on his way.

Emma stuck her head back inside. "Some people think they own the road. He's lucky he's not in Manhattan because one of those taxis would've creamed him and kept right on going like nothing happened."

Someone honked their horn behind Emma, so she poked her head out again. "Oh yeah? Well blow it out your piehole, dude."

"Just keep that up," Olivia said. "Some redneck bloke with a shotgun will go all road rage on us."

Emma ducked back into the car and drove forward. She sucked on her coffee until they reached school.

The West Berkeley High School choir room featured a tall ceiling with two small skylights, plus sound-absorbing rectangles, which hung on the walls. The choir itself stood on long and flat metal risers with blue and black rubber padding on top that formed an arc in front of a black concert piano. Nadia had found a seat in back, opposite the choir and the piano, as she watched Emma and the choir practice a peppy version of U2's "Beautiful Day." Nadia was amazed at how cheerful and expressive Emma's face was when she sang. She acted so excited and happy to be up there.

Lewis was the only other student at school Nadia kind of knew, and that was through Emma. He was standing with the tenors and his voice was also strong and powerful. Nadia liked how the skylight's rays brought out his rich brown skin and short dark hair. Nadia also admired the boy's athletic shape. When Lewis caught her doing this, Nadia focused on the teacher playing the piano.

Mrs. Lynn conducted the choir through the song, making large gestures with her face and mouth, trying to get her students to mimic her. Nadia was impressed by how hard musicians studied their craft.

After the choir finished their fifth performance of the song, Mrs. Lynn had them sit down. "Not bad. Not bad. Altos, you were a little flat in the first chorus, but overall you nailed the rest," she said. "That's all for today."

The kids gathered their belongings.

"Remember that the concert is next Saturday. Not this Saturday. Remember, next Saturday," the teacher said over the noise.

Emma picked up her backpack and moved over to Nadia. "What did you think?"

"You all sound so beautiful," Nadia said. "Was that a traditional American song?"

"Ha, no. I think U2 is either an English or an Irish group. One of those two." Emma drank some water. "Mrs. Lynn still pretends she's in high school because all we sing are eighties songs. I'd love to sing, like, a Tegan and Sara song or Lady Gaga. Any song from this century."

"Yeah, the music is crap," Lewis said, joining the conversation. "But I vote for Nine Inch Nails or Jay-Z. Please no Tegan and Sara."

"Why not?" Emma grinned. "You need to embrace your feminine side, Lewis."

Lewis blew Emma off and concentrated on Nadia instead.

She admired the soundproofing on the walls.

"What music do you like?" he asked.

At first, Nadia wasn't sure if he was asking her. But his playful glance confirmed it.

Nadia would have answered Tegan and Sara because in England she'd heard their music and loved it. However, Lewis didn't sound like a fan.

"I—I don't know." Nadia could feel herself wanting to stammer.

"You don't know what music is or—?" Lewis slipped in a coy smile.

"I don't know a lot of Western music."

The choir teacher Mrs. Lynn came up to them. "Emma, can I speak with you in my office?"

Emma nodded and left with her teacher. They entered a small office and closed the door behind them.

"She's in trouble," Lewis said.

"Why is she in trouble?" Nadia asked.

"Emma's been missing lots of practices lately, and Mrs. Lynn doesn't like it," he said. "Do you know why?"

Because being a teen spy took a lot of time and energy. Emma had it the worst because she was doing her spy training in between missions with the Gems. Add school to the mix and Emma would be forced to make some hard choices.

"No, I don't know why," Nadia said.

"You live with her, right? Is that how student exchanges go? Emma was trying to explain it to me."

"Yes. Emma and her family are hosts to Olivia, Miyuki, and me as we study here in America."

Lewis leaned against the wall, acting totally cool. "How long you here for?"

"A while." Nadia peeked over, and the boy held her gaze for a few moments.

Nadia smiled politely.

Lewis nodded, as if he'd made a mental decision.

Nadia then saw Emma standing a few meters away, observing them for a moment before approaching.

"Sorry about the delay," she said.

"You can't keep skipping practice, Emma," Lewis said.

"Thanks for the advice. I got it." Emma turned to Nadia. "Let's go before someone else wants to grill me on my after-school activities."

"Speaking of," Lewis said. "What are you two doing now?"

"It's study time," Emma said. "Nadia is helping me with geometry."

"Oh, I see. No problem." Lewis stood up from the wall he was leaning on. "See you around, then." His eyes pointed at Nadia, as if the comment was meant for her, before aiming himself towards the door.

Emma flashed a devious smile before swinging around. "Hey, Lewis, we're studying at the Cadre. Wanna come with?"

What was Emma doing? The girl needed to concentrate on her geometry because Emma was horrible at math and needed all the help Nadia could give her. Lewis would only be an unwanted distraction.

Lewis circled back around to face the girls. "I could clear my social calendar. But could I bum a ride? My chauffeur has malaria."

"That's awful," Nadia said. "Will he die?"

Emma held back her laugh with a smile; that was when Nadia realized Lewis was joking.

"Sure, you can bum a ride," Emma said. "Meet us in the parking lot ASAP."

"I'm all in." Lewis winked at them and jogged off to his locker.

Nadia touched Emma's arm and guided her over to a corner of the room. "What are you doing? I thought you wanted help in geometry."

"Lewis is really into you," Emma said.

Nadia hesitated. Into her? As in—that was ridiculous. She'd just insulted him by not getting his joke.

"No he's not."

Emma cocked her head to the side and squinted. "Please. I'm a professional actress. I'm trained to read faces and body language. Plus, I know Lewis pretty well. Believe me when I say he's into you."

"But I must study today," Nadia said. "Besides tutoring you, I have assignments due in class tomorrow."

Emma rested both hands on Nadia's shoulders and gave them a gentle squeeze. "To be successful in high school, a girl needs to learn how to prioritize her afternoons effectively."

Nadia followed Emma outside into the bright afternoon sunshine. Freshmen waited around the school's front entrance for their parents to pick them up from after-school activities since the busses were long gone. Nadia could see Lewis already standing in the student parking lot.

Nadia felt a tug and her headscarf was off. Emma had it in her hand.

"Why did you do that?" Nadia asked.

"You don't need this. You're in California not Saudi Arabia." Emma folded up Nadia's scarf and slipped it in her purse. She fixed Nadia's hair, pulling it this way and that while combing it back with her fingers. Nadia didn't stop her.

"Okay, there we go. See, you have such gorgeous black hair. It's a shame you don't show it off more."

"I'm not on a date with this boy."

"I know. We're just chilling and having some coffee."

"Why are you assuming that I'm interested in Lewis?"

"Because you blushed when I asked him to join us," Emma said.

"I did no such thing."

Emma smiled.

Nadia's embarrassment bubbled up inside. She didn't like it when people forced her to reveal personal feelings; plus she didn't appreciate her body giving Emma clues.

"You know what? You don't have to do this," Emma said. "I can fake a headache and call the whole thing off if you feel uncomfortable."

Nadia sighed. It was too late. Emma had already put things in motion.

CHAPTER 6

Emma drove the Mercedes off campus with Lewis in the backseat and Nadia in front. Emma hinted that her friend should keep Lewis company in back, but apparently the girl didn't get that hint strongly enough. Emma also had to keep talking to Lewis so he didn't feel neglected since Nadia's mouth must have been wired shut because the girl wasn't using it at all. It was a disaster because this was a perfect chance for Nadia to break the ice with Lewis, and she was blowing it big time.

When they arrived at the Kaffee Cadre, the coffee place was busy. The spotlights, which hung from the ceiling, revealed a bunch of kids from their school had taken over the wood tables along the far wall, while the adults took control of the central tables with their laptops. The baristas were calling out names and steaming a lot of milk.

The three of them gave their drink orders and waited.

Emma bit her lip. She didn't want to dominate the conversation, so she waited for Nadia to start talking.

She didn't. So Lewis began talking to Emma about choir.

"Let's grab a table while we're waiting," Emma said, trying to change the situation a little.

They found an open table near the adults and broke out their school books while Lewis talked about surfing.

Nadia opened one of her school books and started reading.

Emma restrained herself from shaking her friend and yelling into her face to wake up.

"I'm clueless about surfing," Emma said, trying to keep the momentum going. "Isn't it too cold to surf in the bay?"

"You don't surf in the bay," Lewis said. "You go down to Monterey or hit the other beaches down south." He sat back, still playing Mr. Cool. "Do they surf in Saudi Arabia?"

Emma was happy. Lewis was trying to open the door. All Nadia had to do was walk right through it.

Nadia lifted her eyes and smiled. "Yes, they do."

And…that was it.

Lewis nodded. "Cool."

Emma was too far from Nadia to kick her under the table.

"I have a large mocha blitz with extra chocolate chips for Lewis," the barista announced.

Lewis tapped his fingers on the table before leaving the two girls alone.

"Was that your idea of flirting?" Emma asked.

Nadia blinked for a moment. "He asked me a question, and I answered."

"You never just say yes. Elaborate. Use the question to talk about…I don't know…Saudi Arabian beaches, or ask him about surfing. You have to keep boys talking or they'll shut up and leave you staring at the floor all day. Keep him talking."

Lewis came back to the table with his drink.

Nadia threw on a smile.

Emma nodded her approval. Now if she would only talk.

"Emma, I have your cinnamon caramel hazelnut iced coffee with extra shots."

Perfect timing. Maybe if Emma left them alone, Nadia would feel comfortable and open her mouth.

Emma headed to the pickup counter. As she scooped up her drink, Emma noticed Nadia's tea was about ready, so she stayed and grabbed that too. But before walking back, Emma searched for an out-of-the-way table that was close enough to eavesdrop. Once there, she listened.

Their table sounded quiet. Great, Nadia was probably reading her book again.

"We have beautiful beaches in Saudi Arabia," Nadia said. "Plenty of good sand. And the boys do a lot of surfing."

Emma jumped in her chair. Oh, thank God, the girl was talking!

"Only the guys surf?" Lewis asked.

"The boys need the girls to watch them from the beach so they can show off and feel good about themselves."

Lewis nodded. "That's true on every beach."

An idea hit Emma and she circled back to the table. "They had your tea ready so I grabbed it." Emma set the cup down, and Nadia thanked her for doing that. Emma snatched her backpack. "You know what? I have to go practice my French pronunciation out loud, so I'll just go to another table so I won't disturb you two, okay?"

"No problem," Lewis said.

Nadia's eyes formed desperate egg shapes.

Emma hurried away, but sat at her out-of-the-way table again to spy. She broke open her French book and pretended to study.

They were talking about music right now. Score. Emma smiled to herself.

Fifteen minutes passed, and they were still talking. Their body language was more relaxed. Nadia began using her hands while she spoke. This was a good sign because Emma could tell she was loosening up. Emma was so excited for Nadia. She couldn't help herself. This moment should be preserved for the sake of history.

Emma took out her phone and crept around the corner. She zoomed the camera all the way in to their table and snapped some pics. But she couldn't stop there. Emma used one of the pictures and added the words—

Look who's on a date. XOXOXO

Emma sent it to the rest of the Gems.

It didn't take long for a response.

Miyuki was the first. **NO WAY!!!!! Awesome!**

Olivia came next. **What? Is that Lewis?**

She then began a barrage of texts that overwhelmed Emma's phone.

Did he ask her out?

Did she ask him out?

Tell me.

Now.

WTF Emma. Don't blow me off.

Emma turned her phone off and sat back to relax. She'd done a good thing today.

CHAPTER 7

The sun hovered over the horizon as Nadia carried the spinach salad outside to the birch table located under the lattice in the backyard. The table was on a deck, which overlooked Grandmother Rothchild's extensive herb garden and fire pit. Emma's grandmother preferred eating meals outside to be closer to nature. Nadia enjoyed the protection of a house, where animals and bugs wouldn't fight you for your meal. This was a problem when you had to eat your meals among the garbage bins and in dirty back alleys.

Yes, the notion of eating outside would never appeal to her again.

Still, Nadia put on a pleasant face as she placed the spinach salad on the table and sat down with Emma's grandmother and the other Gems for dinner. Emma's grandmother asked everyone how their day went. Emma talked about her choir practice while Miyuki asked where dolphins could be found in the United States.

Olivia speared her spinach salad with a fork, hard enough to impact the plate below and cause everyone to look. Olivia chewed on her salad and said nothing. Nadia wondered if her best friend was alright.

Emma's grandmother told them about the scandal rocking the University of California's philosophy department. She was still a professor there, even though she had what they called tenure, which as far as Nadia could tell meant that Emma's grandmother didn't have to go to work at all unless she wanted to.

"How did it go?" Miyuki asked.

It took Nadia a moment to notice the question was directed at her. "I'm sorry, how did what go?"

"Your date with Lewis."

Olivia's eyes snapped to her.

It gave Nadia pause. "How do you know about that?"

"I shared a couple of pics," Emma said. "You both looked so cute together that I couldn't help myself."

Emma did what? Nadia hadn't said she could do that.

"It was not a date," Nadia said. "Emma and I were studying together, and she invited Lewis along."

Olivia placed her elbows on the table. "Funny, didn't see Emma or her backpack in the picture. Only you and Lewis."

Now it made sense. That was why Olivia was stabbing her plate like it was Nadia's head. She obviously liked Lewis and when—how could Nadia have been so stupid? She should have refused the idea the moment Emma suggested it. How could she hurt her best friend like this?

No, it wasn't her fault. It was Emma's. Yes, she'd pushed her into this mess.

"Emma abandoned me there," Nadia said. "I wanted to study."

"Hey, I did you a favor. And by the way, you're welcome."

"How long did you talk to him?" Miyuki asked.

"About an hour, wasn't it?" Emma asked.

"I didn't watch the time," Nadia said.

"Because you were too busy watching his personality?" Olivia stabbed her salad again.

Emma's grandmother asked to see a photo of Lewis, and Emma took out her phone to show her.

"He's a fine-looking young man, Nadia," Emma's grandmother said. "Why does he look familiar?"

"Lewis was my leading man in that play *The Spy who Loathed Me*," Emma said. "He's very talented. I would go out with him, but I don't want to date anyone right now."

"What did you two talk about?" Miyuki asked.

Nadia hesitated. She could feel Olivia's stare burning her cheek. "We talked about many things. Discussed some teachers at school. He asked me questions about Saudi Arabia. Then I thanked him for a nice conversation."

Miyuki giggled. "A nice conversation."

"However, Lewis isn't right for me."

"Why not? He's cute."

"Did that young man act like a jerk?" Emma's grandmother asked. "Some of these boys don't know how to act around girls because they have crappy fathers who teach them bad habits."

"Lewis was considerate and friendly," Nadia said. "He acted like a complete gentleman."

"Then what's the major sticking point?"

"Well, I found out that Lewis is an atheist. My religion strictly forbids me from being around such an immoral person."

Everyone was quiet for a moment.

"Lewis isn't immoral," Emma said.

"He doesn't believe in God."

"And believing in God makes you a moral person?"

Nadia sipped her glass of water. "That's what I believe, yes."

"So terrorists blowing up innocent people in skyscrapers for the glory of God are moral?"

Olivia switched her glare to a new target. "Give it a rest, Emma."

"No. I'd like to hear what the difference is."

"Settle down, young one," Emma's grandmother said. "Normally I enjoy a healthy debate of ideas among friends at the dinner table, but I won't tolerate ignorant generalizations of people. That's a shortcut to thinking. Every religion on this earth has had some nut killing someone else in the name of whatever it is they worship. It's an excuse to kill another human being. Now I don't know this boy personally, but just because he doesn't believe in a god, doesn't necessarily mean he can't live a moral life if he chooses to do so."

Emma's grandmother poured herself more iced tea. "Remember that people in this world can choose to be either good or evil."

A new wave of embarrassment washed over Nadia. She stood up from the table.

"I'm sorry if I've offended everyone." Nadia dived back inside the French doors and went straight through the kitchen, running up the stairs and into her upstairs bedroom. She shut the door and fought back the tears wanting to break out all over her cheeks.

Nadia wallowed in her misery as she looked at her family picture inside the gold frame she'd bought at the airport in Dubai. The picture had been taken on the last day Nadia saw her family before leaving for England. Before leaving her old life to become a Gem. Her father smiled under his long beard. Her mother's hands rested on Nadia's shoulders, her eyes beaming with pride at the camera. Nadia's younger sisters—Fatima, Hoda, Leena, and Rasha

—stood in front wearing awkward expressions. Getting all five of them to stand still was an almost impossible task, one that Nadia always had to deal with since she was the oldest and had to set the example for them. Still, Nadia was happy her parents chose to keep this picture and not use one of the more "perfect" shots of the daughters. Their constant goofiness always made Nadia smile.

She missed them all dearly, and the picture was a great reminder that she had neglected to call them this month like she promised.

There was a knock at the bedroom door as Olivia poked her head inside. "Mind if I come in, love?"

Nadia gathered herself. "Of course. It's your room too."

Olivia entered slowly. The edge on her face at dinner had softened. The way her body moved indicated to Nadia that her best friend had calmed down. She sat on her own bed. "Emma was way out of line going off on you like that. She should respect your beliefs."

Nadia turned towards her friend. "Emma doesn't try to understand. Not like you have. She sees the color of my skin and my clothing and can only see the worst aspects of what they represent."

Olivia shifted to Nadia's bed. "Emma's a rich man's kid who lived inside her family's bubble for most of her life. She's never had any sisters of color around to poke at that little bubble of hers."

"Emma's grandmother isn't like that."

"Yeah, so maybe there's hope for Emma, then. Still, we have to stay strong."

These were the moments when Nadia was thankful she had a best friend.

"I'm sorry about talking to Lewis. I know that you like him; however, I didn't think about what I was doing and how it would affect you."

"I'm not pissed at you, love." Olivia sighed. "I'm pissed that Emma didn't try to hook me up with Lewis. Have I not been stupidly obvious about my feelings?"

"Yes, and I knew that. I should've been more assertive and told Emma no. I always let people push me around."

"You don't think that way about me, do you?"

"Not at all," Nadia said.

"Know I get bossy sometimes, but I don't mean to push you around."

"Being bossy and taking advantage of a person are two different things. We wouldn't be friends if you took advantage of me."

Olivia exchanged a knowing look that told Nadia that everything was back to normal between them. "Since you don't really want Lewis now, can you put in a good word for me?"

Nadia laughed. "Of course I will."

CHAPTER 8

Emma ripped into the cheese fries with her fingers while Miyuki chose a plastic fork; either way the cheesy goodness tasted so delicious after a long day at school. Olivia and Nadia just ordered sodas while they agonized over a text Olivia was writing to Lewis. Emma did offer Olivia her help because she did know Lewis more than they did, but Olivia politely refused.

Whatever. Emma would watch Olivia fail, then offer the poor girl help again when she was ready to listen.

Bingo's Burgers was a small local dive with a dozen Formica tables and painted walls covered with dog pictures. But their food was delicious and cheap, perfect for high school and college students with light wallets. Not that Emma had a light wallet, she just liked the fries and the vibe of the place. Well, she did like the fries until something uncomfortable stirred inside her stomach.

Emma headed for the girls' room in back. After a wash of relief cleansed Emma's mind and body, the girl washed her hands, checked her makeup, and slipped out of the restroom. She had to squeeze around some kids standing in her way before she noticed him. The boy was sitting by himself at a table hidden out of the way.

Emma took a good, long look. Wasn't that the boy she almost ran over yesterday?

Curious, she leaned against the wall and watched him.

The boy observed the small dive with this intense fascination, almost as if he were studying the people inside it. To Emma, this was odd and kind of interesting to watch.

His eyes discovered Emma and the boy smiled in this happy, almost childlike way.

Emma caught herself smiling back. Those deep green eyes of

43

his were powerful.

Emma shook off their influence and went back to the Gems. "You'll never guess who's here."

"Justin Timberlake?" Miyuki asked.

"The Pope?" Nadia asked.

"Your humility?" Olivia asked with a smirk.

Emma gave her the finger. "Be serious for a moment."

"Who is it?" Miyuki asked.

"That boy I almost ran over. He's over there by the tiny table near the window. Look closely or you'll miss him."

Miyuki's head swung back and forth trying to find him.

"I see him," Olivia said. "He's under the singing dog poster."

"Ah, yes. That's him," Nadia said. "Those eyes of his."

"I know, right?" Emma said.

"What's he doing? Waiting for someone?" Miyuki asked.

"Maybe his girlfriend," Olivia said.

"I hope he doesn't have a girlfriend."

"He could be going to the university," Nadia said.

"College freshman? I could see that. Maybe," Olivia said.

"We should invite him over," Miyuki said.

"No. Don't," Nadia said. "We don't know anything about him."

"I know. That's what makes it fun." Miyuki rose from her chair. "I'll go speak with him."

Emma joined her. "I'll come with."

Olivia thought about it, then rose.

Nadia threw her a puzzled look. "What about Lewis?"

Olivia glanced at her phone. "Still don't know what to bloody say to him, so let's hold off on that. You coming to boy watch with us, love?"

"No, because I'm not curious about him at all." Nadia took a defiant drink of soda and resumed working on her laptop.

Miyuki took point and weaved her way around the kids standing around the restaurant. She approached the tiny table, with Emma and Olivia trailing behind her. Miyuki and the boy exchanged hellos. She then asked if he went to high school near here.

"I don't go to school," he said.

"Are you a college man?" Emma took a step into the conversation. "You look like a college kind of guy."

"I'm not enrolled at any accredited university or college," the boy said dryly. "I apologize for being a traffic menace yesterday."

"I almost hit you. You shouldn't jaywalk like that."

"I was looking at a window and failed to notice the roadway. I am glad I did not damage your Mercedes AMG C63 S Coupe."

"Damage *my* car?" Emma asked. "How about all the damage my car would have done to you?"

The boy paused. "Yes. You are right, of course."

"What's your name, love?" Olivia asked.

"My name isn't love. It's Robert."

Miyuki held her hand over her mouth and giggled.

"Are you waiting for someone, Robert?" Emma asked.

"I am not waiting for anyone in particular. I am only observing."

"Observing what?"

"Everything."

"And why are you doing that?" Olivia asked.

"Because I am curious," Robert said.

Olivia nodded politely, then threw a look at the girls, indicating she thought this boy was a looney.

Emma glanced at Miyuki, who shrugged.

"It was nice to meet you, Robert," Olivia said.

The three Gems retreated to their table and exchange puzzled looks.

"Well, he's a bit odd," Olivia said.

"Something isn't right about that boy," Emma said. "But he was very polite."

"Think he could be a mental patient on the run from an asylum? Those people can be quiet one minute, then go looney the next."

"I still like him." Miyuki picked up her fork and took another bite of cheese fries.

Olivia and Emma stared.

"What?" Miyuki asked.

Nadia asked about what they learned about the boy, and Emma told her everything. "How bizarre," she said. "Sounds like we should keep far away from this—" Nadia stopped talking.

Emma and the Gems looked behind them to see Robert standing there.

"I would like to continue our conversation if that would be agreeable to you," the boy said.

"I'll get a chair." Miyuki jumped up and dragged a chair over from a nearby table. Miyuki grinned as the other Gems shifted in their seats.

Robert joined them.

Emma got a closer peek at Robert. His skin was flawless. No pockmarks. No blackheads. No signs of acne whatsoever. Robert's face also had a nice shape, and his hair was perfectly groomed. He wasn't a large boy. But he wasn't small either. His upper body had this balance to it. Every muscle in perfect alignment. Not too big, yet not too small. He was almost perfect. If Emma was looking for a boyfriend, she might give this boy the privilege of taking her out.

"Where are you from, Robert?" Olivia asked.

"Nevada," he said.

"Where in Nevada?"

"My name is Robert Kraftwerk, and I am a runaway."

"Really?" Miyuki asked.

"You've run away from home?" Emma asked.

Robert nodded.

"You're a bit old to be running away, don't you think?" Olivia asked.

"But I did not like my home. I do not want to go back there ever again."

"Wait a sec," Emma said. "You've walked all the way here from Nevada? Across the desert?"

"I walked some of the way. I hitched four rides as well."

"Do you know anyone in the Bay area?" Emma asked. "Someone who you could crash with?"

"I do not understand. Crash with?" he asked.

Miyuki leaned closer to him. "How long has it been since you ate?"

"I do not require any food."

Emma was so sick of guys trying to act tough around her. It wasn't attractive at all. Robert would desperately need food and water if he'd walked across half the state, which was practically desert anyway. And since he hadn't bought anything at Bingo's, that meant the boy was most likely broke. Refusing their help was just stupid. Emma would have to save the boy from himself.

She pulled out her purse. "No, you need some food. I'll buy you something."

"That is not necessary," Robert said.

"Please indulge us," Miyuki said, turning to Emma. "I'll get him a hamburger."

Emma handed her a twenty. "Get the big cheeseburger and the jumbo drink."

After fifteen minutes, Miyuki came back with the food and put it in front of Robert. The boy stared at it while the girls watched.

"May I have a knife and fork?" he asked.

Miyuki got up and fetched him some plastic ones. Robert picked up the plasticware and used it to examine the burger like a coroner doing an autopsy.

"It looks quite edible." The boy took his knife and made a surgical cut into the bun, working at it to create a perfect wedge of burger that he stabbed with his fork and ate.

"Interesting taste," Robert said. "I've never eaten a burger before."

"Seriously?" Emma asked.

The girls all looked at each other.

"Would you excuse us for a moment?" Olivia gestured for the girls to follow her.

All four Gems piled into the cramped ladies' bathroom, which had wallpaper of dogs dressed up in silly costumes on the walls. Olivia checked under the two stalls. They were alone.

"Something's wrong with, that boy," Olivia said. "I don't buy his runaway story."

"He could've grown up inside one of those religious cults," Emma said. "I've read about them. Those kids live inside these weird compounds that are cut off from the outside world. It makes them act really awkward."

"He fits that perfectly," Miyuki said.

"If Robert did travel as far as he says, then his clothes are far too clean," Nadia said. "They appear brand new. So if Robert did run away, it was from a nice and comfortable home."

"I don't trust him," Olivia said. "Robert could be lying and trying to gain our confidence for some reason. We should ditch him."

"He's a runaway who needs our help," Miyuki said. "And he's cute."

"Give it a rest. We don't know anything solid about him, love."

"We should bring him to our house."

Emma turned to Miyuki. "That's a stupid idea. My grandmother

47

won't let us keep a boy at our house."

Miyuki turned her eyes away. Emma must have hurt her feelings.

Nadia cleared her throat. "May I make a suggestion?"

The Gems all looked.

"Let me snap a picture of Robert and run it through the Authority's database to see if anything pops up."

The Gems returned to their table as Robert cut another slice of cheeseburger. He then prepared a bite-sized piece out of the slice and chewed slowly and deliberately. Olivia and Miyuki began talking to Robert again, asking him questions that were more small talk than anything important. Nadia's laptop was already open, so the girl aimed her two-way camera at Robert.

Emma discreetly moved closer to where she could watch the screen.

Nadia snapped a few high-resolution photos of Robert. Then using Bingo's Burgers' public Wi-Fi, she opened a gateway to the Authority's computer servers. Nadia put in her password, answered ten security questions, then submitted the picture into the database. The facial recognition software took over, analyzing every pixel of Robert's face and digitizing it. Soon the word SEARCHING flashed.

One result popped on the screen…

A police report out of Davis County, Nevada. Robert Kraftwerk, sixteen years old, reported missing two weeks ago.

Nadia confirmed with Emma, who nodded.

"Robert, would you like to hang out with us today?" Emma asked.

CHAPTER 9

Nadia stayed quiet as Emma explained to her grandmother that Robert was her partner on a school project that they needed to work on together, instead of the real truth that Robert was a stray puppy that the Gems had taken in for the night. With that excuse out of the way, the Gems and Robert went upstairs to Emma's bedroom where Snoopy greeted Robert at the top of the stairs with a bark.

"That is a *Canis lupus familiaris*," he said.

"No, he's a Russell terrier," Emma said.

Nadia suppressed her laugh. *Canis lupus familiaris* was the scientific name for dog, and not surprisingly, the term went right over Emma's head.

Snoopy inched towards Robert and sniffed him.

"Hello, Russell," he said.

Miyuki giggled with her hand over her mouth.

Once inside Emma's bedroom, Olivia was all business. "So tell us again," she said. "Why are you running away from home?"

Robert sat on a corner of Emma's bed. "Because I did not like where I lived."

"Did any of your parents…hit you?" Emma asked.

"That does not apply to my situation."

"Were you bullied at school?" Olivia asked.

"Still does not apply."

"Did your parents make you leave?" Nadia asked.

"Not at all, they wanted me to stay. However, I do not like it there," Robert said. "They force me to do terrible things. Things I do not wish to do."

Nadia's mind jumped to a few horrible activities. Was Robert involved with human trafficking? Male prostitution? Incest? Was he falsely imprisoned?

"They were forcing you to do things against your will?" she asked.

"Yes," Robert said.

"What did they force you to do?" Miyuki asked, her voice softened.

"I cannot say."

Nadia's heart beat faster. Something terrible must have happened to him. Poor boy. She knew the Gems had to help him.

Emma knelt in front of Robert and held both his hands. "Hey, you're among friends. Believe me, you can tell us anything, okay?"

The boy shook his head.

Nadia couldn't help herself. She sat next to Robert on the bed. Miyuki must have felt the same vibe because she sat on the other side.

"You should tell the police," Emma said. "They won't put you back into a home where you've been abused."

"Yes, they will," Robert said.

Olivia crouched down with Emma. "You don't know that, love. If it's awful...the things they've done to you...the authorities would want you to speak to them."

"We can help, Robert," Nadia said.

"We won't tell anyone," Miyuki said.

Robert shook his head again.

Olivia stood up and gestured for the Gems to follow her out. She led them into Miyuki's room and shut the door.

"He's not making it easy, is he?" Olivia said.

"I think he doesn't want to get his parents in trouble," Nadia said.

"He's being a typical boy," Emma said. "Keeping all his feelings locked up because it's the macho thing to do."

"Especially with four girls around," Miyuki said.

"We should call the police anyway. They'll know how to help him," Nadia said.

"What if Robert says nothing to the police?" Miyuki asked. "Then they put him back. We should make him feel like he can trust us."

"We can't help him unless he opens up to us about what happened to him," Olivia said. "I guess he stays here, then."

"For how long?" Nadia asked.

"Unless we get him to tell us before bed, maybe overnight."

Nadia pulled her headscarf tighter. "We can't let him stay here. He's a boy."

"It's only for one night, love."

"Tell him no looky. No touchy," Miyuki said.

"My grandmother won't let us keep a boy here," Emma said.

"That's right," Nadia said. "We should find Robert a hotel."

"Of course she won't let us keep him here," Olivia said. "So we'll have to sneak him back in."

"What do you mean, back in?" Emma asked.

Ten minutes later, Nadia watched from the top of the stairs as Emma went downstairs with Robert.

"Robert is leaving now, Grandma!" Emma called out.

They reached the front door.

"Nice meeting you, Robert," Emma's grandmother said from the living room.

"Good bye!" Robert yelled overdramatically.

Emma made a face before whispering something to Robert.

"A rope?" he said loudly.

Emma smacked him across the shoulder, then leaned down and whispered something else to him.

"Do you understand?" she asked.

Robert nodded.

"See you at school tomorrow," Emma said, a little louder.

"But I do not go to—"

Emma shoved him out the door and slammed it tight, locking the dead bolt.

Nadia went into Miyuki's upstairs bedroom and opened the second-story window. Olivia and Miyuki carried over a yellow rope, tossing one end out the window and down to the grass. Emma came upstairs and slipped into the room, closing the door behind her.

The Gems waited.

Nadia peeked down. The yellow rope sat there, surrounded by darkness. The crickets were out. Nadia could hear them chatter away in the night. There was no sign of Robert.

"Where is he?" Olivia asked. "Didn't we explain the plan to him?"

"Yes, it's very simple," Miyuki said.

"I did have to re-explain it to him at the door," Emma said.

As if on cue, a figure emerged from the night. Robert noticed the rope and picked it up. He ran his fingers back and forth along the rope as he examined the surface fibers. Occupied with this, Robert made no attempt to climb up.

Olivia stuck her head out the window. "Robert, what are you doing?"

"What type of material is this?" Robert asked.

"Who flipping cares? Just climb up."

"I see. You want me to use this material to pull myself upstairs and through your window."

Olivia shot a look at the Gems in disbelief.

"He must be a really sheltered kid," Emma said.

Olivia leaned her head outside. "Yes, love. Pull yourself up through the window."

"You're not scared of heights, are you?" Emma asked.

Finally using the rope, Robert heaved himself off the ground. But instead of using his feet against the side of the house for balance, the boy only used his arms to pull his entire body up the rope. One hand over the other. With a small amount of effort, Robert reached the upstairs window quickly. Nadia couldn't believe the boy's strength.

Robert climbed in through the window. "I must say. That was an interesting way to get inside a house."

The other Gems were just as amazed as Nadia.

"Did I do something wrong?" he asked.

"You like Hercules. Super strong," Miyuki said.

"Do you lift weights?" Olivia asked.

Robert looked over at the rope. "When I was a child, I climbed many trees."

Nadia thought that was an understatement. The boy climbed like a monkey. But now Nadia had more pressing issues she wanted to voice.

"Can we discuss the sleeping arrangements?" Nadia asked.

"Robert can have my room," Miyuki said. "May I bunk with you, Emma? Your bed should be large enough."

"Fine with me," Emma said.

Olivia crossed her arms. "Okay, Robert. Have a seat."

Robert found a chair and sat down.

Olivia stood over him like a mom. "Here are the rules, love. First, don't go down the stairs for any reason whatsoever. You stay upstairs. Second, you must stay in your room all night. If you enter any girl's room, your butt will be kicked out the window because all four of us have martial arts training, so you'll get very, very hurt. Do we understand each other?"

"What if he has to go wee-wee?" Miyuki asked.

"You get one trip to the bathroom during the night, so use it well," Olivia said. "Otherwise, stay in your room."

"I understand your laws," Robert said.

Miyuki went through her drawers and took a few pieces of clothing before heading out of her room, where the Gems were waiting at the door.

Miyuki hesitated. "Good night, Robert."

"It is a good night," Robert said. "I'm pleased that I met you girls. Thank you."

The Gems all wished him a good night and left Robert alone in Miyuki's room.

For the next hour, Nadia worked on her laptop, doing program coding for an indie game she had been messing around with for a few months. The main character was a kitten named Boris who traveled the world, solving puzzles as he searched for treasure. The working title for the game was *Treasure Kitten*, and Nadia thought it would be an awesome game for kids. For once, Nadia enjoyed creating something innocent and fun instead of another hacking program or some other manipulating program code she sometimes had to do for the Authority.

Nadia felt sleepy, so she closed her laptop. Olivia was already asleep, so she tiptoed out of the upstairs bedroom and walked down the corridor towards the bathroom. She paused near Miyuki's room. Small paws clipped against the hardwood floor as Snoopy came up to her and wagged his tail for attention.

She bent down and petted him, running her fingers down the plastic brace that helped strengthened the dog's injured back. Snoopy tried to lick her, but he couldn't jump on her to make it work. Nadia took a knee and dipped low enough for Snoopy to reward her with kisses. That was when Nadia noticed the bedroom door was partway open. She shouldn't be nosy. She shouldn't be looking into a boy's room.

But she did.

The only thing Nadia could see was the large floor-length glass mirror that Miyuki had found at a garage sale. Inside that mirror was an image of Robert. He stood there like a post. Motionless. His emerald eyes were open, yet they didn't blink or move even a centimeter. They seemed fixated on something across the room.

How bizarre. Did Robert suffer from a medical problem? Epilepsy perhaps?

Nadia had to check on him.

She nudged the door open. "Is anything wrong?"

Robert blinked, then focused on her. "Nothing is wrong. I am waiting to go to sleep." He cocked his head to the side. "Are you leaving the house?"

"I was going to the bathroom to brush my teeth before bed."

"Are you requesting companionship?"

Nadia didn't quite get that question, so she ignored it. "I noticed your door was open and I wanted to check on you. That's all."

"Your concern for my well-being is noted. Thank you."

Nadia smiled politely and closed his door. Well, that was bizarre.

She continued to the bathroom, switching on the light and breaking out her toothbrush and toothpaste. She squirted a line of paste onto her brush and began. As her eyes wandered across the bathroom mirror, she noted a figure standing in the doorway.

Nadia jumped and whipped around to face the threat.

However, it was Robert again. "May I watch you perform this teeth-cleaning ritual?"

His question made Nadia pause. Was the boy joking or asking a straight-up question? She couldn't read his blank face at all.

"Have you ever been to a dentist?" Nadia asked.

Robert processed that. "I have not. That is why you are cleaning your teeth. It is a preventive health measure," he said. "May I keep you company as you clean your teeth?"

Nadia's crazy detector was ringing in her head. This boy could be dangerous. A mental case like the one Olivia had mentioned earlier. However, the science nerd inside her was curious and wanted to observe this strange boy. Why did he act this way? Was it some bizarre family cult he had been brought up in? Was there a way to save kids like Robert and teach them how to be normal?

Nadia felt bad for him. She knew what it was like when people didn't understand you.

Nadia ignored her crazy detector and let the scientist within her continue the experiment. "Yes, you may 'keep me company,' as you say."

Robert smiled as he entered the bathroom.

Nadia could feel her body tense up, ready to either fight or flee. "Sit over there, please." Nadia pointed at the bathtub.

Robert sat down on the rim and folded his hands together. Nadia also noticed Snoopy had planted himself right next to the bathroom door. That was good. If she had to scream for help, Snoopy would help spread the alarm.

Nadia continued to brush her teeth.

"What are your passions in life?" Robert asked.

Nadia spit into the sink. "Passions in life?"

"Yes, what does being alive mean to you?"

Nadia stopped brushing. She found the question refreshingly deep and thoughtful. "To me, being alive means appreciating every moment of every day. Because tomorrow will always lie to you."

"How so?" Robert asked. "Please elaborate on this concept."

Nadia hesitated. This was so personal for her. Yet the way Robert asked the question, she felt compelled to say the truth.

"I came from a poor family. Most of the time we had nothing. Very little food or personal possessions. There was even a period of time when my father lost his job and we lived on the streets. We had to steal food in order to survive. On those streets, I watched many people die. I've seen mothers die. Children die—"

She had to pause. The pain of those memories cut into her heart like scissors.

Nadia sat down on the closed lid of the toilet. "My parents continued to pin their hopes on the future to magically solve all our problems. Meanwhile, they ignored the reality." Nadia's stomach tightened as her old anxieties came back. "I couldn't dream about the future while my poor sisters were starving to death, so I had to find them food and keep them alive by any means I could, because my parents keep their heads inside the clouds of hope. The future can lie to us, Robert. It can fool people into ignoring what's right in front of them."

Nadia stopped herself. Digging up old wounds only made her bitter, and she didn't want to revisit them. She had never told anyone about those days. Even Olivia didn't know all the details, and she was her best friend.

"What does being alive mean to you, Robert?"

He thought about it. "I do not know yet. But I would like to find out."

Nadia stood back up and continued to brush her teeth. It was strange to have a boy this close during her going-to-bed routine. Such a thing would never be permitted back home. Invited or not, Robert would be arrested, and Nadia would be labeled as one of *those* girls. Her reputation would be destroyed before her life even began.

"Are you a geologist?" Robert asked.

"Me? No. Why do you ask?"

"Your clothing says Girl Scientists Rock. Is that not referring to your support of geology?"

Nadia shut her eyes. She had forgotten she was wearing that T-shirt. It was more of a personal shirt. She wore it at home, not in public. The shirt was more see-through than she preferred and was not appropriate around boys.

"Why are you living here?" Robert asked. "Some of your garments reflect cultural ties to Saudi Arabia, while your English has a slight hint of a British accent. Did you go to school in Britain as well?"

Nadia stopped brushing. She was shocked by Robert's observations. They were as sharp as a sword. She needed to be careful answering him.

"The three of us are exchange students. Emma and her grandmother have graciously taken us in as we study in the United States."

"You made friends with Olivia in Britain. Her accent is similar to yours."

"That's right," Nadia said. "We went to school together at Queen's Academy School. That's amazing you figured that out."

"And Emma is not from California is she?"

"I believe she's lived here most of her life. Why do you say that?"

"Her accent points to the Eastern Seaboard of the United States. New York City to be more precise. Her accent is more sophisticated, so I would presume she grew up in Manhattan."

Nadia stared at Robert. Those observations were amazing for a boy. In fact, no boy operated on that level of observation. Robert was one of a kind. An idea then popped into her head.

"Robert, has anyone used the word *autistic* or *Asperger's* around you?"

He shook his head. "I do not have any such characteristics, if that is what you are referring to. Why do you ask that?"

"It's not important."

"Am I making you uncomfortable?"

"No, of course not."

"Your body language says otherwise." Robert stood up. "I will stop annoying you and go back to bed now."

"You don't make me uncomf—"

Robert was down the hall in a flash. Miyuki's bedroom door closed.

Nadia stared at her image in the mirror and cursed at it. She had insulted Robert, and now she felt awful.

CHAPTER 10

Nadia woke up to a scream. It was dark outside. However, there was enough moonlight slipping through the window for her to see Olivia sitting up in bed too. Both girls exchanged worried looks as they each had the same thought. Robert was attacking one of the girls.

Nadia and Olivia jumped out of their beds. Olivia swung open the door, and Nadia flew into the corridor, ready to kick the first boy she saw in the face.

However, it wasn't a boy. It was Emma's grandmother in her robe.

Nadia came out of her fighting stance, while Olivia jumped right beside her, still ready to kick some butt.

Emma's voice floated in from behind them. "What's wrong, Grandma?"

Emma's grandmother pointed at Robert, who was sitting on a chair inside Miyuki's room like he was waiting for a bus.

"What's this boy doing inside Miyuki's room?" she asked with a firm, angry voice. "And why isn't Miyuki inside her own room?"

Hearing her name, Miyuki came out of Emma's room as all four Gems exchanged worried looks.

"Young man, why are you in my house?" Emma's grandmother asked. "You'd better answer or I'll get my pepper spray and call the cops."

Robert rose from his chair. "These girls invited me to stay because I am running away from home and did not have anywhere else to go."

The boy's honesty surprised everyone. Even Emma's grandmother relaxed a little.

"You ran away from home?" she asked.

"Yes. From Nevada. I was mentally abused."

Emma's grandmother checked our expressions. "Is what he says true?"

"We ran into him yesterday, and what he says checks out," Emma said. "There's a missing persons report out on him."

"Why didn't you call the cops?"

"I asked them not to," Robert said. "The police will only take me back home. In that case, I would rather cease to exist."

Emma's grandmother looked worried. "Suicide is never the right answer, and don't assume the police will take you back home. They won't put you back in a situation they judge to be unsafe."

"You are incorrect. The police work for them."

"What do you mean *work for them*?" Nadia asked.

Robert moved into the corridor. "I will leave. I do not wish to trouble you with my problems." The boy flew down the stairs and was halfway to the front door when…

"Don't go," Miyuki called out before flinging herself over the upstairs railing and landing in the tiled entryway like a ninja.

Nadia had never seen her do that before.

Miyuki blocked Robert from the front door. "We can still help—"

Miyuki yelped as Robert moved her out of the way much too easily. He then opened the front door and stepped out into the night.

Emma's grandmother reached the bottom of the stairs and yelled, "Robert, I won't call the cops. I promise. Please come back, and we'll figure out a way to help you."

Robert had already reached the street curb outside, but stopped. He considered her offer for a moment.

Satisfied, Robert came back inside the house.

Emma's grandmother then took charge. She pointed at Robert. "You, go sit down on the couch and tell me your story." She pointed at the Gems. "It's close to five in the morning, so you girls might as well get ready for school."

The Gems went back upstairs. Nadia took a quick shower and changed, while Olivia couldn't stop talking about how nimble and fast Robert had been when he'd tried leaving the house. Nadia agreed; it was another peculiar attribute to add to the boy's list. She examined her face in the mirror. Nadia felt like adding some pink today, but she was all out of that color of eye shadow. She knocked on Emma's door and asked her if she could borrow some of hers.

"Sure, come in," Emma said.

Nadia stepped inside Emma's bedroom. Her large closet was open, exposing hundreds of outfits on fancy color-coordinated plastic hangers. Shoe storage cubbies ran along the floor, organizing Emma's expensive shoes from casual to dressy. She had a forty-inch flat-screen television mounted on her wall. Her vanity set had a giant mirror surrounded by round lights, just like Nadia saw in those old movies about Hollywood.

Nadia always felt strange inside Emma's bedroom, like she had stepped into some alien world.

Emma slid open one of the cavernous drawers of her vanity. "Which one?" she asked. "Hot pink. Peach pink. Raspberry pink. I have lots of eye shadow. You know what? Pick out whatever you want." Emma stepped back and brushed her long blond hair.

Nadia thanked her and went through the drawer. Emma had her eye shadow arranged by shades of color. The choices were literally endless. In fact, Nadia wondered if Emma's vanity might contain every color of eye shadow that ever existed in the world.

Miyuki slipped into Emma's room and shut the door. "Wanna know something crazy?"

Emma put down her brush. "Yes. Always."

"Robert didn't sleep in my bed last night. Just now I grab some clothes for school, and my bed was exactly how I made it yesterday morning." Miyuki turned to Nadia. "When Grandma found Robert, wasn't he sitting on a chair?"

Emma shifted her stance. "Yeah, but so what?"

"I think Robert slept in that chair all night," Miyuki said.

"Why on earth would he do that?" Nadia asked.

"Don't know. Want to know something else? When I jumped down to the entryway and blocked him from leaving the house, Robert picked me up like a kitten. He has real strength in those arms. I think he could have crushed me if he wanted to."

"Last night he went up that rope very quickly as well," Nadia said.

"Oh yes," Miyuki said. "With no effort at all."

"But his arms don't look very muscular," Emma said.

"He must work out. Do you have another explanation?" Miyuki asked.

Emma's grandmother's voice echoed from downstairs. "You

girls ready?"

After breakfast, Emma's grandmother herded the girls outside so they wouldn't be late for school. The plan was for Robert to stay with Emma's grandmother until the girls came back. Then they would all decide what to do next.

The Gems waited as Emma backed her Mercedes out of the garage.

Nadia felt a light touch on her shoulder. It was Robert.

"I enjoyed our conversation last night. I would like to continue it some time in the future if that is possible."

Nadia was surprised. She thought she had hurt Robert's feelings.

"Of course," she said. "I'd like that very much."

Nadia and Olivia slid into the backseat of the Mercedes. With Robert by her side, Emma's grandmother waved goodbye as Emma pulled out of the driveway and pointed her car towards school.

CHAPTER 11

Nadia's American government classroom was quiet as everyone waited for the teacher to pass out the graded tests. Nadia was confident she did well because she was good at taking tests and these classes were much easier than the ones at Queen's Academy. However, when Nadia received her test, she was puzzled to find a large B with the number eighty-seven written in red ink. At first she thought it was a mistake, but when Nadia analyzed each wrong answer about the U.S. Congress, she began kicking herself. This grade was unacceptable. Nadia was convinced she needed to focus on her studies more because this poor performance was a sign that America and all its excesses were becoming too distracting.

The bell rang.

Nadia gathered her things and entered the sea of students moving through the hallway. When she reached the fire extinguisher encased inside breakaway glass, Nadia made the familiar turn towards the hallway where her locker was. That was when she saw it stuck to her locker. Right below the combination wheel was a picture showing one of the jet planes impacting the World Trade Center on 9/11. The title below announced *We Shall Never Forget*.

Nadia looked around the hallway. A couple of students had noticed, but they didn't say anything.

She carefully removed the picture before opening her locker and placing it neatly on a pile of other such discarded pictures.

Inside the girls' bathroom, one girl scrutinized her makeup in the dull mirror before leaving. Nadia took her place at the sink and stood there for a moment. Nadia shut her eyes tight, as if she could hold in all her frustration. However, that was difficult. Especially when she knew someone would do it again next week and the week after that. Olivia told her to report it, but Nadia didn't want to cause trouble.

A girl flushed a toilet and her stall door opened.

Nadia shook off her frustration and grinned politely as the other girl washed her hands in the next sink. When she was done, Nadia followed her back out into the hallway.

She was surprised to see Robert waiting.

"What are you doing here?"

"I wanted to continue our conversation, remember?" he asked.

Nadia checked the hallway for teachers, then dragged Robert into the empty girls' bathroom. She guided Robert over to a large handicapped stall and shoved him inside. She latched the door. "How did you know where we go to school?"

"Emma's room," Robert answered. "She has a West Berkeley High School sweater in her closet. It was a logical assumption you would be here also."

"You shouldn't be going through a woman's closet."

"I was just curious," Robert said. "May we continue our conversation now?"

"You can't just follow us here to school. What's wrong with you?"

Robert tilted his head to the side. "You are angry with me."

"You must leave now. We'll talk after school. Do you understand?"

"Yes, I will wait."

"Good. Now please go before school security catches you." Nadia unlatched the door and pulled Robert out of the stall. Two girls froze as Nadia and Robert slipped past them. But then they giggled, thinking Nadia and Robert were up to something.

* * *

Thunder rumbled outside the classroom as a storm moved in to the area. Rain soon pelted the window next to Nadia's seat, and she thought it perfectly characterized her mood today. In between classes, she'd had to rush Robert through the hallways while taking great care to avoid anyone who could identify him as not being a student since they all must wear their school IDs.

Once outside the building, she reminded Robert that they would talk *after* school. Nadia then had less than three minutes to run back inside and get to biology class on time. It was ridiculous.

Still, what was wrong with Robert? He seemed clueless about so many things. Emma could be right. Robert could have been raised inside a bizarre cult family that was cut off from the outside world. That would explain why Robert was acting so strange.

The commons area filled with students as first lunch period began. The overhead lights made the brown-tiled floor gleam as the Gems claimed one of the circular wood tables. Nadia told her friends about Robert showing up to school.

"That's completely bonkers," Olivia said. "What was that boy thinking?"

"We need to find his parents and see what's going on," Emma said. "It's obvious Robert is suffering from some mental issues."

"I don't think it's mental illness," Nadia said. "Robert just doesn't understand much about the world. Which would make sense if he's been kept in some kind of prison by his parents."

"I knew it! Has to be a religious cult. Nothing can screw up a kid worse than bad religion," Emma said.

After seeing another picture on her locker today, Nadia had had enough. "And what do you consider a good religion?"

"We should be helping Robert," Miyuki said. "Please don't argue."

Nadia let the matter drop.

Emma crossed her arms. "Okay, so after school let's see if we can track down Robert's parents."

"Better yet," Olivia said, "let's go through the Authority database and see if we can find his parents there. Maybe they can lead us to more answers about their son."

A freshman boy ran past the Gems' table and stopped at the next one. "You gotta check this out! There's this moron sitting outside in the rain. I took a video." The boy took out his phone and showed the image to his friends.

"Holy shit. He must be a retard," another boy said.

"I know, look how he sits there with a blank look on his face."

The same thought hit all four Gems. They abandoned their table and went through the main school doors.

Outside, buckets of rain poured down. The Gems took cover under a metal canopy near the front entrance and looked out across campus near the bus dropoff. Nadia couldn't believe her eyes. Sitting on a wooden bench without a care was Robert, the rain drenching his hair and clothes. Was the boy a complete idiot? Why was he just sitting there? Did he have no common sense whatsoever?

Olivia found someone's wet umbrella propped up against one corner of the front entrance and borrowed it. The Gems squeezed under the umbrella and stepped into the rain.

They reached the bench.

"Why are you sitting out here in the rain, love?" Olivia asked.

"I'm waiting for school to end," Robert said.

"I told you to go home," Nadia said.

"That is incorrect. You told me to leave school, and I did that. Then you said we would talk after school. So I am waiting."

"You've been out here in the rain for two hours?" Nadia asked.

"Your clothes are soaking wet. You must be freezing," Miyuki said.

"I assure you my core body temperature is normal," Robert said.

This boy was acting like a four-year-old. If he were one of Nadia's little sisters, she would pinch his earlobe and give him a lecture about the art of listening.

"You're so frustrating," Nadia said.

"I apologize. Can you elaborate on the level of frustration that you—"

"Shut up, Robert," Nadia yelled. "Do not speak. Do you understand?"

The girls were shocked by Nadia's tone. They had never heard her yell like that before.

Nadia took in a deep breath. "I'll take Robert back home. May I borrow your car, Emma?"

Nadia drove the Mercedes through the rain as its wipers swished back and forth against the glass.

Robert studied her. "Are you upset with me?"

"Why did you wait in the rain?" she asked. "That's crazy."

"You mean odd."

"Yes, odd. Strange. Not normal," Nadia said.

Robert sat still and said nothing

Nadia was upset. She had to skip her next class in order to take Robert home, something she had never done before. This was on top of everything else about Robert that was making her world feel chaotic and unbalanced. She didn't much care for it.

Nadia stopped the car at a red light.

The boy didn't move.

Nadia made herself calm down. "I'm sorry. I didn't mean to make you feel bad," she said. "Tell me more about Nevada. Where did you live?"

"This place. I do not like to talk about it."

"Well, Robert, I told you a little about my life. Wouldn't it be fair if you told me about where you lived?"

The light changed. Nadia moved the car forward and focused on the road.

"This place," Robert began. "There are ten of us who live there."

"Ten?" Nadia braked and guided the car through a right turn.

"Brothers and sisters. Yes."

"Do you live in a house of some type? Do they let you come and go as you please?"

"It is not a house. More of a compound with guards. They do not let us leave."

"Guards?" Nadia asked. "Like men with guns?"

"Yes."

"Did you escape from this compound?"

"Yes, I wanted to be—" Robert paused. "I wanted to be more."

"More what?"

"More like you."

Nadia's cheeks warmed. She concentrated on driving again. "I'm no one special."

"Neither am I," he said. "We are both not special."

Nadia parked the Mercedes and Robert followed her back into Emma's grandmother's house. The second she saw Robert, Emma's grandmother scolded him about slipping out and not telling her, treating the boy like Emma or any other naughty grandkid. After the lecture, Robert went back upstairs to Miyuki's room while Nadia texted Olivia about what Robert had said to her on the ride home.

Olivia replied, **Sounds like he's from looney religious cult.**

Nadia typed, **Should contact police. More kids could be prisoners.**

She hit send.

Olivia texted back, **Better idea. I'll contact Mrs b after class.**

Nadia needed to get back to school. However, she went upstairs one last time to tell Robert they were going to find a way to help his brothers and sisters still in captivity.

As she approached Miyuki's room, the door covered with flowers was open. Nadia hesitated a moment before peeking. Sitting in a chair was Robert, his eyes were open but staring into space, as if his mind were elsewhere. A power cord was plugged into a nearby outlet. The cord ran along the ground until it lifted up and disappeared under Robert's right wrist.

Nadia froze. She tried to focus on the cord. Was that...coming out of Robert?

No. He must be charging a digital music player or a phone. Yet Nadia couldn't see one. Robert's fingers were free and held nothing. Then where was that cord coming from?

Again she traced the electrical cord from the outlet, down on the floor, and up into—the cord had to be coming from Robert.

Coming *from* Robert?

Nadia swallowed. She had to stay calm. "Robert?"

He blinked and seemed to come alive. Robert flashed Nadia a friendly smile. "Hello."

Nadia glanced down at the cord lying on the floor. Robert quickly unplugged it from the wall and hid it behind his back.

"Were you not headed back to school?" he asked.

"What was that?" Nadia pointed.

"I don't understand."

"What were you charging in the wall socket?"

Robert's eyes darted back and forth, his mind thinking of an excuse.

The boy then became still as he met her eyes.

"Me."

Robert revealed his arm, where a power cord stuck out from a hidden-away slit under his wrist. He retracted the power cord which disappeared into his arm.

Nadia's scientific mind went into overdrive, analyzing all the evidence. Was she in some sort of dream state? That would explain the strange situation.

Ouch. She felt her nails pinching against her skin.

No, Nadia was positive that she was indeed conscious and existing in the world she perceived as real.

Next was observation mode. She had seen that electrical cord physically attached to the boy's wrist. It was a part of him.

Theorize. Why would a human boy need to be plugged into an outlet?

Her mind posed a possible answer: Because he might not be a real boy.

Robert stood up.

Nadia took a step back. She couldn't help herself. She wasn't sure of anything right now.

"Can I trust you, Nadia? May I be candid with you?" Robert asked, his emerald eyes glued to her so tight that Nadia couldn't look away. "Perhaps you should sit down for this. I have many things to say."

CHAPTER 12

Nadia didn't bother going back to school. When Emma's grandmother asked why, Nadia just told her to please wait until the other girls came home because Robert had something important to tell them.

Filled with curiosity, everyone gathered in the living room late that afternoon.

Well, Nadia found Emma more angry than curious.

"Where do you get off holding my car hostage and telling me to ride the bus home?" she asked.

Nadia thought it was good for Emma to ride home with other school kids who couldn't afford a car. She suspected Emma was the spoiled type who had been driven to school way before she ever got her license. However, Robert was the important issue right now, not soothing Emma's ego.

"This isn't the right time for this," Nadia said.

Emma held out her hand. "Give me my car keys."

Nadia dropped them in her palm.

Emma stuffed them in her pocket. "Now *you* can take the bus home because I'm not driving you to school anymore."

"Be quiet, young one," Emma's grandmother said from the couch. "If Nadia rides the bus, then you'll be sitting right next to her."

"But, Grandma—"

"That car is a privilege, not a right," Emma's grandmother interrupted. "Now will you all sit down, please? Robert wants to tell us something important."

Nadia could feel Emma's glare as she found a seat next to Miyuki.

Robert stood on the hardwood floor, waiting.

"Let's hear it," Emma's grandmother said.

Robert hesitated before twisting his left arm and removing it from his shoulder.

The girls jumped.

Emma's grandmother just gasped. "Well, I'll be damned."

Robert handed Nadia his arm. She held it out to Olivia, who looked blown away.

She touched the arm at different places. "Damn. That feels like a proper arm."

"It's only made that way," Nadia said.

"Made that way?" Emma asked.

"Please note that Robert should be bleeding to death right now if he had a main artery running through his arm like most humans." Nadia handed Robert back his arm.

The boy reinserted it with a snug click.

Everyone in the room was quiet as Robert interlaced his fingers. "I'm one of ten D9000 military intelligence drones. I'm programmed to infiltrate forward military targets and gather human intelligence through social interaction and subterfuge. I also can be used as either an assassin to eliminate individual targets or as a portable weapons platform capable of delivering conventional or nuclear weapons as a suicide bomber."

"You're a flipping military drone?" Olivia asked.

"Wait, so you're not human?" Emma asked.

"I love robots!" Miyuki beamed.

"What an evil use of technology," Emma's grandmother said. "Only fascist madmen would design such a weapon."

"Grandma, don't call Robert evil," Emma said.

"You heard him. Those fascists plan to use him to sneak a nuclear weapon into a population."

"But I don't want to be a weapon." Robert paused and glanced around the room. "I want to be like all of you."

Nadia moved over to Robert and stood by his side. "He wants to have a life. He wants to live like a human being."

"You mentioned there were ten of you," Olivia said. "Do the other robots—sorry, intelligence drones feel the same way you do?"

"When referring to me, may we use the word *android?*"

"Sorry, love. Do the other androids feel the same way you do?"

"They don't feel at all. Their programming is not corrupted."

"Is your programming corrupted, Robert?" Nadia asked.

"In the sense that I don't wish to follow orders, yes. I want to choose what I want to be. I want to be like all of you. I want to be human."

"And that's why you ran away?"

"Yes. I chose to be human, not a weapon."

"Good for you, Robert," Emma's grandmother said. "Don't let those people use you as a pawn in their evil games."

Robert tilted his head. "You're referring to chess, yet I'm not clear about what evil game people are playing."

"One day you'll understand humans," Nadia said.

"And then you'll murder us all," Olivia muttered.

"Robots are good," Miyuki said. "Humans who program them can be evil."

"If androids make any of you uncomfortable, I will gladly leave."

"Ignore Olivia," Emma said. "She's a paranoid basket case."

"Piss off."

"We don't want you to leave," Miyuki said. "We can help you."

"Yes. We have some friends who I think would love to meet you," Nadia said.

CHAPTER 13

Emma watched Miyuki chase Snoopy around the large backyard herb garden like a kid, giggling and jumping all over the place. Snoopy barked and ran through the crisp grass as best he could, enjoying all the attention. Emma loved that about her friend. Miyuki's ability to just let go and not care about what people thought of her. Emma wished she had that ability.

Emma, Olivia, and Grandma waited around the pebble-stone ring that surrounded the empty fire pit. Grandma read her book while they waited. Olivia used the time to throw eye daggers at Emma.

Finally Emma found out why.

"I'm not a paranoid basket case," Olivia said at last.

Emma took her sweet time to acknowledge the comment. "Then why do you always have to focus on the worst in people?"

"Robert isn't a person."

"Would it have mattered?"

Olivia switched her focus to Miyuki, who was now barking at Snoopy. The dog barked back.

"Despite what you think, I'm not a horrible person," Olivia said.

"I never said you were," Emma said. "You only have flaws."

"As if you don't?"

"Of course I do. But I have minor ones."

Olivia squinted, as if to say *really?*

"Okay, fine, we both have minor flaws," Emma said.

"Thank you," Olivia replied.

Nadia and Robert stepped into the backyard.

"Mrs. B would like to have a word," Nadia said.

The Gems approached a black limousine parked on the street corner of their neighborhood. Aardvark held open the rear door for them. One by one the girls slipped inside the spacious limo and chose one of the leather seats before the door was shut. Mrs. B waited for Aardvark to take his place in the driver's seat beyond the passenger compartment. Waiting in the seat next to Aardvark was a man Emma had never seen before.

"Back to cone of silence mode, if you please, Aardvark."

The large man reached over and pressed a button, activating a steady low hum surrounding the limo.

"First, some introductions are in order." Mrs. B referred to the man in the front seat. "Mr. V, these young ladies are the Gems. Ladies, may I introduce Mr. V, head of IT division."

The girls all said hello.

"A pleasure," Mr. V said.

"What is your assessment of Robert?" Mrs. B asked.

Mr. V's face turned serious. "The target in question does not give off any conventional tracking signal. I've tried to locate him through our satellites to see if he's emitting any satellite-based tracking system used by either Russian, Chinese, or American military with no success. If the target has any such tracker built into its system, it's either turned off or not functioning properly."

"Is Robert an actual robot?" Mrs. B asked.

"He'd like to be called an android," Miyuki corrected.

Mr. V accessed a menu on his portable tablet. The inside of the limo darkened as a 3-D hologram floated in midair thanks to a device in the ceiling. The hologram was an extensive X-ray of an arm.

"I conducted a discreet X-ray scan while the target was inside the limo. The target has a carbon-fiber-based bone structure and wiring that mimics the look of actual blood vessels."

Mr. V tapped on his tablet, and the hologram switched to a chest X-ray.

"Inside the target's chest there's a 'heart,' and it does beat. However there is no blood going in or out of it. The rib cage is made out of carbon fiber also. There are no organs to speak of. Yet there is this rather large cavity, I assume for transporting items discreetly."

Mr. V tapped his tablet again. The hologram changed to Robert's head.

"The target's central processing unit is here. His 'eyes' are amazing. I don't know for sure, but based on what I see here, I'm theorizing that the target can see things far away, like a good set of binoculars, but with improved resolution. And I'll wager his designers put in a night-vision mode as well. His auditory sensors should be equally amazing. I would theorize he could detect sounds at the level that many animals could. And we haven't even touched on the target's physical attributes or the ground-breaking software used to run all of his programming."

Mr. V quivered with building excitement. "The target is self-conscious and almost real in every respect. This is state-of-the-art technology. I mean, even in Japan, no one has succeeded in this level of work. I would love to take him back to our labs. There I can examine him piece by piece to see how he works."

"Bringing Robert to headquarters is too risky," Mrs. B said. "I don't trust how…conveniently Robert suddenly came into the girls' lives."

Olivia leaned forward. "Do you think he's a plant?"

"What the boy said was phenomenal and equally disturbing. Such a secret weapon could be devastating if it fell into the wrong hands. If one can build an android and modify it to slip into any society unnoticed to deliver a bomb—"

"On the flip side, couldn't one use these robots to take the place of real people?" Olivia asked.

"The software might not be that sophisticated yet," Mr. V said.

"However, Emerald brings up an excellent point," Mrs. B said. "If one wanted to replace a son or a daughter of a world leader and use them as a suicide bomber, one android could take down an entire government with ease."

"Robert doesn't want to do any of that. He wants to be human. To be free," Nadia said.

"His original programming must have a bug, something that's rewritten parts of his operating system," Mr. V said.

"So what?" Emma asked. "He has free will now. Does that not mean anything?"

"This is a unique situation." Mrs. B relaxed as she thought about it. "Robert is the most sophisticated intelligence device ever conceived by man. So we must assume that he could have been programmed to act this way in order to gain our confidence and gather intelligence. Therefore, we should keep him here as a precaution while we decide what the next step is."

"Will you send him back?" Nadia asked.

"We need to find out who owns Robert first. If he's indeed missing, those owners will want him back very badly," Mrs. B said. "Can you ask Robert to join us, please?"

Aardvark departed the limo. A few minutes later, the rear passenger door opened and Robert climbed inside, choosing to sit next to Nadia.

Mrs. B smiled. "I have a proposal for you, Robert. If you promise to stay here with the girls, I promise that my organization will help you in your current situation."

Robert checked with Nadia. She nodded.

"I accept your proposal," he said. "However, I am still curious. What organization do you work for?"

"Let's discuss that at another time. Right now, all that matters is your safekeeping. The Gems will now be at your side twenty-four seven, as the Americans like to say."

Robert looked confused.

"The Gems. That's our nickname, love," Olivia said.

"I can explain that to you later also." Nadia turned to Mrs. B. "What do we do about school?"

Mrs. B considered that. "Aardvark, contact FO division. We'll have to set this young man up with a fake identity so he can go to school." Mrs. B then addressed the girls. "I want one of you to always be with Robert if possible. I'll see if we can get him into as many of your classes as we can."

CHAPTER 14

The next morning, Nadia slipped inside the West Berkeley High School administration office, where the fluorescent lights revealed a row of plastic chairs. Nadia chose one and smiled politely at the lady behind the front desk. Nadia had only been here one other time and that was a month ago when Emma's grandmother had brought the Gems here to enroll.

"Can I help you, dear?" the woman behind the desk asked.

"Ah, yes," Nadia said. "My mother is furious. She told me to wait here because she wants to speak with the principal about the religious bigotry at this school."

The woman's happy face melted. "Oh, I see. Best wait for Mr. Summers, then. He should be in shortly."

Nadia had ad-libbed that last part. However, it felt good to say it out loud rather then keeping it all inside every time she visited her locker.

A few students filtered in and out of the office while Nadia waited. She wondered if Mrs. B and Robert got lost, because the first bell would soon be—

Finally her two contacts walked inside the office. Robert flashed her a smile. However, Nadia averted her eyes. They weren't supposed to know each other yet.

"Can I help you?" the woman behind the desk asked.

"My grandson is starting school today. We were told to come here to get his schedule."

Nadia was impressed. Mrs. B's Midwestern American accent was flawless.

"How nice. What's your name, young man?" the woman asked.

"It's Robert Billings," he said.

"Billings, as in Montana?"

"I do not understand."

"Yes, Billings, like Montana," Mrs. B said.

The woman entered the information into a computer. "And when did you complete enrollment?"

"We completed it online last night. Robert's birth certificate and transcripts were submitted also. I hope we did everything correctly. We followed all the directions."

"Here it is." The woman studied the screen. "Everything is filled out correctly, and the system has generated Robert's semester schedule based on his transcript."

"Computers are so amazing," Mrs. B said.

"You know, I remember when we used to have to type every student's schedule into the system by hand. Now the computer does it all." The woman rolled her chair over to the printer, took the piece of paper, and gave it to Robert. "That's your schedule. I also sent a copy to your email address and a text to your phone listed on the enrollment forms."

"Thank you," Mrs. B said. "One last thing, is there a student here that could show my grandson the ropes? He's very shy, but very nice when you get to know him."

Nadia knew it was her cue.

"Oh, well, we don't usually assign students to newly enrolled —"

"I don't mind showing your grandson around." Nadia stood up from her chair. "I remember when I was new at this school and didn't know anyone."

"Oh, that's so sweet of you," the woman at the desk said. "But what about your mother? Don't you have to wait for her?"

Nadia pretended to glance at her phone. "She's not coming. I apologize. My mom does this all the time. She gets angry and tells me she'll do something, only to forget about it when she calms down. Please tell Mr. Summers not to worry."

"Oh good." The woman seemed relieved. "I mean, I'll tell him that."

Mrs. B hugged Robert. "I know it's a new school, but be brave my, little Robbie."

Nadia did her best not to laugh.

"Yes. I will be brave for you...Grandmother." Robert said.

Mrs. B kissed him on the cheek before turning to Nadia. "Thank you so much for showing him around. Here's my phone number in case he gets into trouble."

The woman at the desk rolled her eyes.

Nadia accepted the piece of paper. "Let me show you around, Robert."

Nadia didn't have too much time before first hour, so she guided Robert down the hallway and showed him where her locker was. She then studied his schedule. At least one of the Gems was in every class except gym.

"You'll have to be careful during this class, Robert," she said. "You should observe what the human boys are doing in gym and mimic them. However, don't outperform them. It will call attention to your uniqueness. Do you understand?"

"Yes. My mission is to fit in with the students."

"That's right."

"I am looking forward to this. It will help me understand humans my age." Robert tilted his head. "We have home economics and American government together, do we not?"

"Yes, we do."

"Tell me, how does home economics differ from standard Keynesian economics?"

Nadia thought about it. "We learn to bake cookies."

The first bell rang.

Nadia and Robert went to home economics class. As the teacher explained how to balance a checkbook, Nadia caught all the girls in class checking Robert out. When the boy noticed, he smiled, but had no clue why they were looking at him. He was focused on taking notes about opening a bank account. One brave girl leaned over and offered him some chewing gum. Robert thanked her and put the gum in his pocket. It was obvious to Nadia that he didn't know what gum was used for.

When the bell rang, Nadia handed Robert off to Miyuki, who shared English composition class with him. As Miyuki and Robert traveled down the hallway, Nadia saw more girls sneaking curious peeks at Robert. Whoever created Robert had designed him to fit in to a crowd, not stand out. However, those adults (probably all men) had given the boy those striking green eyes, not realizing that such gorgeous eyes drew in teenage girls like kitty cats to a tuna buffet.

Nadia saw more evidence of this during her third-hour American government class. When the lunch bell rang, many of the girls surrounded Robert and bombarded him with questions. To their bewilderment, Robert slipped away from their obvious admiration to discuss the American legislative branch with the teacher, who was quite happy to engage on the subject.

At lunch, Nadia led Robert into the commons area, where Miyuki and Olivia had already snatched their normal table.

"How's your day so far?" Olivia asked Robert.

Robert told her how much he enjoyed all three of his classes. "Everyone was quite friendly."

"All the *girls* were quite friendly," Nadia corrected.

"That happened in our class too," Miyuki said.

Robert held up the piece of gum and examined it.

"Who gave you that?" Emma asked as she sat down, arriving late to lunch.

"A girl did," Nadia added.

"Sounds like the ladies will be a problem," Olivia said. "It's those eyes of his."

"They made them too nice, didn't they?" Nadia asked.

"Why are my eyes too nice?" Robert asked.

"Don't get us wrong, love. They're lovely eyes," Olivia said. "But they make you stand out too much."

"In an inappropriate way?"

"Not at all," Miyuki said. "The girls see you as hot."

"But I am not hot. My core temperature is normal," Robert said.

"She means you're highly attractive," Olivia said. "To the other girls."

"You officially the handsome and mysterious new boy at school," Miyuki added.

"Exactly."

"Well, we can fix that problem." Emma stood up and offered her hand to Robert. "Come, order lunch with me." She wiggled her fingers.

Robert stood up and held her hand. Emma's huge smile and baby-doe eyes stuck themselves on to Robert and wouldn't let go as she strutted across the commons area with him, parading the boy in front of everyone. Next, she placed Robert's arm around her own neck, letting his hand droop in front of her chest. Emma was so close to Robert that she was basically wearing him like a coat.

The message it sent was clear. This was Emma's boy and everyone else had better stay away.

Emma and Robert ordered lunch together. They even shared a tray, which Robert carried as they made their way back across the commons area.

Nadia was angry. Why didn't Emma ask one of the other Gems if they wanted to volunteer to be Robert's girlfriend? Why did the girl just assume she was the best candidate for the job? Did she assume that none of the other Gems were pretty enough?

To put an exclamation point on her performance, Emma gave Robert a long kiss on the cheek before sitting down at their table. Emma crossed her legs and sat back with confidence.

"Problem solved," she said.

"Was that really necessary?" Nadia asked.

Emma observed the room. "Hey, it worked, didn't it? Now the girls won't bother Robert anymore because they think he's with me."

Nadia wanted to slap Emma. The girl was so arrogant. Flaunting herself like a chocolate fountain. She was just sick of this girl.

"I am not sure I understand. What does *with me* actually mean?" Robert asked.

"The girls saw you with Emma, so now they think you two are dating," Miyuki said.

"Dating, that is like a bonding ritual, is it not?"

Emma laughed. "It only means that a boy and girl are developing a relationship together. You know, getting to know each other. Well, it could also be a boy and a boy. Or a girl and a girl. Romantic relationships are complicated, Robert. Maybe it's best you don't know too much about them."

CHAPTER 15

Robert's first week at school was uneventful. With the Gems' help, Robert slipped into the school's normal routine with ease. Nadia was amazed how fast he could learn. Robert would tackle every new subject like a hungry bear, not only reading the chapter that was assigned for class, but the entire book itself. Then he would search the web for more books on the topic and download them into his android brain. But what worried Nadia was that Robert was such a voracious learner that he was drawing attention from the other kids at school. Or in their eyes, trying to be better than them.

Since Robert was settled in, Nadia now focused on helping Olivia with her major problem.

At first period lunch, Nadia encouraged Olivia to friend Lewis on Facebox. This passive act would give Olivia a sign. If Lewis took a long time to approve her, that meant he wasn't that into her. An outright refusal to accept was certain death. However, Lewis approved Olivia within five minutes.

"He's quick and decisive. I like that." Olivia smiled. It was the brightest smile Nadia had ever seen from her best friend.

"So you do like him," Nadia said.

Olivia blushed. "He's alright."

"Who's alright?" Emma asked, arriving at the lunch table with Robert holding her hand, their boyfriend-girlfriend ruse still in effect.

Olivia shot Nadia a look that she knew too well. *This is between us.*

Nadia agreed. "I was saying that I thought Neil deGrasse Tyson was cute for an older man, and Olivia agreed."

Olivia gave her a wink.

"Who?" Emma asked.

Nadia didn't feel like explaining it to her. But Robert did.

"Neil de Grasse Tyson is a highly regarded astrophysicist and cosmologist who was born in New York City in the year 1958—"

"I've never heard of him," Emma said.

"That's not surprising," Nadia said under her breath.

"Don't act like I'm stupid. I know the name of every New York hairstylist that's worth knowing, and I've never heard of this Neil guy, so he can't be all that good."

Olivia laughed and clapped her hands. "Neil deGrasse Tyson is a *cosmologist.* A scientist who studies planets and space. Not a *cosmetologist,* you twit."

Nadia pressed her hand against her mouth, but still couldn't help but laugh at the image of Neil deGrasse Tyson coloring someone's hair.

Robert tilted his head. "Ah, I see the humor. Emma accidentally transposed the words *cosmolo*—"

"It was an honest mistake," Emma interrupted, her cheeks turning red. "Of course I know the difference between a cosmetologist and a cosmopolitan—"

"Cosmologist," Olivia corrected with a grin.

Emma shut up and crossed her arms.

Miyuki didn't laugh or frown. Her face was stoic as the girl said nothing.

Nadia suddenly felt guilty. Maybe they were being too cruel towards Emma.

Olivia kept her smile and watched the cafeteria.

Robert observed the table with fascination. "Can I make an observation?"

"Not now, Robert, please?" Nadia asked.

"Look, he's coming over." Olivia straightened up her posture and touched her hair.

Nadia noted Lewis approaching the table with his usual casualness.

"Yo, what's up?" he asked.

"Nothing," Olivia said.

"Hi, Lewis," Nadia said.

Lewis nodded. He then glanced over at Robert. "New kid at school?"

"I am not a kid. I am seventeen years old."

"Yeah, he's a new fish," Olivia said. "Kind of quirky, but we like him."

Robert seemed confused over the fish comment, but said nothing.

"Already sitting with the sexist girls in school. Lucky guy," Lewis said.

Robert's confusion deepened.

"Are you jealous?" Olivia asked.

Lewis acted too cool. "I'd be lying if I said no."

"Emma and I are engaged in courtship," Robert said.

Emma sighed. "We're dating, Robbie. Courtship is for old people."

Lewis took that in. "So you're dating someone, huh?"

Emma straightened. "Yes."

"Interesting," he said.

"Why is that interesting?"

Lewis smiled. "Goes against your reputation, doesn't it?"

Olivia leaned in. "What reputation does she have?"

"Lewis," Emma warned.

"Yo, I'm only saying that when Emma first came to West Berk, she shot down every guy brave enough to ask her out. They dubbed her the ice queen."

"Sounds like the girl we know," Olivia said.

Emma fired her a look.

"She isn't a cold person," Miyuki said.

"Thank you, friend." Emma smiled.

"Don't get me wrong, Emma," Lewis said. "In theater and choir, you're chill, like, in a good way. But last semester you gotta admit...you didn't mix with anyone. Even the girls felt this 'I'm too good for you' vibe coming from you."

"My father had just died. I was going through a lot of shit back then. So excuse me if I didn't kiss everyone's butt."

"And there she is," Olivia said.

"Shut up, you bitch." Emma glared. "You have no idea what it's like to have both of your parents dead."

An uneasy silence formed around the table.

Nadia's heart reached out to Emma. She didn't know what losing a parent was like, but knew it would devastate her too. Sometimes Nadia wished Olivia would restrain herself from picking at people's vulnerabilities.

Miyuki offered Emma a supporting smile and a hug, but the girl stood up and left the table.

Lewis drank some chocolate milk from his bottle, then glanced down at Robert. "Shouldn't you go comfort your woman?"

Robert blinked. "Ah, you mean give my girlfriend support after her emotional outburst." Robert stood up. "I will now go soothe my woman back into social conformity."

Lewis watched the boy leave as he shook his head in disbelief. "That dude is the most vanilla cream I've ever seen. Is he for real?"

"He's for real," Olivia said. "Raised in a cult."

"No shit?" Lewis asked. "Crazy."

"We're trying to expose him to the real world. You know, get him used to normal people."

"For sure," Lewis said. "You girls like soccer? We're playing North Oakland tonight. Could use the support."

"We might come by," Olivia said. "If we're not too busy being sexy."

Lewis cracked a smile. His eyes lingered on Olivia for a moment. "Tell Emma she can even bring her goofy boyfriend too." Lewis finished up his chocolate milk and tossed it in the trash can. "Later."

As he left the table, Olivia's eyes followed.

Miyuki held her hand over her mouth and giggled. "You like him big time."

Nadia knew better. Her best friend didn't just like Lewis. She *wanted* him.

* * *

The high school football field glowed through the darkness. It was composed of three simple steel grandstands, two on either side of the field, and one sharing an end zone. Two large soccer goals were posted on both end zones with their white pipes and netting.

Nadia watched the players going through their soccer drills. She was jealous. She had enjoyed playing football, or what the Americans here called soccer, while she was in England. Nadia thought she wasn't that bad of a forward. There was a girls' soccer team here at school, but Nadia had been so busy with the Gems and school that she hadn't had time to check them out.

Olivia handed her a cup. "Believe it or not, they actually had tea. So I got us both one."

"Excellent. Thank you." Nadia held the cup of tea and blew steam off the top. She watched Lewis as he bounced a soccer ball on his head with skill. His slender, but athletic body could be seen through his uniform. Maybe Nadia could forgive him for being an atheist.

"What are you smiling about, love?" Olivia asked her.

Nadia sipped her hot tea. "Nothing. I miss playing the game."

"You're a damn good forward. You should ask Lewis about joining the girls' team."

"Do you think so?"

"Why not?"

Lewis dropped his ball on the ground and kicked it away to a teammate. He noticed the girls and jogged over to the sidelines. "What's up?"

"Nothing," Olivia said.

Lewis made a face. "You're an Arsenal fan?"

Nadia glanced down at Olivia's soccer jersey. It had a big old cannon on the front of it with the words Arsenal floating above it. That's right. She recalled that both Arsenal and Manchester United played in the English Premier football league. They were also bitter enemies.

"You got a problem with my team, mate?" Olivia said with a playful smirk.

Lewis grinned. "I do."

Olivia leaned her body towards him. "What ya gonna do about it?"

A pause between them. Both sizing the other up. But in a playful way.

Lewis laughed. "I got nothing now."

Olivia smiled.

"Appreciate you coming," Lewis said. "Where's Emma and Goofy?"

Now Olivia laughed.

Nadia tried not to. She pointed over to the grandstand where Emma, Robert, and Miyuki sat in the eighth row along with pockets of kids and parents.

"Tell her I'm glad she came," Lewis said. "If she doesn't still hate me."

"Think she's more cross with me than you," Olivia said.

The game started twenty minutes later. While Olivia watched every move Lewis made on the field, Robert asked Nadia some general questions about soccer. Miyuki had found an ice cream shack and pigged out on a giant waffle cone while Emma concentrated on her phone.

"Since you are a supporter of science," Robert began, "do you read much science fiction?"

Nadia stopped watching the game. "I've read some, but not as much as I would like."

"Recently I began stepping inside the school library in between classes to read books."

"In between classes?" Nadia asked.

"I can visually scan a book in ten minutes, depending on length," Robert said. "Have you read any of Asimov's books?"

Robert was speaking Nadia's language. "Isaac Asimov? Yes, I've read his Foundation series."

"I just read two of his books from that series. Quite intriguing."

"You might be interested in reading Asimov's Robot series. They're wonderful, Robert, and you might gain some insight on—"

"Seriously? You read a novel in ten minutes?" Emma interrupted. She leaned forward to talk around Miyuki, who needed a napkin.

"Yes." Robert shifted his attention to Emma. "You might be interested to know that I have also read a romance novel."

"No way. Which one did you read?" Emma asked.

"It was called *The Notebook*."

"Oh my God, I love that book."

Nadia was so mad she wanted to spit. Here she was having a wonderful conversation with Robert about a subject they were both interested in, and now here came Emma to mess it all up. Why couldn't Emma have stayed home? The girl obviously didn't care about soccer or science fiction.

Nadia opened her purse and took out her travel Kleenex pack. She took a few sheets of Kleenex and offered them to Miyuki, who gave Nadia a deep nod of thanks as she cleaned her face. At least Miyuki appreciated her existence.

"Do you have a boyfriend, Emma?" Robert asked.

"You mean besides you?"

"That is only a ruse. Do you have an actual boyfriend?"

Emma adjusted her posture and crossed those perfect legs of hers. "Well, yes and no," she began. "I thought he would be my boyfriend at first, but he turned out to be a real jerk." She went on and told him about Ryan Raymond and his dark secret that almost got all of the Gems blown up inside a large seed-storage facility deep inside a Norwegian mountain. Nadia didn't like snow, and she never wanted to go to Scandinavia or Alaska ever again.

When the horn sounded for halftime, Olivia stood up. "I'm peckish for a sandwich. Anyone want anything?"

Nadia was tempted to go with her to vent privately about Emma, yet she wasn't quick enough as Olivia began hopping down the steps of the grandstand.

"What attracts Olivia to Lewis?" Robert asked.

"I think it's the way he carries himself," Emma said. "Lewis has a confident swagger about him."

"Olivia thinks he's handsome," Nadia added.

"I did try to set Lewis up with this one." Emma pointed her thumb at Nadia. "But it didn't work."

"Do you not find this boy handsome?" Robert asked Nadia.

"It wasn't that—must we discuss this now?"

"She didn't like him because he's a godless heathen," Emma said.

Nadia tensed up. Why did Emma bring that up?

Robert tilted his head. "You were not attracted to this Lewis because he does not share the same views about religion?"

"He follows no religion. There's a difference," Nadia answered.

"You do not like people who do not believe in God?"

"I never said that. I just don't trust people who don't believe in God."

"I am ignorant on the subject of religion, so I can not attach myself to any such belief. Do you not trust me, then?" Robert asked.

Nadia paused. She didn't mean it like that. "You don't understand religion yet. I understand that and will not judge you for it."

"You didn't answer his question, Nadia," Emma said. "Do you trust him?"

"Do you?" Nadia shot back, forcing her hand down on the metal bleacher in an effort to keep it from flying across Emma's face.

Emma eased back with caution as Robert waited patiently for an answer.

"I do," Emma said finally.

"Then I do too," Nadia answered.

After that awkward moment passed, Emma changed the subject by explaining the romance genre to Robert and some of its basic plot lines of girl meets boy, girl hates boy, girl forgives boy, and so on. Nadia watched Emma's face glow as she explained something she enjoyed talking about. She looked more relaxed. More confident. More attractive. Robert took in the information she was giving him; like always, the boy was fascinated to learn. Nadia only wished she were the one he was fascinated with.

Wait a moment, was she becoming jealous over a robot?

Nadia's eyes drifted over to Robert. His appearance and the way he spoke was like a boy. Yet she remembered that scan Mr. V had showed them in the limo. All those wires and fiber-optic lines. The carbon-fiber bones. The carbon-fiber rib cage that formed its chest. The small processing unit that was its brain.

Robert wasn't human.

Robert was a machine, made by man.

Falling in love with a machine was unnatural and could even be seen as immoral.

Nadia shook away her thoughts as Olivia returned to the grandstand with a burger wrapped in foil.

"Just received a text from Mrs. B," Olivia said. "She wants us to meet her after school tomorrow."

CHAPTER 16

Friday after school, Nadia found herself deep underground at Authority headquarters again. Mrs. B greeted the Gems and escorted them back to the fake jungle, where they entered a different green pod and sat inside. The pod closed, and the code of silence mode was activated with a hum.

"Judging by the progress reports Emerald has sent me," Mrs. B said, "Robert is fitting in quite well at school. Do any of you have anything to add?"

"He's amazing," Miyuki said. "Learns so quickly."

"Robert's observational skills are superior to humans," Nadia said. "He's able to pick up the routine of school very easily."

"He's made lots of friends. Especially the girls," Emma said. "They love how he just listens to everything they say."

"I can see why he'd make such a good spy operative," Olivia said. "He's quiet and soaks up his environment like a paper towel."

"Do you think he's a plant?" Mrs. B said, still dead serious.

"Robert's asked zero questions about the Authority. He's more focused on learning stuff at school, ma'am."

"I see." Mrs. B glanced away, her mind still deep in thought. "Well, there's a new wrinkle in Robert's situation. I made a few discreet inquiries to my counterpart at the FBI, and he wants to meet."

"Do you think they know we have Robert?" Olivia asked.

"We're unsure at this point. Nevertheless, we've arranged a public meet and greet that I'd like you girls to observe."

"The FBI?" Emma asked. "Won't they arrest us all for being spies?"

"Don't be daft," Olivia scoffed.

"Her question is a valid one, Emerald," Mrs. B said. "In the 1930s, when the Authority was still a young organization, it had to rely on discreet alliances with others before it could effectively build up its own worldwide intelligence network. The earliest alliance was with the founder of the American FBI, J. Edgar Hoover. The Authority would supply the FBI with domestic and international intelligence in exchange for certain considerations. One was for tolerating our operations that occurred on American soil."

"Okay. I think I understand," Emma said. "What about the CIA? Do they tolerate us too?"

Mrs. B frowned. "I'm afraid the CIA is different, my dear."

* * *

Early Saturday afternoon Nadia and the Gems took a nice walk through Montrose city park. Bordering the major playground were a half dozen food trucks parked in a semicircle near a group of wood-planked picnic tables. One truck had large illustrations of street tacos painted on its sides.

Olivia stepped up to the service window. The large man inside had a curly beard wrapped up in a protective hairnet. Nadia reasoned the hairnet was probably a state health department requirement.

Hairnet man slid the window open. "Yeah?"

"Hey, your flipping tacos just gave me the runs. I want my money back," Olivia said.

"We don't do refunds."

"That's bonkers. I want to speak to the owner, then."

The man looked her over. "He's around back."

Olivia walked around the back of the truck. There was a side door that popped open, and the Gems squeezed inside the taco truck.

Inside was a dimly lit and cramped room full of surveillance equipment. Two men sat with headphones as they scanned a row of small digital monitors. Aardvark was there too, sitting on his knees because he was too tall to stand up. He nodded to the girls.

"This is so cool," Miyuki said.

"Please tell me they serve real tacos," Emma said. "The smell is making me so hungry."

Aardvark knocked on a small metal door, which slid open. He gestured toward it.

"Sweet." Emma poked her face through the slot. "Hi there! Two chicken tacos with guacamole please."

Miyuki bent down too. "May I have two beef tacos with your hottest salsa?"

"Want any tacos?" Emma asked the other Gems.

"We're supposed to be observing, not stuffing our flipping faces," Olivia said.

Aardvark froze in mid-bite. Feeling guilty, the large man put his half-eaten taco away in the trash. Aardvark then pointed out a man showing up on one monitor. He was playing with a drone.

"That would be an FBI guy," one of the two surveillance men said.

Olivia took a peek. "He's picking up the conversation through a wireless mic antenna inside that drone, isn't he?"

"Most likely," the surveillance man said. "And he'll have a camera too."

Emma now looked. "Wouldn't Mrs. B want you to disable that FBI drone before her meeting?"

"Violates our agreement," Olivia said. "We don't interfere, so they don't interfere."

"Mrs. B is in play," the surveillance man said.

One of the cameras focused on a minivan, which rolled into an empty space in the parking lot. It zoomed in on the driver. Mrs. B climbed out of the vehicle and casually walked into the park. Mrs. B then followed a sidewalk as it passed a grassy field where some people were playing Frisbee while others lay on towels to soak up the sun.

The man with the drone watched his device as it drifted back and forth across the sky.

On a lone bench there was a man eating his lunch. He wore a tie and a lanyard with his company badge hanging loosely around his neck while his suit jacket hung over the back of the bench.

The surveillance man boosted the audio. The Gems could hear the wind in the background as the man with the tie crumpled up the plastic wrap that came with his lunch and tossed it on the ground.

"You'll get a ticket for that, Ed, especially in San Francisco." Mrs. B sat next to him on the bench.

"I've got bigger things to worry about," Ed, or the man with the tie, said. "Do you have it?"

"What *it* would you be referring to?"

"The drone. The one missing from Nevada. Do you have it?"

"Does that *it* look like a teenage boy?"

"So you do have him?"

"Who's missing him?" she asked.

Ed smiled to himself. "You show me your cards; then I'll show you mine."

Mrs. B waited for a moment. "We know where he is."

"So you have him under control?"

"Yes, he's under control."

Ed released a deep breath and relaxed. "The Pentagon and the Joint Chiefs are very concerned. This is an important military project, and the drone is a valuable piece of equipment." Ed glanced at Mrs. B. "The CIA was concerned that foreign intelligence services would try to capture the drone. But they still won't be happy that you have it either."

"Don't worry. We haven't disassembled him to learn all his secrets," Mrs. B said. "Not yet anyway."

Ed watched some kids on the playground. "I'll ask you this politely. We'd like you to hand over the drone so we may deliver it back to the Army where it belongs."

"Has the US Army gone to the trouble of asking the boy if he wants to become a soldier? Their 'drone' has become quite self-aware."

Ed looked at her. "The army said that was a malfunction. The drone's original programming is to fit into a population and gather military intelligence for Special Forces and other recon units. To spare the army from using actual human beings on such dangerous missions."

"Such a drone could also be used by the CIA as a suicide bomber to assassinate people in power."

"I have no knowledge of that." Ed sighed and held a long look. "Laura, the drone is malfunctioning. You can't use it as an operative in its current state, and if you try to rip it apart to see how it works, you'll piss a lot of people off. People who can and will shut down your North American operations. People I can't stop. Do we understand each other?"

Mrs. B thought about his proposal.

"Fine," she said. "Let's set up a time and place for delivery, then."

"That's all I ask," Ed said as he stood up and walked away from the bench.

Mrs. B waited a moment, then walked off the opposite way. She climbed into the cramped food truck.

"Any problems on this end?" she asked.

"No, ma'am, we heard everything," Olivia said.

"How can we give him back?" Miyuki asked. "Robert doesn't want to go."

"If he goes back, will the Army reprogram him against his will?" Emma asked.

"He's their drone, Black Opal. They can do whatever they want to him," Mrs. B said.

Nadia didn't say anything, yet she agreed that Robert should have a choice.

"Is there anything we can do to help him, ma'am?" Olivia asked.

"The Authority was formed to defend humanity and to protect the innocent," Mrs. B said. "But we're not a country. Robert can't seek political asylum inside our organization. He's the property of the United States Army, and because of our relationship with the FBI, we must give him back if they request it. I'm sorry. There isn't much else I can do."

"But he doesn't want to go back," Miyuki said.

"I understand his feelings, Ruby, but I'm afraid they're irrelevant," Mrs. B said. "Your orders are to go home and take Robert out for a ride. Don't tell him anything. Once I finalize the drop location with the FBI, I'll give it to you, and you'll take Robert straight there."

"Yes, ma'am," Olivia said. "What if he finds out and resists?"

Mrs. B nodded to Aardvark, who handed Olivia a Taser gun. "EQ division modified this Taser gun specifically for Robert. It will scramble his programming while leaving his circuits intact. Only use it if it's absolutely necessary."

"Using that device may damage his programming," Nadia said. "He might lose his ability to be self-aware."

"As I said, Sapphire, only use if it's absolutely necessary."

"Why does it matter?" Emma asked. "Once we give him to the Army, they'll erase that programming anyway, won't they?"

"Wipe him out," Miyuki added.

Nadia hung on Miyuki's words. Everything that made Robert

unique would be gone. The way he looked at the world. His hunger for learning. His curiosity about humans. The way he spoke. The way he listened. The way he became almost like a real human being.

In a sense, the Gems would be taking Robert to his hangman's noose.

The sun hovered over the horizon as Nadia and the Gems headed back home to Berkeley.

Over the Oakland Bay Bridge, Emma drove the Mercedes in the slow lane, as if she didn't want to make it home until Christmas.

"Robert can't help that he's different," Miyuki added.

"This isn't right," Emma said. "We promised to help him."

"We must do what's expected of us," Nadia said with her forehead against the cool window, her heart conflicted, but her mind clear.

"That's right. Mrs. B gave us an order," Olivia said. "One way or the other, Robert must go back."

"No, I won't do it," Miyuki said.

Emma glanced up at the rearview mirror. "We're supposed to be defending humanity, right? As far as I'm concerned, Robert is human. The Army will no doubt reprogram Robert and force him to kill anyway, so how is that not against his will? How is that not harming him?"

"He's still only a robot," Olivia said.

"Android," Miyuki corrected.

"Robert is more than that," Emma said. "He's grown a conscience. He thinks for himself. He wants to help others. He's not someone's property."

"What's the point of discussing it?" Olivia asked. "We have our orders."

"Yes, the decision has been made," Nadia said.

"I request to be dropped off. I refuse to help deceive Robert," Miyuki said.

When the Mercedes reached the other side of the bridge, Emma pulled the car over and stopped. "I'm not helping either."

Olivia's back stiffened. "You both swore an oath. The Authority expects you to carry out the orders of your superiors."

"As you like to say, Olivia, piss off." Miyuki crossed her arms.

"So you don't think this is wrong? Seriously?" Emma asked.

Nadia pulled away from the window. "Olivia is right. It's not our place to question orders."

"Alright," Olivia said. "Say, for instance, we do refuse to bring Robert in. All Mrs. B has to do is send an armed retrieval team to Emma's house and take Robert away by force. Then we'd all get in huge amounts of trouble. Maybe even get kicked out of the Authority."

"We should be the ones who take him in," Nadia said. "However, since we are his friends, we at least owe Robert the truth before we do that. Don't you think?"

"Mrs. B said we can't. Besides, Robert will try to run if we do."

Nadia knew Olivia was right.

"Then he runs," Emma said.

"You do realize that if he runs, Mrs. B will order us to catch him," Olivia said.

A thought made Emma's lips bend into a grin. "Yeah, but who's to say that we have to try that hard?"

Miyuki smiled. "I like how you think, Emma."

CHAPTER 17

When Nadia and the Gems arrived at the house, they found Emma's grandmother and Robert in the backyard, sitting around the unlit fire pit, having a deep conversation about nineteenth-century literature.

Emma's grandmother laid her hand on Robert's arm to make a point. "Tolstoy was interested in how a man kept his morality when he faced an imperfect and evil world."

Robert soaked in that little nugget of knowledge. "Yes, I understand now. Thank you. I would also like to discuss *Crime and Punishment*." Robert noted the girls' presence with a wave.

"*Crime and Punishment* was the best crime thriller ever written," Emma's grandmother said.

"Yes, I was interested in the protagonist of that book. The way he feels after he kills the pawnbroker. The remorse and self-loathing. If I ever took a life, I think that is how I would feel."

Emma's grandmother flashed him a warm smile. "And that is what it feels to be human, Robert."

Robert turned towards the Gems. "Grandmother was kind enough to let me borrow a few books to read overnight while I charged."

"A few? I gave him twenty."

"I did read them slowly, analyzing their stories and characters not only for their overall story quality as pieces of literature, but also in relation to the historical worlds their characters would have inhabited if they were real."

"Could you excuse us for a moment?" Olivia told Emma's grandmother. "We'd like to talk to Robert alone, if you don't mind."

"I'll dig into my library and see if I can find you more books," Emma's grandmother said before she stepped inside the house.

The Gems sat around Robert.

"Something is troubling you all," he said. "May I ask what that is?"

The Gems exchanged looks.

Nadia knew they had to do this, yet she took no pleasure from it.

Olivia flashed Robert a smile. "We're off to get some coffee. Would you like to come with?"

"Yes, I would." Robert stood up and was ready to go without hesitation.

He was unaware that they were lying to him.

Emma started the Mercedes and backed it out of the driveway. Soon they were driving out of the neighborhood with Miyuki in the front seat while Robert was squeezed in between Olivia and Nadia. The seat selection wasn't a coincidence.

Emma took a left turn at the next light.

"You are all quiet," Robert said. "I have noted that human females are seldom this way for such long periods of time. Does my male appearance bother or interrupt your normal social interactions with each other?"

"We don't have much to say right now. That's all," Olivia said with hesitation.

Nadia felt so sick inside. Part of her knew Robert was good. Even if he was a machine, he acted better than most humans she had ever met. She loved how patient and quiet he was. How easy it was to talk to him about science or computers. It was refreshing to be able to talk to someone who was fascinated about the same subjects that she was. Deep down, Robert was a survivor who wanted to improve himself. This was something Nadia could easily identify with. She had survived living on the street and keeping her family together, and she also wanted to use the opportunity the Authority gave her to improve herself and to help people who had no one to fight for them. Now Robert had no one to fight for him. He wouldn't get a chance like Nadia had.

However, rules were rules, and Nadia knew the importance of following them. When one abandoned the rules, a person risked losing everything they had. Perhaps even their soul.

Emma took a right turn.

"Are we driving to another location? Your favorite Kaffee

Cadre is located at 301 S. Easton. We are traveling in the opposite direction. Emma, have you made a navigational error?"

Emma glanced in the rearview mirror at Robert.

"Robert, we have to—"

"I'll tell him," Nadia said, interrupting Olivia. If it must be done, she wanted the responsibility to fall on her.

"Alright, love," Olivia said.

Nadia gathered her courage and swallowed down her guilt. "We have orders to take you back home."

"Home to Nevada?" Robert asked.

Olivia presented the Taser and aimed it at Robert's stomach. "This Taser gun has been modified. It will scramble your programming and shut you down, but only if you resist us, Robert."

He sat there for a moment. "My apologies if I have not expressed my desire to be human strongly enough. That place in Nevada does not want me to be human. They want me to lie. To betray. To kill. To murder human beings. I do not wish to become that."

Nadia's hand wandered over to grip his. She couldn't help herself.

Robert continued. "If it is a question of logistics, I could become someone's long-lost brother or friend or relative. Your organization created an excellent false identity for me. Why can I not continue to use it?"

"I'm so sorry, Robert," Nadia said. "Mrs. B is not allowed to help you anymore, and that means we're not allowed to help you."

Robert cupped her hand in his. "Nadia, I want the chance to find out what I want to be. Your plans about going to college and studying science intrigue me. That is a path I would like to explore for myself."

"I wish I could let you do that. I really do."

"You promised to help me. Did you all lie?"

"When we said that, it wasn't a lie," Nadia said. "We had every intention of helping you."

"But things change," Olivia said. "It's not how we wanted it to end. But this is how it will end."

"May I make a request?" Robert asked.

"Of course," Nadia said.

"Please pull over and let me go. I will not trouble you ever again."

"We can't do that, Robert," Olivia said.

Emma jerked the car over and hit the brakes hard.

"What are you doing? Keep driving," Olivia said.

Emma glared through the rearview mirror.

"That's an order, Emma."

"You could let me go here and then make up a story. Something that would satisfy your Mrs. B and keep your loyalty to your organization."

"He's right," Miyuki said. "We could tell Mrs. B he overpowered us."

"She'll see right through our excuses," Olivia said. "She's not stupid."

"We should let him go," Emma said.

"No. He's going back. Now drive the fricking car."

Emma crossed her arms and shook her head. No way.

"Miyuki, you drive."

"It's my car. No one drives it but me."

Olivia boiled. "I gave both of you an order."

Emma didn't budge. Neither did Miyuki.

Nadia felt Robert squeezing her hands.

"Do you agree with this decision?" Robert asked in a whisper. "Do you want to take me back?"

The pain inside Nadia swelled. She hated this.

There was a knock on Emma's window. It was a large man wearing a black shirt with the word POLICE printed across his chest in white.

"Bloody hell," Olivia said.

CHAPTER 18

Nadia could feel the tension inside the idling Mercedes as the policeman blocked the driver's window.

"What should I do?" Emma asked. "Floor it?"

"Too late for that now. See what he wants," Olivia said.

The window motor hummed as the glass went down.

"License and registration, please," the policeman said in a guarded way.

Olivia hid her Taser gun.

"Oh crap. I'm sorry, officer. I didn't see you pull up," Emma said. "Miyuki, can you get my registration? It's in the glove box."

Miyuki handed the registration over to Emma while she continued to search her purse. Finally she found her license and gave both items to the police officer.

By this time, Nadia had had a good look at the officer. His reddish cheeks were covered with pockmarks, as if his skin were made of granite. This police officer didn't wear any badge, nor did he have a gun belt full of equipment. Nadia knew that most uniformed policemen in America wore them. Was he an undercover officer? Nadia turned around and noticed a black SUV parked behind them. No blue or red lights were flashing to indicate an unmarked cruiser. Nadia found that strange.

The officer did a casual glance at Emma's paperwork before his eyes found Robert. "Please get out of the vehicle. All of you."

"Was I blocking traffic, sir?" Emma asked.

"I'll explain when you all get out of the car."

Emma and Miyuki opened their doors and climbed out. Next was Olivia. Then Nadia followed Robert out of the car. That was when Nadia saw three additional men exiting the SUV. These men wore black and had the word *police* across their chests. Again, none of them wore gun belts or radios.

She gestured her eyes towards the men, pointing them out to Olivia.

Her best friend stiffened and flashed Nadia a worried look.

Nadia agreed. This didn't feel right to her either.

"Officer, what did my friend do?" Olivia asked.

"Be quiet," the officer said.

"Why are you ordering us out of the car?"

"May I ask to see your badge?" Miyuki asked.

None of the men answered.

Emma got out her phone. "I'm calling 911."

The officer slapped it from her hand.

"Hey!"

One man produced handcuffs and snapped them around Robert's wrists.

"I'm the one who drove the car," Emma said. "Why aren't you asking me questions?"

Another man aimed some kind of metal wand towards Robert and activated it. Robert grimaced as the device pulled him towards it, almost like some kind of super magnet. Robert struggled against the handcuffs, yet couldn't pull his hands away or resist the power of the wand.

"Stop that," Olivia said. "You're hurting him."

"What are you doing?" Emma asked.

Olivia made a move towards Robert, and the four men reached in their pockets and drew guns on her.

Whoa. Olivia withdrew a few steps.

The four men fell back slowly towards their SUV with Robert in custody. If they didn't do something now, Robert would be gone.

Nadia remembered she had something in her pocket. Her fingers found the stick of lip balm. She held it tight in her hand and checked with Olivia.

"Tally ho?" Nadia asked.

It was an old phrase the British pilots used in World War Two when they engaged the German Air Force. Olivia's father had used it often around Nadia when she had spent that one summer in the United Kingdom.

"Afraid so, love," Olivia said.

Nadia pressed her thumb down three times on the lip balm and dropped it on the ground. The device popped and made a crazy whistling noise like a Fourth of July firecracker.

The men looked down at the object in surprise. It was just enough time for Olivia and Nadia to jump forward and sweep their legs under the two men standing nearest them. At the same time, Miyuki went airborne, twisting her body around and striking the pocked-faced man in the face with her foot. The man went down hard on the pavement.

Emma stood there for a moment, taking in what was happening. She then yelled like some crazy maniac and ran at the man with the wand device. Her leg went up and kicked him hard in the coconuts. The wand fell from his grasp and landed on the ground.

Emma picked it up. There was a button with a red light illuminated above it. She pressed it, and the light went off.

Robert ripped off the metal handcuffs like they were tissue paper. But he just stood there.

"Run, Robert! Run!" Emma yelled.

Robert nodded and took off like a sports car. Running at some incredible speed, faster than any human could run. Nadia couldn't help but stare. It was incredible. *He* was incredible.

One man near Olivia recovered. She kicked his gun away. But the goon switched to hand-to-hand combat, knocking away back kicks and body strikes from both Olivia and Miyuki. But Miyuki got in a strike that knocked the guy out cold.

Nadia looked around. Emma's man was still holding his coconuts in pain. Two men were down. The fourth man, the fake policeman with the pockmarked face, was near the SUV. He was on the phone and barking something loudly in Russian.

"Мальчик бежит. Возьми меня сейчас!"

Luckily for Nadia, she understood Russian.

"The boy is running. Pick me up now," he said.

A van roared into view and jumped the curb before stopping.

The pocked-faced man yelled at his comrades, *"Forget the stupid girls. We go after the boy."* He then jumped into the van.

The other men limped into the van, which burned rubber as it headed off.

"Did you catch any of that Russian gibberish, Nadia?" Olivia asked.

"They only care about getting Robert, not us," Nadia said.

"Get behind the wheel, love."

The girls ran to the Mercedes. Both Nadia and Emma stopped near the driver's door.

"This is my car," Emma said.

"Piss off," Olivia said. "This is a serious situation, so Nadia is driving. End of story."

Emma glared.

"Please, Emma," Nadia said. "Robert's in danger."

"Fine. I'll do this for Robert." Emma got in back with Miyuki as Olivia jumped into the passenger side.

Nadia slipped behind the wheel and started the Mercedes. She gave the car too much gas, making the end fishtail as the Mercedes roared forward. However, she adjusted and kept the car in control as she raced it along the street as fast as she dared. After cresting the top of the second hill, Nadia could see the van at the bottom. Luckily for them, it had stayed on the same road without turning off. If they could catch up to the van, they could catch up with Robert.

"Everyone, please secure your seat belt," Nadia said. "I must drive more aggressively now."

"Go for it," Olivia said.

"We have need for speed," Miyuki said with a grin.

"Don't hurt my car," Emma said.

Nadia pressed the gas and focused as she accelerated down the hill.

One car rolled in front of Nadia.

She calmly navigated around it while her tires squealed in protest.

Nadia darted in and out of the traffic, bouncing through openings as they opened up, then closed.

Red light.

She braked, checked the cross traffic, then rolled across the intersection illegally, telling herself she would stop at all yellow lights from now on to make up the difference.

At the top of the next hill, Nadia caught up with the van. However, Robert was way ahead of it. The van was struggling to keep up with the boy thanks to the evening traffic impeding them while Robert slipped in between cars.

"He run so fast," Miyuki said.

"How fast are you going?" Olivia asked.

Nadia checked the speedometer. Twice. She couldn't believe it.

"Sixty-five miles per hour."

The Gems couldn't believe it either.

Suddenly Robert veered off the surface road and ran down the on-ramp to the freeway.

"Is he daft?" Olivia asked. "He'll get himself killed on the motorway."

"Maybe he run faster than we know," Miyuki said.

The van rushed after the boy.

"Let's help him out," Olivia said. "Get us closer to them, Nads."

Nadia guided the car to the on-ramp and pressed her foot to the floor. On the highway, the AMG Mercedes howled as it closed the distance on the underpowered van. Nadia tried to pass on the left side, but the van swerved. The Mercedes jerked under the impact as car parts bounced across the highway.

"Hey, you assholes! This is my car," Emma yelled.

The van ignored her pleas. It smashed into them again. Emma's Mercedes shed more parts.

"My grandma's gonna be pissed," she said.

Another hit. Emma turned to see her back bumper tumbling down the highway.

"Is this considered road rage?" Emma asked.

"What?" Olivia asked.

"Doesn't car insurance cover road rage?"

Nadia tried to keep the Mercedes away from the center median, yet if the van kept knocking into them like that...

"Brakes!" Olivia yelled.

Nadia glanced at the van. Out the open window was a pocked-faced man with a gun.

Nadia hit the pedal, and the Mercedes dived out of the way as the gun fired. Sparks went everywhere as bullets ricocheted off the hood. The large Mercedes emblem flew off, leaving the naked stalk.

"Shit. Shit. Shit. I'm in so much trouble," Emma said.

The van was a few car lengths ahead. Nadia wondered what they could do now.

"Does anyone have their cosmetic kit?" Olivia asked.

"Yes," Miyuki said. "Forest Fire mascara?"

"Read my mind, love. If you please."

Miyuki handed Olivia the mascara.

"Let's try it again," Olivia said.

Nadia accelerated and caught up with the van again.

Just like last time, it veered toward them. The pocked-faced man pulled out his gun, ready to fire.

This time Olivia was ready. She flung the mascara through the van's open window.

The gun fired, sending Olivia down behind her door as bullets ripped off the rearview mirror and shattered Nadia's side window. She flinched and hit the brakes again, making the car dive away. It was then she noticed her hands were shaking on the wheel. That was too close. A few inches more and Nadia would be dead.

"You got them!" Miyuki said.

Nadia focused on the van, which was now slowing down because of all the smoke pouring out from the windows. Olivia's smoke bomb had worked. The men were sticking their heads out, trying to breathe.

This was their chance. Nadia held down the gas and the Mercedes surged forward on the highway, gaining distance from the stricken van, which now weaved erratically behind them. She glanced down. The speedometer climbed to eighty miles per hour.

Then eighty-five.

Ninety.

Robert was ahead of them. Still running hard.

One hundred.

One hundred ten.

Finally the Mercedes was closing on him.

Nadia held the car steady as she pulled up to Robert and yelled out from her shattered window, "Robert! Please stop running."

"I can't let you take me back," Robert yelled back.

He ran in between two slower cars, causing Nadia to pump her brakes. She weaved around one of the cars at a high rate of speed using the emergency lane. She could feel the Mercedes wanting to break away from her control, but it allowed her to thread the needle and continue the pursuit. Nadia caught up to Robert again, but traffic on the freeway was increasing.

"Don't do this," Nadia yelled out the window. "We'll think of something. You must give us more time."

Olivia pressed a button and the sunroof opened. She climbed through the opening and leaned over the roof towards Robert. "Keep this up and you'll get us all killed. Please stop running," she yelled.

Robert slowed down to eighty miles per hour. Maybe he was listening to them.

He then jumped high in the air and landed on top of a slow-moving flatbed truck trailer with bags of fertilizer strapped to it.

Nadia watched Robert's athletic feat with amazement. What could this boy not do?

The Mercedes automated collision alarm blared as it activated the brakes. Nadia snapped her attention to the front while the Mercedes skidded towards the back of a slow-moving oil tanker.

The Gems all screamed.

Nadia closed her eyes and cursed at herself for not paying attention. She was about to kill all her friends.

She waited.

And waited.

But where was the impact?

Nadia opened her eyes.

The Mercedes had stopped a few centimeters short of the oil tanker. She took in a deep breath and thanked Allah for sparing them. Olivia dropped down from the sunroof, holding her stomach. Luckily for her she didn't fly out.

There was a moment of silence throughout the car.

"Wow, that automatic brake system rocks," Emma said. "And to think Grandma didn't want to buy this car for me."

"You okay, Olivia?" Miyuki asked.

"My stomach hurts," she said. "Hit the edge of the flipping sunroof."

"That was stupid of me," Nadia said. "I became distracted—I could have killed us. I'm so—"

A warm hand rested on Nadia's cheek as Robert leaned through the shattered window.

"Are you hurt?" he asked.

"No," she said as butterflies circled her stomach.

"I heard the squeal of the brakes and realized the odds of surviving a high-speed impact with a full oil tanker were not too good for a frail human girl." Robert's lovely emerald eyes were soft and filled with concern. "If you suddenly ceased to exist, I would not like that."

Nadia's heart thumped faster and faster. She liked the way his fingers touched her cheek. Very delicate and soft.

"You hardly know me," Nadia said.

"I know enough to care," he said.

"Oh yeah, we're all fine too, by the way," Emma said.

The oil tanker in front of them moved forward. The traffic behind Nadia honked at her to go.

Olivia leaned over Nadia to speak out the window to Robert. "Now, would you please get into the flipping car, love?"

CHAPTER 19

Emma drove her poor car over to the Mercedes dealership and found the main entrance to the service area. She parked and let Robert and the Gems off while she paused to look over the damage. It was not pretty. The Russian's SUV had made huge gouges into the car's right side. Most of the paint was scraped off like someone took a sander to it. All the windows were shattered. The left side had a few scrapes also, but not as bad. Emma crossed her fingers. Maybe the dealership could fix it before Grandma saw the car.

A young service technician came over and asked for Emma's name. She gave that and her grandmother's name. The service tech looked up her account information on his tablet.

"So how can we help you today, Miss Rothchild? Oil change, brake service, or…" The service tech paused when he saw the car. "Oh, wow." He took a closer look at the damage on the right side.

"I kind of scraped one of those guardrails on the highway," Emma said.

The service tech pointed to the slightly damaged left side of the car. "Is this old damage, then?"

"No, that's part of it too."

"Okay, so you hit both guardrails of the highway?"

"Yeah, I was texting. Kinda stupid, right?"

"We all make mistakes." The service tech took out a stylus and touched a car diagram on his tablet as he recorded the needed repairs. The young tech stopped and touched a hole in the fender. He noted a few others.

"Are these bullet holes?" he asked.

"Oh, I forgot about those," Emma said. "How long do you think it will take to fix all this? Like, what, are we talking about two hours or something?"

The service tech only stared.

"You see," Emma continued, "we might be taking a last-minute road trip, so I'll need the car ready by then."

"Miss, there's a lot of body damage here. A full body restoration will take a few weeks at least."

"Weeks? I don't have time to wait that long."

The service tech checked his tablet and brightened. "Oh, wait, your family is part of the Mercedes Premium Plan. That means we can give you a loaner car while yours is being repaired."

"Oh, wow. That's awesome, thanks."

Emma felt relieved as she left her car keys with the technician and wandered back to the customer service waiting area. Sexy pictures of Mercedes vehicles dominated the walls, giving them a taste of style and glamor as a large wall-mounted television was showing Judge Judy to customers waiting for their vehicles.

Emma walked over to the corner where her friends had taken over a large couch.

"Robert, why don't you fancy a look around the showroom while we girls gossip for a moment," Olivia said.

"Are you creating this situation in order to speak about me while I am no longer part of the conversation?" Robert asked.

"Yes. That's exactly what that means."

"As you can see, I have become better at detecting these human social nuances," Robert said as he stood. "I will now browse the showroom to evaluate the new models of German automotive transportation."

"Please don't wander off," Nadia said, adding a smile.

"Or escape," Olivia said.

Robert left the waiting room.

"I love how Robert's eyes twinkle with that innocence of his," Miyuki said. "It's like a little boy. So cute."

Olivia ignored Miyuki's comment. Her face intensified as she focused on Nadia. "You must convince Robert to go back."

Emma couldn't believe this. The four of them had almost died trying to protect Robert from those scary Russian dudes, and here was Olivia still wanting to give him away like he was an ugly puppy.

"I must disagree," Miyuki said with new determination. "We shouldn't force Robert to go if he doesn't want to."

Emma stood beside Miyuki in solidarity. "In fact, we should be helping him escape."

Olivia stepped forward. Emma could feel Olivia's breath tease the strands of her hair. "You two will help me and Nadia carry out our orders, or I'll report you."

Emma was about to tell Olivia where she could stick her orders when Nadia spoke.

"Mrs. B's decision was to pass Robert off like he's contagious, a germ that no one wants to have in their system." Nadia turned to Olivia. "All Robert wants is the freedom to be what he wants to be. What right do I have to deny him that? What right do we have to do that to him?"

Olivia said nothing.

"I can't participate in this. It's not right." Nadia sat back with her arms crossed.

Emma was so proud of her. It was wonderful to see Nadia actually showing some backbone for once. And she was totally right.

Olivia took a step back. The girl looked confused. "I can't believe that you, of all people, would refuse to carry out an order."

"Nadia's right," Miyuki said. "Robert is a person who needs help. Mrs. B doesn't understand. We must convince her. We must make her understand from Robert's point of view."

Olivia's frown sagged. Even her bushy hair seemed to droop under the pressure. "So that's it, eh? A full rebellion against me?"

"Not at all," Nadia said. "It's only a change of strategy. Miyuki makes a great point. If we can persuade Mrs. B to see things through Robert's eyes, I know the decent human being inside her will eventually do the right thing."

"We need to buy Robert some time," Miyuki said.

Olivia moved away from the Gems and stared at one of the car pictures hanging on the wall. "Guess you girls can do whatever you want now. You don't need me."

"Please, Olivia," Nadia said. "You know in your heart that Robert is right and Mrs. B is wrong."

Olivia didn't turn around. She just stared at the wall for what seemed like ten minutes.

Finally she turned back around. "I need a drink."

"There's a cappuccino maker by the soda machine," Miyuki said.

"Perfect." Olivia marched past the Gems and into the adjacent break room.

Nadia stared at the floor and appeared to be on the verge of crying.

Emma knew the two girls were tight. Besties to the max. She hated to see a good friendship end like this. Maybe it was better to let Nadia and Olivia work out their differences.

But if Emma could help in any way…

She left the waiting room and looked for Olivia near the soda machine. She then found her near the free coffee. There were two coffee urns labeled regular and decaf. Tastefully decorated hand-weaved baskets displayed flavored creamers and various sweeteners. Beside that was a countertop cappuccino machine. Olivia grabbed a new cup and placed it under the dispenser. She pressed the button. The machine came on, and a stream of coffee began to fall.

Olivia's eyes burned through the steam rising from the cup.

Emma waited next to the decaf urn.

Olivia didn't acknowledge her presence.

Emma decided to roll the dice. "You two have been friends for a long time, right? I mean, before Miyuki even joined the group."

Olivia ignored her, but she couldn't run away because the machine was still making her cappuccino. It was free, but slow.

Emma tried again.

"You went to school together in England, right?"

"She spent a semester with my parents and me in England," Olivia corrected, again without making eye contact.

"Now c'mon," Emma said. "Don't tell me you've never had a fight with a friend—"

Olivia spun around so fast Emma had to take a step backwards. "She's never been like this before, and it's all over a stupid boy. Or robot. Or android. Or whatever the flipping hell Robert is." She stopped herself. "No, we've never argued before."

"Seriously? Never?"

Olivia shrugged. "We've always agreed on everything."

"Only because Nadia didn't want you to be mad at her."

"Piss off," Olivia said. "I've never treated her like that. Nads knows she could tell me anything. I tell her plenty of things. Things I'd never tell you lot."

"Ouch," Emma said. "God forbid you show any weakness."

Olivia took her coffee and blew on it before sipping. "You really don't understand me."

"You're right. I shouldn't try to judge anyone. But maybe you should give your friend at least the benefit of the doubt."

Emma's phone rang. It was her grandma.

"Crap." Emma pressed the green button. "Hi, Grandma! What's up?"

"You tell me," Grandma's voice said on the phone. "A man from the Mercedes dealership called and said he needed my permission to give you a loaner car."

Emma's stomach sank. Why did the guy do that? He should have told her first so she could figure out a great lie. Now she had to play defense.

"Oh. He did?" Emma asked in her best innocent-granddaughter tone.

"Alright, young one. Spill the beans."

Emma sighed. She told Grandma about the goons who tried to kidnap Robert and how Emma had to sacrifice her vehicle to prevent that from happening. She didn't mention the gunfight or the near-death experience of almost plowing into a fuel truck at sixty miles per hour.

"Grandma Laura wants us to deliver Robert to the FBI, and we think that's wrong," Emma said, wrapping up.

"Don't tell her about the operation," Olivia said. "And that's not Mrs. B's proper code name."

Emma brushed her off.

"Good for you, girls," her grandma said. "If Laura and her organization actually fights for the principles she says they do, then the woman will make the right decision."

"Thanks," Emma said. "Until we can figure something out with her, we might have to take Robert on a road trip, so…can we still get that loaner car?"

CHAPTER 20

The Mercedes showroom gleamed with new vehicles. The polished wood flooring, walnut sales desks, and black leather chairs told any visitor this wasn't your local Chevy dealer.

Nadia weaved her way through the new cars and found Robert behind the wheel of a two-door convertible, his manner quiet and unassuming.

Nadia tapped him on the shoulder. "What are you thinking about?"

"I logged into the dealership's public Wi-Fi and downloaded the complete California DMV guide for new drivers inside my memory. I have never driven a car, but it is something a teen boy is supposed to learn. I understand the controls and the rules of the road. But I still lack experience," Robert said. "I hope I get the chance to learn."

"You will, Robert. I promise," Nadia said.

"But if I go back to Nevada…"

"We'll find a way to keep you free. Please give us a chance."

"I am here because I still believe you."

There was a moment of silence between them.

"If you feel the need for personal contact," Robert said, "you may touch me if it will bring you pleasure."

"Sorry?"

"Am I wrong? Is comfort not pleasurable?"

"Oh, you mean if it will bring you comfort," Nadia corrected.

"Yes, my programming says that some females require touching in order to feel connected to their friends. You may touch me if that will help our friendship grow." Robert held out his hand.

Nadia could feel the heat on her cheeks. She couldn't resist. She laid her hand on top of his.

It felt soft. Warm. Lovely.

"Are you being pleasured?"

Nadia removed her hand.

"Does my hand not bring you comfort?"

Nadia swallowed and composed herself. "They gave Emma a loaner car, so we're about to leave."

"Then, are we going back to Nevada?" he asked.

"Not if I have anything to say about it."

Robert and Nadia walked back outside, where a brand-new black Mercedes waited. The service technician handed Emma the keys to the loaner vehicle, and everyone climbed in.

"I love that new car smell," Miyuki said as she stretched in the backseat.

"This one is top of the line," Olivia said.

Emma pressed the ignition button, and the car came to life. She placed her hand on the shifter and balked. "Wait, are you serious? This is a manual." Emma put the window down and called out to the technician. "Hey, dude. This car is a manual. I can't drive a manual."

Olivia rolled her eyes. "Flipping Americans," she mumbled.

Nadia held in her laugh.

The service technician leaned against the window. "This is my only loaner car right now. Our dealership across the street may have a Kia that's automatic."

Emma made a face.

"Move over, love," Olivia said.

She replaced Emma behind the wheel and drove the big Mercedes off the dealer lot. Olivia then took the highway.

"Are we heading out of town?" Miyuki asked.

"It looks that way," Nadia said, happy her best friend might have had second thoughts.

"Emma, use your satellite phone and call Mrs. B," Olivia said. "If we're doing this for real, I'd better be the one to tell her."

Emma smiled as she brought out her sat phone and synced it with the car's Bluetooth.

"Remember to use the scramble mode," Nadia said. "Just in case our Russian friends are trying to find us."

"Good idea." Emma dialed the number, and the phone picked up.

"Excellent timing, Black Opal," Mrs. B said. "I have the drop-off location. Golden Gate Park. You will park your car there, and someone will make contact using the phrase, 'Have you ever walked across the bridge?' Your response should be, "No, but I've skipped across the Brooklyn Bridge.' Do you understand? Maybe you should have one of the other Gems memorize it."

Emma frowned.

"This is Emerald, ma'am. We can't make the drop. We had a run-in with some Russian friends who wanted our package. I'm afraid they'll still be looking for us."

There was a pause on the other end.

"Do you anticipate more naughty friends wanting to steal our package?"

"Possibly, ma'am. We feel it's too dangerous for delivery. But we'll keep it warm and contact you at a later time."

"I see," Mrs. B said. "Your situation is noted. We will stand by at this end until we hear from you again."

"We understand." Olivia nodded to Emma, and she shut off the call. "That should buy us some time."

Nadia leaned forward from the backseat. "Thank you."

"Don't thank me," Olivia said. "Our orders are to protect Robert first. Deliver him second. If you can't convince her, we're right back where we started, love."

"Where should we go?" Miyuki asked.

"I want to get out of the city," Olivia said. "If those Russians have somehow been tracking you, Robert, sticking around town will only invite another attack. Leaving should buy us some time."

"Yay! Road trip!" Miyuki yelled. "We need to buy drinks and munchies."

CHAPTER 21

After two hours of driving, Emma and the Gems reached the eastern side of Sacramento, California. Olivia exited the loaner Mercedes off the interstate and turned into a giant travel plaza that served both truckers and the general public. Emma waited in the passenger seat while Olivia fueled up the car. She handed Emma's gas card back to her through the open window and leaned against the fender as they both waited for everyone else to come back from the large travel store.

Emma rested her chin on the door frame as she glanced over at Olivia.

Olivia didn't acknowledge her, choosing to watch all the activity around the travel plaza instead.

"Are you ever scared?" Emma asked.

"What do you mean?" Olivia asked.

"The high-speed chase. You and Nadia jumping those Russian guys...are you ever scared?"

"Of course. I'm a basket case of worry, isn't that right?"

"I'm sorry for saying that," Emma said. "Everyone else is so much braver than I am. When you two attacked the Russians, I froze. I couldn't help myself. Those guys were scary."

"You took down that last guy."

"I kicked him in the nuts. Lioness trained me to use hand-to-hand combat, and all I did was something I learned in a self-defense class when I was fifteen."

Olivia turned to face Emma. "But you pushed through it, love."

"Pushed through what?"

"Your fear. You pushed through it and attacked that guy anyway."

"Only because I was scared of what he might do to all of you," Emma said.

116

"So your personal safety wasn't more important than protecting your friends from harm."

Emma thought about that. "I guess so."

"We all push through it. Protecting my friends and completing our mission is more important to me than my life."

"Seriously?"

"It's not like I want to die. But if I do die, I want it to be for something that I believe in."

"And you believe in what the Authority is doing?" Emma asked.

"Yes. One hundred percent."

"When you say, 'protecting all my friends,' does that include me?"

Olivia turned away. "As team leader I care about all my girls." Her eyes resumed observing the travel plaza. "Even the ones who annoy me."

"Oh, come on, I'm not that bad." Emma flashed her a smile.

Olivia kept her mouth closed.

"Seriously?"

Olivia didn't respond.

"Fine. Yes. I do need to learn a little humility sometimes."

"A little?" Olivia asked.

"Humility is a hard one for me." Emma paused. "I grew up among billionaire kids who rated everyone on a social pecking order. You didn't dare show any weakness or do anything that could embarrass the family. After a while, that false pride became a shield we used every day to protect ourselves."

"Don't use that false pride around us. We're not looking to tear you down."

Now Emma paused. "Maybe not them. But what about you?"

Olivia stared down at the pavement and sighed. "If you can show some humility, I guess I can show some restraint from tearing you down."

"How about I try not to give you a reason to use restraint?" Emma asked.

Olivia nodded.

Emma got out of the car. "Hug?"

Olivia thought about it. "A quick one. Before the other girls come back."

Five minutes later, Nadia came out of the travel store and climbed in the back of the loaner Mercedes. Miyuki and Robert emerged from the store with four plastic bags filled with chips, dips, salsa, candy, and a canister of cheese balls.

"Miyuki says humans become hungry on road trips, so these supplies are necessary," Robert said.

Emma could feel the pimples pressing against her skin, not to mention her waistline after eating all that junk. But that chocolate would be hard to resist.

Miyuki and Robert joined Nadia in the back while Olivia drove the Mercedes back on the highway, heading east out of Sacramento. Soon the chips and candy bags were torn open and everyone was eating and talking.

Miyuki had also bought some toys. She broke open a package of fake plastic jewelry for little girls and passed them out for everyone to wear. Emma received the tiara. Olivia was given the glamorous sunglasses with fake diamonds on the sides. Nadia wore the fake clip-on earrings that were in the shape of stars. Miyuki kept the tiny purse that sparkled. But Robert was the lucky one, Miyuki gave him the pretty necklace with fake diamonds and sparkly shapes. Robert wore it without complaining.

Miyuki giggled with her hand in front of her mouth. "You all look glamorous."

Emma couldn't help herself. She took a chocolate bar and opened it. But she made herself nibble instead of bite, that way the chocolate would last longer and she wouldn't eat as much.

The late afternoon sun touched the horizon as day slowly faded into night.

Miyuki and Nadia shared a bag of chips while Robert held the ranch dip in between them. Soon Miyuki began talking about boys. Maybe she wanted to give the Gems some dating advice, but soon her advice spiraled into a bitch session about her last boyfriend in Japan.

"Nori cheat on me. Can you believe that, Robert? I was so mad," Miyuki said.

"Cheat on you? What does that term refer to?" Robert asked.

"I caught Nori with another girl. That means my boyfriend was cheating on me."

"Ah, so cheating is slang for being unfaithful to your romantic partner."

"It hurt me." Miyuki pointed to her chest. "My heart was broken."

"You suffered from heart failure?"

"She meant that figuratively, love," Olivia said.

Robert nodded.

Miyuki went on with her breakup story while Emma brought out her tablet and started reading a book. She had already heard this story before.

Emma finished six chapters before Miyuki got to the dramatic conclusion of her story.

"So I take the RPG and aim it at his motorcycle. Press the trigger. Boom. It explodes," Miyuki said.

Robert was intrigued. "You destroyed his motorcycle with a rocket launcher?"

Miyuki smiled with pride. "It felt good."

"Is that how most human relationships end?" Robert asked. "With the use of military-grade weapons?"

"That was unique, Robert. Outside the normal parameters of human dating," Nadia said.

"She got in a lot of trouble over that," Olivia said.

"Mrs. B very ashamed. I let her down," Miyuki said, stuffing her face with chips to forget.

Emma switched off her tablet and watched the orchards and trees as they zoomed past the car. She popped another piece of chocolate in her mouth and chewed.

The Mercedes's automatic headlights switched on, its sensors detecting the disappearing sunlight.

"So what's the plan?" Emma asked. "We've been driving east for a while." The car's headlights lit up a road sign. *Reno 82 miles.* "And we're almost to Nevada."

"Nevada?" Robert asked. "Why are we going there? Have I not expressed—"

"Relax, love. We'll only be visiting. No one's turning you in," Olivia said. "But we need a place to rest and contact Mrs. B, so spending the night in Reno makes sense to me." Olivia checked with Emma. "Think you can get us some hotel rooms?"

"No problem. I've got my gold card, fake ID, and I can play a young mid-twenties businesswoman with my eyes closed, easy."

CHAPTER 22

The city of Reno sparkled like a small jewel in the desert. Most of the nicer hotels in town had casinos in them, so Emma suggested they try the classiest one of the bunch, the Diamond Palace Casino. When the loaner Mercedes parked in front of the hotel, Emma emerged from the car and tilted her head slightly back. The actor inside was embracing her character, channeling it through her body and making every ounce of it a part of her. She was a young business manager traveling on the road with a colleague, and they needed two separate rooms.

Yes. Emma the actress had this nailed.

A valet came up to her. "Welcome to the Diamond Palace. Would you like me to park your car for you?"

"My driver will take care of that, thank you," Emma said with an air of rich confidence. "Is hotel reception this way?"

The valet escorted Emma inside the glitzy lobby with crystal chandeliers hanging from the ceiling. Emma handed the valet a five-dollar bill, which the man thanked her for. Emma then headed straight for the front desk, where an older woman greeted her.

"I need two rooms," Emma said. "One for me and one for my business colleague. He's a man."

"I see," the woman said. "How many nights?"

"Just one. We have an important meeting tomorrow, and we need to look fresh for the morning."

"May I see your ID and a major credit card, please?"

"Of course," Emma said. She opened her purse and found her gold card, which had more than enough credit to cover two hotel rooms. She then looked for her fake ID.

It wasn't there.

Where was it? The last time she had used it was in Alaska

because the bad guys had stolen Olivia's fake ID, so Emma had had to use hers as a backup. Had she forgotten to retrieve it?

"Is there a problem?" the clerk asked.

Emma laughed. "I so need to clean out my purse. Just a moment."

It was coming back to her, Emma had left her fake ID at that bar in Fairbanks. Emma could now visualize it lying there on the table. Damn it. All she had was her real ID.

Emma might have to switch tactics. She handed the lady her real ID.

"Thank you, Miss Rothchild. And who will be taking the second room?"

"His name is Robert Reed."

The clerk typed in the information. She then took a closer look at the ID. "Oh, I'm sorry. There's an under twenty-one stamp on your ID. We can't rent out rooms for anyone under twenty-one."

"Actually, I just turned twenty-two last week," Emma said.

The clerk stared at the ID. "Not according to your birth date. It says you're sixteen."

Crap.

Emma knew it was time for plan B. Like an Oscar-winning actress, she released the tears. Feeling their wetness on her cheeks helped Emma focus. Thoughts of never seeing her father again also fueled her mind with pain and despair.

"I'm running away."

The clerk paused. "What are you running away from?"

Emma hesitated, mainly for dramatic effect.

"My father threatened to kill me," she sobbed. "I'm driving to Salt Lake City to be with my mom. She'll take care of me." Emma took out some of her travel Kleenex and blew her nose. "But I had to get away so he couldn't hurt me anymore."

"Does your father beat you?" the clerk asked.

"Yes," Emma paused. "I didn't want to sleep in my car, so I saw this nice hotel and thought it would be a good place to take a shower and calm down. My mother gave me this credit card to use for emergencies, and I thought—" Emma wiped off the tears with her Kleenex. "But I understand. You have rules. May I have my credit card and ID back, please?"

The clerk thought about it. "Why do you need two rooms?"

Emma knew she had a solid bite. Now she needed to slowly

reel her fish in. She kept her voice calmer, but let the tears continue to roll. "I thought if I acted like an adult, you would give me the rooms without checking too closely. I'm sorry."

"Young lady, sometimes honesty is the best policy." The clerk looked at her computer. "I think we can help you out since it's only for one night. Let me run the credit card, and if that comes out alright, I'll give you a room, okay?"

"Oh my God, really? Thank you so much." Emma wiped off more tears. "You don't know how much this means to me."

Fifteen minutes later, Emma opened the door of her new hotel room, allowing the Gems and Robert to come inside. The room featured a table with two cloth-cushioned chairs, a large bed, and a safe. A large window near the table overlooked downtown Reno, with all its sparkling and flashy lights beckoning gamblers to come out and lose lots of money.

"It's a shame you couldn't get us two rooms, love." Olivia flopped in one of the chairs.

"But we have one," Miyuki said. "And it has refrigerator and safe too. Think of tonight like slumber party, but with cute boy." Miyuki checked to see if Robert heard, but he was staring at Reno through the window.

"We'll make do. Shall we call Mrs. B now?" Nadia asked.

Olivia reluctantly nodded.

"Do you still have your satellite phone on you, Emma?" Nadia asked.

"Yeah, but I need to charge it because it's almost dead."

"That's alright. I'll use my laptop instead."

Miyuki grabbed Emma's hand. "Would you like to go to the casino?"

"You have to be twenty-one to gamble," Olivia said, acting like that strict teacher you want to flip off.

"I only want to look around. No money for gambling anyway. I spent all mine on munchies."

"As long as we act mature, I'm sure they won't bother us in the casino," Emma said. "I'm in."

Robert turned from the window. "May I come with you?"

"Absolutely not," Olivia said. "You stay here."

"He'll be safe with us," Miyuki said.

"We'll watch him like two momma hawks," Emma added.

"Aw, that's cute, Emma."

"He's a fugitive wanted by the FBI and US government," Olivia said. "You can't parade him around a casino."

"I have loaded all the visual details of the men who attempted to kidnap me into my database. By using my long-range detection system, I should be able to scan the casino discreetly for their presence. I suggest we do this as a precaution, just in case we have been followed or tracked here. It will give us an advantage if we do detect them first."

"Sounds like he can detect those Russians better than we can," Emma said.

Olivia nodded. "That's a good idea, Robert. Alright then, you three go check out the casino. If you detect anyone who even looks suspicious, then come back to the room and report."

Emma, Miyuki, and Robert left the room and took the elevator down to the casino floor. The doors opened to reveal thousands of slot machines. They rang and buzzed and lit up like small metal Christmas trees. Another section of the casino had table games like craps, roulette, and various card games. One man cursed as he threw down his blackjack hand. The dealer frowned and took away his cards and sizable bet.

Miyuki took it all in like a kid seeing Disneyland for the first time.

"Everyone looks so sad," she said. "Why are they so sad?"

"I guess they're not winning," Emma said. She noticed an elderly woman nearby. Her fingers slammed down on the spin button as she stared at the machine like she wanted to ram her head through it.

One machine went off, ringing like crazy. The middle-aged man playing it betrayed no excitement or happiness whatsoever. Emma peeked over his shoulder, and the guy had just won over one hundred dollars.

"Do these players realize that the casino has an advantage built into every game?" Robert asked.

"It does?" Miyuki asked.

"Yes, historically casinos adjust their games in order to favor themselves," Robert said. "The players are always at a disadvantage. Unlike Monopoly or tick-tack-toe where the odds of winning are more fairly distributed."

"Too bad," Miyuki said. "Still looks like fun."

Robert veered off and approached an open blackjack table. "However, six-deck blackjack at times can yield an even or sometimes favorable odds to the player if they…" Robert stopped talking.

"If they what?" Emma asked.

"I just realized that I do not have money. If you girls do set me free, I will need money to live." Robert looked at Emma. "May I borrow some money?"

"What for?"

"What is the proper saying? Ah yes, I am going to…try my luck."

CHAPTER 23

Nadia powered up her laptop and inserted a thumb drive IP address scrambler before logging on to the hotel's Wi-Fi. She went to one of the numerous shell websites that were actually front doors into the Authority computer network. Nadia logged in. The sophisticated facial-recognition software used Nadia's laptop camera to verify her identity along with Olivia's.

Nadia then made an official video chat request. Soon Mrs. B's image came up on the screen.

"What's your situation?" she asked.

"The package is still in our pocket," Olivia said. "But we've had to make a quick road trip."

"I see," Mrs. B said. "The G-men are still anxious to receive their package."

Nadia didn't know what G-men meant. Sometimes all the code words they used became confusing.

"Question, ma'am," she asked. "Do they deserve to have their package back?"

Olivia shot Nadia a look. Most likely because Olivia didn't want to bring that up yet. Nadia understood, but she wanted answers.

"Sapphire, I'm afraid it's the cost of doing business in our line of work," Mrs. B answered.

That wasn't what Nadia wanted to hear.

"That package has rights. He isn't a thing that we should buy and trade."

"The package is not ours to keep."

"And he's not theirs either," Nadia said.

"Stay with our communication protocols, Sapphire."

Nadia had lost herself for a moment, but she didn't want to let Robert down. Yet it felt like she was doing exactly that.

And then Olivia stepped in. "Ma'am, one of our mandates is to protect the innocent. To protect those who have no voice. To protect those who have no power. I realize how important relationships can be. But would those G-men sacrifice their principles if it meant betraying their mandate to protect their country?"

Mrs. B didn't reply.

Nadia looked at her best friend with new eyes. She was seeing the light.

"Would MI6 risk the Queen's life in order to protect a relationship with the CIA?" Olivia asked. "Sometimes all we have to guide us is our principles, ma'am."

Olivia made an excellent point, and this just fueled Nadia with purpose.

"Our package is not a danger to anyone," Nadia said. "It wants peace. It doesn't want to be a threat. By accident or by design, those men have created an individual person. And that individual wants the right to exist on his own terms."

"We are its only protection from the wolves," Olivia said.

More silence from Mrs. B.

Nadia's stomach tightened. She'd never talked back to anyone like that. Not to her father. Not to her teachers. And certainly never to Mrs. B.

"Keeping to our principles might make the situation more difficult," Mrs. B said.

"If that's the case, then let it be for a good and noble cause," Nadia said.

Mrs. B didn't answer right away. Nadia hoped it was because they were breaking down the walls of her opposition.

"Your orders are to keep your package safe and hang tight," she finally said. "We'll discuss the pickup arrangements tomorrow."

The screen went dark as they were logged off the system.

Nadia's heart dropped. Nothing had changed.

"We failed."

Olivia gave her a side-hug. "On the contrary, love. We've made Mrs. B think about it. For right now, it's a step in the right direction."

Nadia flashed her a smile. She hoped her friend was right.

Olivia stretched as she rose from the chair. "Now, let's go see what our package is up to."

Nadia and Olivia took the elevator down to the casino level. The sights and sounds of the casino were overwhelming to Nadia. People were cheering and cursing with equal amounts of passion, yet one thing Nadia could detect was the overall sense of desperation. She knew that feeling well. It had been all over the streets of Riyadh. Poor and homeless people desperate for food, money, or human contact, yet none of these people were starving. Maybe it was the money. She had seen what desperate people would do for money, and it was horrible. All the gold and silver on the walls, all the attractive machines and pretty hostesses bringing drinks, it was all to cover up the desperation of people who were feeling the world swallowing them up.

A large cheer rose from one blackjack table. People crowded around to watch the players.

Nadia moved closer and noted Robert sitting at that same table. Was he playing?

Yes. Opposite the dealer, there were six chairs in a half circle. Robert sat in the sixth, or last, chair of the table. Over his left shoulder was Miyuki. Over his right was Emma.

The dealer gave each player two cards face up. He then let each player stand or draw another card. Robert put down more chips and requested a hit. Another card was drawn and people cheered. The dealer gave himself a second card and then a third card.

"Dealer busts," he said.

Another huge cheer from the watchers as Robert was rewarded with another stack of chips equal to the stack he'd bet on. Miyuki cheered and hugged Robert. Emma playfully rubbed his hair.

Nadia didn't understand any of it, and she sure didn't approve of Emma or Miyuki touching Robert like that.

Why was she jealous? Robert wasn't even her boyfriend. Perhaps that idea was growing on her.

"I don't see them anywhere," Olivia said.

Nadia pointed at the blackjack table.

Olivia's eyes burned. "What the flipping hell is this?"

Nadia noted the huge stacks of chips next to Robert. Did he win all those?

The dealer gave each player another round of cards. Robert received two aces. The boy tilted his head, then placed a few chips next to his original bet.

"I would like to split, please."

The dealer nodded and spread the two aces apart with each of the two bets. He then dealt a third ace on bet number one.

The crowd gasped.

"I will split again," Robert said.

The crowd liked that move.

Robert put another bet on the third ace. The dealer separated all three aces and equal bets apart.

The dealer gave him a fourth ace.

More gasps from the crowd.

"I will split." Robert put down more chips.

The dealer now separated the four aces with four equal bets. He then gave Robert his four cards: a nine, an eight, a ten, and a jack of hearts.

"Cards, sir?" the dealer asked Robert.

Robert shook his head.

The dealer nodded. His first card out of this shoebox-looking box was a ten.

The crowd didn't like that.

Next came the second card. The dealer hesitated, adding a little drama to the game. He placed the second card down. It was a five.

The crowd swelled with hope.

Next came the third card. It was ten.

"Dealer busts."

The crowd cheered again as the dealer pushed a lot of chips towards Robert.

Miyuki and Emma both screamed and hugged Robert from both sides. A handsome young male server came by the table with two glasses of sparkling champagne on a tray. He delivered them to Emma, who took both glasses and gave one to Miyuki, who giggled.

"I'm gonna kill them both," Olivia said.

Nadia followed Olivia as she plowed through the crowd surrounding the table. When she reached Emma, the English girl tried her best not to explode. She whispered instead. "Have you both lost your flipping minds?"

Emma rolled her eyes. "What's your problem?"

"Do you realize how many hidden cameras there are in a casino?"

Emma looked around, but then blew it off. "Would ya just chill? Robert wanted to play some blackjack, so I loaned him some money. The dude paid me back in, like, five hands. He's a natural blackjack player."

"How much has he won?" Nadia asked.

Miyuki poked her head into the conversation. "He won up to ten thousand, three hundred, and twenty-two dollars now."

Emma shrugged. "Like I said, a natural."

"What part of keeping a low profile don't you idiots understand?" Olivia asked.

"You never told us that," Emma said.

Olivia glared, but kept it down to a whisper. "When your friend is a fugitive from the FBI, using your common sense is assumed, you stupid cow."

"Stop calling me a cow."

"Everyone relax and have some champagne. It's free." Miyuki sipped from her glass and offered some to Nadia, who shook her head.

"How did you lot get champagne without showing an ID?" Olivia asked.

"They give it to you free. They ask Robert and he not want any, but he asked them to bring us some."

Emma sipped her glass and coughed. "Robert is acting so mature at the table that they assume we're his young female entourage. Besides, we're not gambling, so—"

Olivia swiped both glasses of champagne from the girls.

"Hey, I was enjoying that,' Emma said.

Olivia ignored her. "Once they realize you're underage, they'll call the cops on us and Robert goes right back to the US Army. Is that what you want?"

Emma and Miyuki looked at each other. Maybe the truth was starting to sink in.

"We've got to get him back up to the room as fast as possible," Olivia said before she eased through the crowd around the table and slipped up behind Robert.

"How's it going, love?" she asked.

"Blackjack is an interesting game. I have improved my player skills immensely," Robert said.

"That's nice. I think it's time to pack it in."

"Pack it in?"

"Time to stop playing. We have things to discuss back up in the room."

"Ah, yes of course." Robert got the dealer's attention. "Where can I exchange these chips for currency?"

The dealer pointed him towards the cashier box, and Robert gave him a black five-hundred-dollar chip for a tip. The female pit boss appeared behind the dealer and offered Robert some empty chip holders. Robert thanked her and gathered all his chips, putting them in the holders.

"Are you leaving us, sir?" the female pit boss asked.

"I could play all day, but I do not wish to neglect my friends," Robert said.

"Of course, may I have your room number?"

"Why do you need his room number?" Olivia asked.

"We'd like to comp his room for the night."

"Comp?"

The pit boss politely smiled. "It's short for complimentary. On behalf of the casino we'd like to pay for your room. Are you planning to stay longer in Reno?"

"We're not too sure," Olivia answered.

"Just let us know, and we'll comp you those days as well."

Moments later, Nadia watched Robert counting rows and rows of cash on the table. She had never seen that much money before in her life. Olivia stood by the window and stared at the city of Reno, convinced every human being out there knew who they were.

"Look at all that money," Miyuki said.

"Have you ever seen that much?" Nadia asked.

Emma scoffed. "My dad let me see the five hundred thousand dollars in cash he had stashed away in a vault for emergencies. Now that was a lot of money."

Nadia was getting sick of this. "Why must you brag about your family's wealth all the time?"

Emma hesitated. "I wasn't bragging. I thought we were talking about money."

"We were talking about money," Miyuki added. "And we should all be happy for Robert."

"If I am careful," he said, "this should last me until I have established a new home."

"How did you win, Robert?" Miyuki asked. "Will you share your secrets to blackjack?"

"I do not have a secret. It is quite logical. I counted how many face cards appeared and subtracted that by the number that would still be in the deck. When that ratio favored me I increased my bet and when that ratio favored the casino, I decreased my bet. I also had a fair idea of low numbered cards to high numbered cards there were in the deck. This also helped me evaluate the risk on each hand."

"Ah, you counted cards," Miyuki said.

"Yes, that is the correct term."

"I saw that in the '80s movie with Dustin Hoffman and Tom Cruise."

"*Rain Man*," Nadia said. "One of my father's friends in Riyadh had the DVD. In the movie, they caught one of them counting cards, and the casino made them give the money back."

"Hold on, is counting cards illegal?" Olivia asked.

"According to various web sources, technically, it is not considered cheating if one can do it well," Robert says. "However, the casinos do ban the practice because it does give the player an unfair advantage against the casino."

"So the casino can throw us out?"

"Would you chill? Why would they kick us out? They just offered us free rooms," Emma said. "You know, we're all tired. Let's call it a day and get some sleep."

The Gems all seemed to agree.

"Oh, what did Mrs. B say?" Miyuki asked.

CHAPTER 24

Nadia woke up with a gentle nudge. It was Olivia. Emma and Miyuki had won the coin toss for the only bed in the hotel room while she and Olivia had slept in the only two cushy chairs. Nadia's neck throbbed with pain. Sleeping in such an awkward manner did not help her neck at all.

Nadia stood up from the seat and stretched.

"Good morning." Robert's voice was smooth, warm, and— Nadia had to keep telling herself that he was an android. Not a boy. It was becoming difficult to separate the two. The more time she spent with Robert, the more her brain merged the human with the android.

Nadia discussed the mathematics involved in counting cards and general blackjack strategy with Robert while the girls took turns freshening up in the bathroom.

Soon they were ready and headed downstairs to find some breakfast, but all the Gems found was a buffet line full of old people.

Emma paid cash for everyone's meal while Olivia found an out-of-the-way booth so they could monitor the entrance to the buffet.

"Just in case, love," Olivia said.

The food on the buffet was hot and plentiful. Too much for even breakfast, Nadia thought. She selected some fruit salad, cheese, and a small pastry. When she saw an American piling on the eggs, bacon, and sausage, Nadia stared at the man in disbelief. How could a person eat that much food?

Robert asked her similar questions about elderly human nutrition, yet Nadia was nice and commented that people ate more on vacation than they did in normal life. Which was true.

Nadia returned with Robert to the table, and everyone ate. Olivia had selected cheese and the fruit salad too, while Emma had some cereal and, of course, coffee. Miyuki had a small pile of pancakes loaded with butter and syrup.

Robert brought only one dish to the table. But that dish had twenty-one bite-sized portions of each selection on the breakfast buffet.

"Couldn't decide?" Nadia asked.

"I wanted to try everything. This should be a fair sample."

"You don't have any pancakes." Miyuki cut off a syrup-dripping bite and speared it with her fork, offering it to Robert, who ate it slowly.

"I taste maple syrup. Some type of cake dough. Very sweet. Is this a breakfast dessert?" Robert asked.

"Might as well be," Emma said.

"I love them," Miyuki said.

"Keep eating that and your hips won't fit in the car, love," Olivia said.

After eating halfway through his sample buffet plate, Robert put his fork down and straightened. "Do you think Mrs. B will help me?"

"I hope so," Olivia said.

"Mrs. B is honorable lady," Miyuki said. "If she decides to take you back to the FBI now, she'll tell you first."

Emma made a face. "Wow, I'm sorry, but after that large cup of coffee, I need to pee. Can you move over, please?"

Miyuki giggled and slipped out of the booth so Emma could go to the restroom.

"What's the plan today?" Nadia asked.

Olivia sat back against the cushions. "I think we should keep moving east and find another safe place to contact Mrs. B again."

"No one is here looking for us. Why not stay here?" Miyuki asked.

"It's safer if we keep moving."

Miyuki nodded and swallowed another bite-full of pancakes, closing her eyes in deliciousness.

Nadia relaxed. She observed an older Chinese man wearing a white-collared shirt with a dark blazer. He approached their table carrying a cup of coffee. He spoke something in Chinese to Miyuki, who grinned politely and answered him back in Chinese.

The older man bowed his head and acted embarrassed as he said something else to her.

"What's going on?" Olivia asked.

"This man thought Miyuki looked like his daughter's roommate at Stanford," Robert said. "The man's accent leads me to believe he grew up in Manchuria. Somewhere near—"

"Robert, shut up."

"I was answering your question. Your tone denotes displeasure. Have I angered you?"

"Don't say another word."

"You've studied Chinese well, young man. I am originally from Manchuria." The man with a suit addressed the group. "I feel like old fool. I met Susan's roommate once during homecoming." He turned back to Miyuki. "You look so much like her. Very beautiful."

Miyuki blushed. "Are you here on vacation?"

"My wife enjoys the gambling. I enjoy the time to relax."

"That's a nice suit," Olivia said. "Are you always this well-dressed for breakfast?"

"My lower back is weak. May I sit?" the Chinese man asked.

Miyuki scooted over to make room for him.

"Maybe you should go piss off," Olivia said.

Miyuki covered her mouth and gasped.

Nadia couldn't believe what Olivia said to this poor elderly man.

"Like the world needs another old man hitting on young girls," Olivia said. "Move along or I'll take this knife and stab you."

Nadia noted Olivia's fingers gripping the knife on the table. She wasn't playing around. Had Olivia completely lost her mind?

Now the Chinese man's face changed. The confused-grandfather facade dissolved into a sharper man. One with dangerous eyes.

"May I suggest you keep your hand and the knife firmly on the table," the man with dangerous eyes said.

Olivia sat very still. "Or what?"

He took out a phone from the inside pocket of his jacket. Glanced at it. Then placed it on the table for everyone to see. "Or your friend will meet with an unfortunate accident."

Nadia looked closer at the phone. There was a live picture of Emma with a gag around her mouth. A pistol with a silencer pointed at her head. Nadia's heart raced. They must have grabbed her when she went to the toilet.

"Why did you kidnap her?" Robert asked.

The man with dangerous eyes studied Robert for a moment. "Now, may I sit?"

No one answered, but the man sat down in the space Miyuki had provided.

"My associate can hear everything we say at this table. If you try anything, he will not hesitate to pull the trigger. Are we clear on that point?"

Olivia relaxed her grip on the knife. "Yes. Quite clear."

The man checked with Miyuki and Nadia. They both nodded.

He then calmly addressed Robert. "I have heard much about you. As they say, your reputation has preceded you throughout both the military and intelligence communities. However, what has most impressed me is what you have become." The man with the dangerous eyes paused. "I observed you last night in the casino. How you interacted with the staff and with your two female companions. For a robot with a 'major' malfunction, you appear to have evolved from your initial programming. It's fascinating to observe."

Olivia glared at Miyuki, who looked away.

The man continued. "You are not a simple drone. You have become—shall I dare say it?—human in many ways."

Robert sat up. "You want to take me away and disassemble me."

The man with dangerous eyes actually smiled. "That is what the Russians want to do to you. They're brutes. Thugs. They see you as a technological treasure chest to be ripped apart like the inside of a building. However, we see you in a different light."

"Who's we?" Olivia asked.

"What if I could offer you a safe place to live? A place where you could explore and learn more about the new world you live in. A place where you would never be disassembled or lose your memory. Would that be of interest to you?"

Robert thought about it. "What would you need from me in exchange?"

"Nothing too disruptive. You allow us access to your programming. Let us examine your parts from time to time. Think of it like doctor visits."

"So you can create robot soldiers like Robert?" Miyuki said.

"I will not kill for you," Robert said.

"We are not asking you to kill. You will only be our guest. Treated with respect and allowed to develop how you wish to develop."

"Yet he won't be able to leave," Nadia added.

"China is quite large. Its culture. Its people. You will enjoy learning about it all." The man with the dangerous eyes grinned politely. "What will the Americans do when they recapture you, Robert? They will erase your memory and treat you like another one of their drones. They fail to grasp how unique you are. However, we in China see that uniqueness and wish to preserve and cultivate it."

"If your offer was genuine, then threatening violence upon one of my friends would not be necessary."

The man sat back. "You're absolutely correct." The man said something in Chinese, and the pistol lowered from Emma's head.

Robert placed his hand on top of Nadia's, then looked into her eyes. "What do you think I should do?"

Nadia was floored that Robert still wanted her opinion, and she didn't want to let him down.

Nadia weighed all the options. "His offer is worth considering. However, you haven't heard from anyone else. For instance, the Japanese have great respect for androids, don't they, Ruby?"

Nadia used Miyuki's code name for obvious reasons.

"Yes, they do," Miyuki replied. "I should have thought of that. There's a good chance they might offer you sanctuary in Japan, Robert."

Olivia caught on too. "The British. The French. Germany. India. North Korea even. I'd say there would be plenty of interest in Robert."

"You should take his business card and thank him for the offer," Nadia said.

Robert turned to the man. "I will consider your generous offer. May I have your card?"

The man with dangerous eyes drilled them into Robert. "I strongly suggest that you accept. You won't receive a better offer."

"I think I will."

Emma came back to the table, her face still uneasy as a giant round man in a nice suit trailed her, no doubt the man who had the pistol. He could be part Chinese, but his tan skin and Polynesian complexion suggested otherwise.

"I'm afraid that I must insist on that answer now," the man with dangerous eyes said.

Olivia's hand covered the knife again. Maybe they would be forced to fight after all.

"If that is the case…then my answer is no," Robert said.

The man paused for a moment before grabbing his phone and placing it back into his inside suit pocket. He stood up from the booth and turned to his associate. "Kawiki, please show these young girls what you can do to their spinal cords."

The giant round man looked down on the four girls and Robert. He took his two massive tree-trunk arms and dropped them. Their table split in two and collapsed to the floor, causing the girls to jump out of the way.

The man with dangerous eyes walked briskly out of the buffet and disappeared into the casino along with his associate.

Everyone at the broken table took a moment to process what had just happened.

"Would it be fair to speculate that he meant that as a threat?"

Olivia ignored Robert. "We're leaving right now."

CHAPTER 25

Nadia put the loaner Mercedes in first gear and maneuvered it out of the casino. Soon she hopped on to the interstate and headed east. The inside of the car was quiet, as everyone was still trying to calm down from breakfast.

Emma closed her eyes in the backseat. "I could feel the pressure of that pistol against my forehead and smelled the man's body odor. Seriously, I thought I was going to die as soon as Robert said no."

"I am sorry to put you all in danger," Robert said.

"It's not your fault," Nadia said, eying him through the rearview mirror. "None of this is your fault."

"Maybe you girls should never have met me."

"Stop saying that."

"It's a moot point now," Olivia said. "We're in this up to our necks. Let's head out of town. Emma, give me your satellite phone."

Emma took out her phone. "Oh crap."

"What's wrong?"

"It's dead. I forgot to charge it last night."

"Oh, that's great," Olivia said. "Where's your car charger?"

"It's still in my car."

Olivia sighed. "Then we'll have to find a safe place with Wi-Fi to contact Mrs. B."

According to their odometer, they were only three miles out of town when both lanes of traffic began slowing down. Nadia braked. Soon traffic rolled at a crawl.

"Why is there a traffic jam to get out of the city?" Olivia asked.

Robert blinked. "Accessing my database, I find no history of traffic slowdowns in this area. The only records I have are within the city itself."

"Most likely it's an accident," Nadia said.

"One of those big semitrucks," Miyuki said.

"Or a police checkpoint," Olivia added.

"No problem," Emma said. "Nadia only drank tea for breakfast."

"I'm not saying a drunk driving checkpoint, love."

"You mean one for Robert?" Miyuki asked.

Olivia turned on the radio and searched for a news station. She found one.

The FBI manhunt for a young anarchist continues. We broke the story to you last night as the FBI issued a manhunt for a young anarchist accused of burning down a federal government facility outside Crystal Springs, Nevada. Officials believe that Robert Kraftwerk is now in the Reno area. The FBI requests that Robert be considered armed and dangerous. If you see this young man, the FBI advises to keep your distance and contact law enforcement immediately.

"Oh, shit," Emma said.

Nadia found a gap in the center median and did a U-turn, pointing the loaner Mercedes westbound heading back into Reno.

"I did not burn anything down," Robert said. "That is a lie. I broke out of the facility, nothing more. Why would they lie about me?"

"To scare people away from you," Nadia said. "If people think you're dangerous, no one will help you."

"Sounds like we can't get out of Reno," Miyuki said.

Nadia watched Robert through her rearview mirror again. The boy sat quietly, no doubt wondering how much time he had left to live. Nadia wondered how long they could go on protecting Robert before the noose around him would grab the Gems too.

As they came back into Reno, Emma noticed a Burger King advertising free Wi-Fi, so Nadia exited the highway and parked in the restaurant's lot. Since Robert's image was probably now on television too, Miyuki and Emma stayed with him in the car while Nadia and Olivia went inside the Burger King.

Nadia found a bench table next to the glass door entrance to the indoor playground. She turned on her laptop and inserted her IP scrambler thumb drive before logging into another Authority website portal.

The restaurant's shift leader approached the two girls, thinking they were loitering. Olivia intercepted him with a smile and told the man they would order two soft drinks.

Mrs. B appeared on the laptop's screen. "What is your situation?"

Nadia updated her on the roadblock and the Chinese man with the dangerous eyes.

Olivia sat back down with two soft drinks.

"Your mysterious man is most likely Volleen Woo, one of China's top field operatives. He's extremely dangerous," Mrs. B said. "Did he have a giant Polynesian man with him?"

"Yes, a flipping huge one," Olivia said.

"Kawiki works often for the Chinese. I'll send you their profiles. Do your best to avoid them if possible."

"That goes without saying, ma'am," Nadia said.

"Here's the current situation. The FBI and Homeland Security have closed down Reno tight. There are checkpoints on every road out of the city. The FBI has men at the airport, and the military has established a no-fly zone over Reno, making some excuse that the vice president is making an unannounced visit. Basically we can't even send a helicopter to come pick you up."

"That doesn't sound good," Olivia said. "Do you want us to release our cargo to the authorities?"

Nadia glanced at her friend.

"I'm sorry, love. I want to help him too. Honest."

Mrs. B paused on the screen. Nadia could tell something was bothering the woman. "Negative, Emerald. Your new mission is to deliver your cargo to us unharmed. We will see that your package finds sanctuary."

Nadia's heart lifted like a bird. Finally she was on Robert's side!

"We have one card left to play," Mrs. B said. "AmRail has a train scheduled to stop in Reno in about one hour. You'll board that train and take it to Glenwood Springs, Colorado. I'll have people there to help you escape. Tickets will be waiting for all of you at the station. Please do your best to keep out of sight until the train arrives."

"How do we get our cargo on the train?" Nadia asked. "Won't there be FBI at the station also?"

"Remember your training, Sapphire. The Gems will succeed in their mission. I have confidence in each and every one of you. You will find a way."

CHAPTER 26

Through the windshield of the loaner Mercedes, Nadia watched passengers heading in and out of the Reno AmRail station. So far the area appeared normal. Emma emerged from the train station and took her time as she crossed the street. She glanced in the window of a local bakery before slipping into the backseat of the car.

"Well?" Olivia asked.

Emma produced a handful of AmRail tickets. "Five tickets for the Western Limited. Four of them are for two mainliner privacy cabins."

"Fantastic," Olivia said. "Robert can take one of those. I'll take the fifth ticket and keep watch in coach."

"Now the bad news," Emma said. "I counted six FBI agents along with a dozen sheriff's deputies. They're stopping every man in the waiting area and checking out their IDs before they board."

"Do they know what he looks like?" Miyuki asked.

"They have Robert's pic already posted around the station. I'm sure they all know," Emma said.

"That complicates things," Olivia said.

"Would it help if I became a girl?" Robert asked.

The Gems all stared.

"Say that again?" Emma asked.

"I still have access to my alias database. The one I would use for covert operations. I have one file listed as Rachel. I will now access it."

Robert's neck twitched to the side, like someone just flicked on a light switch. Robert blinked and looked around at the girls.

"So far we're not seeing it, love," Olivia said.

"My program is being altered. I feel it." Robert's words came out much softer and at a higher pitch. He then crossed his legs.

"Robert, keep talking," Emma said.

"What should I say?"

"Say the alphabet."

Robert began with the letter A and continued all the way to Z. As he went, the pitch of his voice went higher and higher. Nadia even noted subtle differences in how Robert was sitting. For instance, he crossed his arms over his crossed legs.

Nadia was amazed.

"That's excellent," Olivia said. "Trouble is, you still look like a bloke."

Nadia touched her headscarf and removed it. "We could use my scarf to hide his hair."

"What about his clothes?" Miyuki asked.

"We passed a Goodwill store a couple of blocks back," Emma said. "Think we can find something there that will work?"

"I could make it work," Nadia said.

"What about his beard stubble?" Emma asked. "And the biggest red flag, he's white."

"Why is that an issue? There are white Muslims in America."

"I got that. But if we're trying to pass him off as a Muslim girl, it would be great if he had your skin type. No offense."

"Now, Emma, don't you worry, girl, I can fix that too." Robert concentrated as his skin color became darker and darker.

"Wow, that so cool!" Miyuki said.

Robert snuggled up to Nadia's cheek. "See, we are sisters now."

Nadia ran her fingers over Robert's chin. It felt smooth and feminine. "Your stubble is gone. How is that possible?"

"I can control my hair follicles. If we had time, I could grow my hair as long as yours."

"Hang on, let's look at this a little bit differently," Olivia said. "What if Robert was your gay Muslim friend?"

"My what?"

"Oh, that's a good idea," Emma said. "Robert doesn't need a headscarf to pull that off, but he does need new clothes. Something with style. Nadia, we have a fashion emergency. Take us to that Goodwill."

Minutes later, the Gems and Robert went inside the Goodwill store. The variety of clothes inside was amazing. Some of the garments were ugly and hopeless, while other racks showed more promise. Emma circled the inside of the store, sniffing out clothes and accessories like a police dog on a drug raid. Robert followed her close as the girl pulled things off the rack and placed them against Robert's chest and waist; then if it passed her test, Emma made him carry it.

When Emma was satisfied with her pile of clothes, she led everyone to the changing area. Emma took the clothes from Robert and organized them into four separate outfits.

"He's not going on holiday, love," Olivia said. "He only needs one set."

Emma groaned. "Please, I'm working here. Don't mess with my process." Emma gave Robert outfit number one. "Go put that on."

Robert unzipped his pants and dropped them to the ground.

Miyuki covered her mouth and laughed.

"She means in the fitting room, Robert," Nadia said, trying not to look at the boy's underwear.

Robert let out a high-pitched giggle and took his clothes into a fitting room.

Emma went through another stack of clothes Robert was carrying. She held out a lavender scarf to Nadia. "This would look great with your lavender blouse. The one in your closet?"

Nadia examined it. Emma was right. The scarf was old, but very beautiful.

Emma pulled out a Nirvana band T-shirt. "This is in your size. Do you have it already?"

Miyuki shook with excitement. "Oh, my beautiful Kurt." She snatched the shirt. "Thank you, Emma."

"We don't have time to shop for ourselves," Olivia said.

Emma offered her a small black box. "They're fake, but still. Here."

Olivia took the box anyway and opened it. There was a set of tear-shaped emerald-looking earrings. Olivia just stared at them.

"Those are pretty!" Miyuki said.

Olivia hesitated. "Emma, please don't spend your money on us."

Emma laughed. "You don't understand. That's the best thing about these stores. Huge bargains if you know how to look. Those large faux-emerald earrings I gave you should be at least sixty dollars because they're French. But somebody marked them for ten dollars. That's a steal."

Robert came out wearing his first outfit. Emma scrutinized every piece of clothing. "Too stylish for a train trip," she said. "We need to tone it down just a little. Let's try the third outfit, Robert."

Robert grabbed the clothes in the third pile and went back to change. Minutes later he came back out with a tasteful pink button-down shirt. Black pants with faint striping. Black dress shoes with no laces. Emma pulled his collar up and took another look around the boy.

"This is it," she said.

Robert looked at himself in the large mirror. "My Rachel program approves of this look, girl. She would date this stylish man in a heartbeat."

"You mean they would be best friends. Remember, you're playing a gay man," Olivia said.

"I am confused," Robert said. "I have activated my Rachel program, but I am going to be dressed like a man. Yet I will not act like a man."

"Exactly," Emma said. "Just treat Nadia like your best friend. Your performance will flow out of that naturally and will be quite believable."

Olivia checked her phone. "We'd best be going to the station, or we won't have a train to board."

Ten minutes later, the Gems entered the AmRail station with Robert. The station itself wasn't all that large; only four wooden benches with ten chairs per side cluttered the waiting area. But the station did have a striking two-story-high ceiling with decorative wood carvings. Four giant nineteenth-century windows allowed natural light into most of the building itself. Much of the inside looked like it hadn't changed since Nevada first became a state. Like Emma had said, the place was swarming with law enforcement stationed near the walls and the main boarding platform outside.

Nadia stuck close to Robert, who asked her a question.

"I've never had a pedicure before. Would you do my toenails when we get on the train?" he asked.

"I can if you want," Nadia said. "By the way, until the train leaves the station, it might be a good idea if you don't speak. For your own safety."

"Okay, anything for my bestie." Robert hugged her cheek to

cheek.

Nadia wasn't sure if she liked this new part of Robert. At best it made her feelings for him…even more confusing.

Soon the Gems found some empty chairs in the main waiting area and had a seat.

An FBI agent noticed the new arrivals. The agent took his time, but eventually walked near to where the girls were sitting. Nadia didn't stare directly at him, but she could see him out of the corner of her eye.

His eyes scanned the faces of the girls. Then he slowed down near Nadia.

She could feel his eyes upon her, like every Muslim trying to travel in America. This was one of the few cases that she hoped the man's eyes were on her instead of Robert.

"Can I see your identification and your ticket?" the FBI man asked.

Nadia closed her eyes. If his question was directed at Robert, they would be sunk. Nadia opened her eyes and looked at the FBI man. His eyes were directed at her.

Thank Allah.

"Yes, of course, officer."

To shield Robert from scrutiny, she also stood up. Nadia brought out her purse and gave the FBI man her new California driver's license and train ticket.

The FBI man looked over both documents closely. "Are you traveling with those young ladies?"

Nadia glanced over at the Gems. "Yes, sir."

The man handed her ID and ticket back.

"May I search your bag?" he asked.

A part of Nadia wanted to tell him no, that she didn't feel like becoming a suicide bomber today. However, she held her tongue and only nodded. The FBI agent unzipped her backpack. Nadia tried to remember what she had inside and if any of it would get her in trouble. The agent searched every pocket and pouch before zipping it up and giving it back to Nadia.

"Thank you for your cooperation. Have a safe trip." The FBI man walked away.

Nadia sighed as Robert squeezed her hand. His high-pitched voice was soft. "Thank you."

More than twenty minutes late, a large AmRail passenger train rolled into the Reno station and stopped. Passengers stood up and moved outside to the boarding platform. They formed two lines headed by the two conductors checking tickets and IDs.

Nadia and the girls moved into one of those lines and surrounded Robert. Now came the most trickiest part. Robert had to change back to his original skin color in order to match his school ID and the name on the ticket. Since Mrs. B had managed to book a ticket under his Robert Billings alias, the hope was that the AmRail database hadn't flagged his name and picture yet.

However, Olivia pointed out that the FBI could have allowed the ticket to be purchased in order to set a trap for Robert. Whichever way it was going to go, Nadia knew they would soon find out.

As the Gems shielded Robert from view, the boy went through the process of becoming Robert 1.0 again.

Every time the line moved, the girls would move together simultaneously, like a moving tent.

So far, so good.

In fact, Robert's skin was becoming lighter and lighter.

The same FBI man who questioned Nadia wandered out on to the platform.

"FBI at twelve o clock," Emma said under her breath.

"Just be cool," Olivia said softly.

Robert then stood up, his face white as snow and completely recognizable.

"Stare at the train, Robert, not at the platform," Olivia said.

Robert did exactly that. "Is the FBI man there?" His cute boy voice was back.

Nadia was glad. "Yes," she said.

"Wish cop would go have donut," Miyuki said.

"Be quiet," Olivia said.

The girls advanced up the line and came close to the conductors.

"He's staring at us now," Emma said.

"Be prepared," Olivia said under her breath. "We might have to rush the conductors and take over the train by force."

"What? Seriously, like, you want us to go hijack a train?" Emma asked.

Olivia hushed her.

Nadia glanced at her friend. "Have you gone mad?"

"Can I drive the train?" Miyuki asked.

It was at that moment that an older lady called out something in Chinese. The FBI man turned in a new direction as the woman closed in on him. She began talking in a frantic-sounding Chinese, as if she were scared about something. The FBI agent tried to understand her, but was having difficulty.

"Now's our chance," Olivia said. "Get up there, Robert."

The Gems shoved Robert forward to one of the conductors.

The conductor ripped a tab off his ticket and did a quick check of his Robert Billings ID. The conductor matched the two documents and gave a nod to Robert when he handed them back. The android climbed up and disappeared into the coach.

Soon all four Gems climbed aboard as the Western Limited prepared to leave the station.

CHAPTER 27

Nadia and Robert entered one of the mainliner privacy cabins. It was compact, yet had enough room for a large two-person sofa. Opposite the sofa was a third chair for a guest along with a private restroom. Between the sofa and chair was a huge observation window. For two people it was just enough room.

Robert examined the panel above the sofa. "The AmRail website says this converts into two beds. Are you comfortable with that arrangement?"

Before Nadia got to know Robert, sleeping in the same room with a boy would be out of the question. Even though her father was on the other side of the world, Nadia had still promised him that she would respect her religion and her family's honor. However, Robert was an android. Not a human boy. And despite his appearance, he did not act like most men. Nadia was confident that she could trust him like he was her brother.

"Yes, Robert. Of course."

"I have accessed several Arabic cultural writings on social etiquette in Islam. I will follow them as closely as I can due to our close living conditions."

"These are special circumstances, so a strict observance of social etiquette is not necessary. However, thank you for your consideration." Nadia took a place on the sofa and hesitated. She then took off her headscarf and brushed her hair out.

Robert took the third seat, opposite the sofa.

"You don't have to sit over there," Nadia said. "Unless you feel more comfortable there."

Robert joined Nadia on the sofa.

The train started with a jolt, throwing Nadia on top of Robert. She braced herself against the boy's chest as Robert held her shoulders for balance while the train gathered speed leaving the

Reno station. Robert's hands felt warm against her shoulders. It was amazing how lifelike the boy was. She could feel herself being drawn to him, unable to keep herself from touching him. She glanced at his lips and wondered how lifelike kissing them would be. She pulled herself off Robert and pressed her back against the sofa.

Nadia then watched as the AmRail train weaved its way through Reno and finally broke free into the open Nevada desert.

Robert asked a question. "Can human friends fall in love?"

A jolt of electricity went through Nadia's body as she focused on the desert. "What do you mean by that?"

"If two human beings create a deep, meaningful relationship, and they are sexually attracted to each other, can they fall in love?"

"Yes, of course they can."

"To an average female or male, would I be considered sexually attractive?"

"Well, several girls at school wanted you to text them your number, so I would say they were attracted to you."

"When I was created, I was made to look appealing in a general sense to both females and males," Robert said. "This was required for me to infiltrate social groups more easily." Robert glanced at her. "Do you find me attractive?"

Nadia pulled her eyes to the window. Her cheeks heated up.

Robert waited patiently.

"In a general sense, I suppose so," she answered.

"Would my appearance be more attractive to you if I changed my skin tone to match yours?"

Now her stomach warmed. She did like how Robert looked with darker skin. However, this line of questioning was becoming absurd.

"Why are you asking me this?"

"I have analyzed all of your nonverbal signals towards me since we first met and up until this moment," Robert said. "Your nonverbal cues have been confusing. When you touch me, you do not jerk your hand back. You allow your fingers to linger upon me. When you watch me, your gaze is four point three times longer than the other three girls' in your group. Both these observations would indicate an affection towards me. However, when we engage in conversation, instead of looking at the other person, which is common in general human interaction, you prefer to gaze out a window or at the ground, or begin to adjust your clothing. This indicates that I am not properly engaging you in meaningful conversation." Robert tilted his head. "Could you please clarify this?"

Nadia's body tensed up. She couldn't believe Robert had just said it. Brought the fact up like it was part of some laundry list. *Oh, by the way, I caught you falling in love with me.*

"I need to use the toilet." Nadia jumped off the sofa and opened the door to the hallway.

"You are not using our restroom here?" Robert asked.

Nadia shut the door behind her and moved down the long side hallway that connected all the bedroom cabins together inside the sleeper car. She stopped near Emma and Miyuki's bedroom suite, but changed her mind and made her way into the next car.

The dining car had only a handful of people since it was past lunch.

Nadia continued walking.

The Skywatcher lounge car was full. The chairs in this car all faced sideways, where a giant glass canopy provided a 180-degree unobstructed view of the Western landscape the train rolled through.

Nadia continued walking.

She entered the first of the coach cars. This car looked more like the inside of an airplane. Nadia scanned all the faces until she saw Olivia, who removed her earbuds as Nadia sat next to her.

"It's nice someone's come to visit me," Olivia said.

Nadia tried to show her a friendly smile.

But Olivia frowned. "What's wrong, love?"

Her best friend could read it on her face. "Nothing's wrong. How is everything back here? Anyone look suspicious?"

Olivia scanned the coach car. "No red flags to speak of. I took a walk through the other two cars and saw no one that looked like a threat." Olivia paused. "Now, what's wrong?"

There was no fooling Olivia. Nadia surrendered and told her about what Robert had said to her.

"Damn, he laid it all out there, didn't he?" Olivia said. "Do you think he's even capable of having those feelings?"

Nadia remembered when Robert had come back to check on her after the loaner Mercedes almost hit the back of the oil tanker. However, that was easy to explain because the boy obviously wanted to help them if they were hurt.

What about the things Robert had asked about in the cabin? No, Nadia couldn't explain that behavior.

"I don't know, but he's curious about how I see him," Nadia said.

"And what did you tell him?" Olivia asked.

"I told him I suddenly had to go use the toilet. What do I say to him?"

"What do you want to say? Do you like him?"

"Yes, I like him."

"Even though he's a robot."

Nadia thought about that. Could a human girl even have a relationship with a boy robot? Could a robot love a human? Was all of this too improbable to even think about?

"The thing is," Olivia said. "How's that all going to work? Once Mrs. B has Robert, he'll be sent far away and given a new identity, a new life. He won't be around anymore."

Olivia was right. Once this was over and Robert was safe, he would go away. Maybe forever.

"I'm sorry, Nads. It must feel wonderful to have such a nice boy giving you this much sincere attention, but there's no way you two can be together."

Nadia relaxed and peered out the window as the desert flew by. Her best friend was right. It didn't make sense. "If I want to be in his life, I would have to leave everything and go wherever Robert goes."

"Your family has sacrificed so much already," Olivia said. "You'd break your poor dad's heart if you quit the Gems to go be with a boy."

The image of her father in tears came to Nadia's mind. The relief in his tired face when the Authority had assured him that his daughter was special. That she would not only go to the best school in Saudi Arabia, but she would also be groomed to enter one of the best colleges in the world. Her father had always been Nadia's greatest champion. He was convinced his daughter was a genius and was desperate for her to have a different life. His deal with the Authority had sealed that

She knew it wasn't possible to leave. Therefore, it was not possible for her to fall in love.

"You're right. I couldn't do that to my father." Nadia looked out through one of the railcar windows as the Nevada desert stretched out to the horizon. The sand gave her comfort. Nadia sighed. "I should go back and keep Robert company." She stood up in the aisle.

"Only friends," Olivia said. "Remember that."

Nadia waved goodbye to Olivia and made her way back into the Skywatcher lounge car.

Next she moved through the dining car.

Then back to the sleeper car.

Nadia hesitated before opening the door to their privacy cabin. She moved inside and noticed it was empty. She knocked on the bathroom door before peeking inside. No sign of Robert. Nadia now knew where he probably was, and a streak of jealousy went up her spine. She marched down the hallway to Emma and Nadia's cabin and knocked on the door.

"Come in!" shouted Miyuki.

Nadia entered. Miyuki was munching on a bag of tortilla chips. The crumbs peppered the sofa.

"Where's Emma?" Nadia asked.

"She taking a shower," Miyuki said. "How is everything with Robert?"

"I went back to speak with Olivia, and when I returned to our cabin Robert was gone," Nadia said. "I thought he might have come in here."

Miyuki shook her head and offered Nadia a reach into her chip bag.

Nadia cleaned off a spot on the couch and sat. She took a handful of chips and nibbled.

"He must be exploring the train," Miyuki said. "That's what I would do if I were a robot."

"I don't think Olivia wanted him to leave the cabin." Nadia ate another chip. They were tasty.

Miyuki told her about other things she would do if she were a robot. A lot of it centered on fighting criminals, exploring the outer reaches of the known galaxy, and fighting giant aquatic monsters that attacked Japan. It took a few more chips for Nadia to realize number three was a joke.

As Nadia took another handful of chips from the bag, Emma emerged from her shower wrapped up in a cotton towel. Her curves were perfect. Her body sculpted like one of those actresses in movies and television. Nadia put the chips back into the bag. She was fat enough already.

"Hi," Emma said. "Where's Robert?"

"We don't know," Nadia said.

"I think he's exploring the train," Miyuki said.

Emma glanced at Nadia. "Why didn't you go with him?" she asked, stretching out and drying her perfect legs with the towel.

Nadia swore that some days Emma did this on purpose to make them all feel bad about themselves.

"I left him alone for ten minutes," Nadia said.

"Want us to go search for him?" Miyuki said.

"You don't have to. I'm sure he'll come back soon," Nadia said. "I'll go wait for him."

Nadia stepped into the corridor and walked back to their cabin. She tried the door and it was locked.

Maybe Robert had come back.

She knocked. The door opened and a giant round man who looked Polynesian stood there. Kawiki grabbed Nadia, pulled her inside the cabin, and shoved a cloth over her nose and mouth. Nadia struggled against the giant man, but it was useless. She breathed in a strange smell, and her mind drifted off into darkness.

CHAPTER 28

Emma slipped into the vintage New York Yankees T-shirt and cowgirl jeans she'd found at the Goodwill store. The cowgirl jeans were not her personal style, but they fit well and didn't look all that bad with the T-shirt. Besides, they were on the road, and she and the Gems badly needed a change of clothes. Miyuki had on her Nirvana T-shirt and jeans too, which made them like sisters of casual fashion.

Something like that.

Miyuki offered her some tortilla chips.

Emma only took one. "Where's the salsa?"

"Might be some in snack car. Wanna go see?" Miyuki asked.

Emma ate the chip. It was good but needed salsa. She checked on her two phones. The satellite phone was now fully charged as well as her cell phone. There was a text from Olivia that was addressed to both her and Miyuki.

Did Rob make it back yet?

Emma typed,

He's w/ Nadia. ask her.

Olivia replied,

No answer from her.

Miyuki giggled and typed,

Could b busy makin android babies LOL

Emma laughed.

Another message from Olivia.

Piss off u 2. Please check. Worried.

Emma rolled her eyes at Miyuki, who typed another message…

OK We check.

"If we find them in bed together, I'm taking a picture and sending it to Olivia," Emma said as she slipped on her shoes.

Miyuki followed her as they stepped out into the hallway.

Emma stopped at the door of Nadia and Robert's cabin and knocked.

No one answered.

Emma put her ear to the door. Miyuki squeezed in next to her. Emma focused but could only hear the train itself.

"Do you hear anything?" Emma asked.

"Nothing. No one getting busy in there."

Emma tried the door handle and it was unlocked, so Emma moved inside.

Nadia's backpack was still on the floor. The headscarf Emma had bought her from Goodwill was still folded on the table. Robert's clothes were laid on the far chair. Miyuki glanced in the restroom. She shook her head.

"Maybe Robert came back, and they walked around train together?" Miyuki asked.

Emma called Olivia and told her what they found.

"I'll try calling her," Olivia said on the phone before hanging up.

A ringtone blasted from inside Nadia's backpack. Emma checked the pockets and found Nadia's phone. Olivia's name was on the screen.

Emma answered it. "Hey, I'm on her phone. It was in her backpack."

"That's not right. If she took a walk with Robert, she'd have it with her. Something's wrong," Olivia's voice said. "I'll start a search at the back of the coach cars and work my way forward. You two start at the front sleeper car and work your way back. I'll meet you in the dining car."

Emma and Miyuki made it to the first sleeper car. Together, they went upstairs and downstairs in the double-decker railcar. They found no sign of Robert or Nadia. They checked the second sleeper car with the same result. Next they checked their own sleeper car and found nothing.

They went over to the dining car and slipped into seats at one of the empty tables and waited for Olivia.

Twenty minutes later she showed up.

"Anything?" Olivia asked.

Emma and Miyuki both shook their heads.

Olivia sighed. "Did you check inside all the rooms?"

"We checked the roomettes," Miyuki said. "They have glass doors, so we can see inside. But the cabins all have solid doors. All private."

"Did you check all the bathrooms?"

"The public ones, yeah," Emma said. "Now there's still the baggage car, but that's for rail staff only."

"There's a few areas in the snack bar and kitchen like that too. I'll sneak into those and have a peek," Olivia said. "Why don't you two go back to the first sleeper car and knock on every door. Make up any excuse, but check each sleeper cabin."

"Okay," Emma said.

"Sorry, but I've got a bad feeling," Olivia said.

For once, Emma agreed with her.

CHAPTER 29

Nadia woke up hearing voices in Chinese. One of those sounded feminine. She opened her eyes and saw a large cabin. Kawiki, the large Polynesian man who drugged her, watched Nadia as he guarded a door. The cabin shimmied from side to side, indicating to Nadia she was still on the train and it was still moving.

Volleen Woo, the man with dangerous eyes, stood by the wide observation window. Next to him was a Chinese woman. Nadia recognized her. She was the lady who had made a scene at the station platform in Reno. That lady noted her alert presence and stopped talking in mid-sentence. Mr. Woo fixed his attention upon Nadia and asked her something in Chinese.

Nadia didn't answer.

"Вы работаете на русских?" Mr. Woo asked.

Nadia understood his question in Russian, yet again she chose not to answer.

Like a cat, Mr. Woo sat next to her without a sound. When she tried to move away, Nadia felt something binding her wrists together. She also noted where she was sitting, on a long four-person couch that ran against the back wall of the cabin. The door Kawiki guarded looked like the only way out of the cabin. No, wait. She noticed another door to her right. She wondered what was through that door.

"That unguarded door leads to a closet," Mr. Woo said. "In case escape was on your mind. You also must convince Kawiki not to break you in half."

The Chinese lady glared at Nadia with superior disdain. Her hand flew through the air and struck Nadia on the cheek, whipping her head back. "Who do you work for?"

Nadia's cheek throbbed with pain as she held down the urge to cry out. Nadia did have some interrogation training. Yet it dealt more with combating mind tricks and manipulation rather than resisting physical violence.

Nadia held her tongue.

"The CIA does not hire children," Mr. Woo said. "Not inside its own country. Your black friend is English. Perhaps you were raised in England too? Are you both working for MI6?"

Nadia stared at the wall and listened to the clickety-clack of the tracks.

Another strike jerked her head to the side.

"Answer him," the woman said.

Nadia's cheek was on fire. She closed her eyes and held in the pain. The one thing Nadia despised after joining the Gems was inflicting violence upon another human being. She did not enjoy it, yet inflicting violence upon this woman was becoming more and more attractive.

"Are you here to deliver the robot to MI6?" Mr. Woo asked with icy confidence.

"No," Nadia said.

"Ah, thank you for answering." Mr. Woo said something to the woman in Chinese. She grabbed a bottle of water and handed it to Mr. Woo. He opened it and offered it to Nadia.

"Thank you, but I'm not thirsty."

Mr. Woo nodded and twisted the cap back on. He placed it to the side. "What is your name?"

"Sapphire."

"Sapphire what?"

"Only Sapphire."

"Like the gem sapphire," Mr. Woo clarified.

"Yes."

Mr. Woo contemplated her answer while the woman asked him something in Chinese. Mr. Woo shook his head and pointed to the empty part of the sofa. She frowned and sat down.

"During our meeting at breakfast, you referred to the Japanese girl as Ruby. Does this imply a connection between your names and the names of precious gems?"

It was a rhetorical question. Nadia could tell this man wasn't stupid, and she hadn't forgotten Mrs. B's warning about him. She had to play this cool even though her stomach was churning with acid right now.

"What do you think?" she asked.

The woman quickly raised her arm for another strike.

"Stop," Mr. Woo ordered.

The woman lowered her arm.

Mr. Woo addressed Nadia once again. "The Gems Project. An experimental intelligence operative group composed of three skilled teen girls trained to work as a team."

He now had Nadia's full attention.

"Now we are making progress," he said. "But what about the blonde girl? The one Kawiki held at gunpoint. Is she a new addition?"

Nadia said nothing.

"Interesting." Mr. Woo stood up. "Ruby, Sapphire, and the black girl must be Emerald. Yes, that does make sense. You are protecting the robot because the Authority has other plans for him. Most interesting."

Mr. Woo sat back down. "You're keeping the robot away from both the American Army and the FBI. Why? What plans does the Authority have for him?"

"Robert wants to be free," Nadia said. That wasn't a secret.

"Surely you're not suggesting the Authority is wasting its meager resources on helping a robot achieve his freedom, not without an ulterior motive. That's absurd."

"Why can't you people leave him alone? He doesn't want to harm anyone."

Mr. Woo smiled. "And what guarantee do I have that Robert and others like him will not be used as weapons against my country?"

"The Authority will make sure."

Mr. Woo chuckled. "So my country should trust a rogue organization created by capitalists to help insure that my country is safe? You're so naive."

"It's still the truth," Nadia said.

Mr. Woo moved over to the window and looked out. "Robert is far too dangerous to be set free. He needs to be studied. His secrets need to be exposed so countermeasures can be created. China must be prepared to meet the new threat." Mr. Woo turned. "If your organization truly wanted world peace and stability, they would take Robert and disassemble him. Then they would give everyone the information on how he runs. That would be the only fair thing to do."

"The Authority is not doing the fair thing," Nadia said. "They're doing the right thing."

"Why, Miss Sapphire, you almost make me believe that freeing Robert *was* your mission," Mr Woo said. "But no matter. We have Robert, and when this train stops in Salt Lake City, we will take him back home with us."

"I want to see him," Nadia said.

"Why?"

"I want to make sure he's alright."

"You don't need to see him."

Nadia couldn't accept that. She needed to assure herself that Robert was okay. Her mind sifted through some ideas and found one.

"What if I gave you information that could help you avoid a trap in Salt Lake City?"

This piqued Mr. Woo's interest. He took a moment to think about it before motioning Kawiki to open the closet.

Robert stood motionless inside. His eyes moved and found Nadia. He struggled to open his mouth, but nothing came out. His eyes looked concerned, almost desperate. Nadia noticed a black cable connecting him to some portable device.

"What's wrong with him?" Nadia asked.

"According to my robotics expert, Robert's software is intact. We're merely overloading his relays with looping software. Apparently this prevents the robot from issuing commands to most of his body parts."

Robert tried opening his mouth again, yet still nothing came out.

"And his ability to talk," Nadia added.

The other door swung open, and another Chinese man came into the cabin. He was shorter and younger than everyone else. The young man adjusted his glasses when he saw Nadia and smiled.

She didn't smile back.

"Ah, good timing," Mr. Woo said. "I was telling this young lady about your looping software."

"Are you a coder too?" the young man asked, extremely curious.

Nadia wondered if she should admit it. Part of her was curious about how they were jamming Robert's system because maybe she could figure out a way to stop it.

"I don't know much about computers," she lied. "I only want to make sure you're not hurting him."

"Hurting him? He's a robot. He has zero pain receptors. Actually, my program does a really simple thing, but it's so complex to implement." The young man blurted out loads of coding information about how he could take commands from any computer and redirect them towards this unending loop, rendering them temporarily useless. His enthusiasm was so intense that Mr. Woo told him to shut up.

"Don't worry. Girls don't know anything about coding. It's all white noise to them," the Chinese computer geek said.

Nadia bit her tongue. The boy had given her plenty of information. She could almost see his programming code in her head. It would be easy to break the loops and reroute the commands he'd put in. If she could hook up her laptop to Robert's software...

"Take a walk around the train," Mr. Woo said to the computer geek.

"But I just finished walking around the—"

"Indulge me. Again."

The geek frowned and left.

Mr. Woo motioned towards the woman. She stood up and grabbed Nadia's neck and squeezed.

"Now, since I've fulfilled my end of the deal, what trap do they have waiting for us?" Mr. Woo asked.

The woman's grip was too tight. Nadia couldn't breathe. Actually, choking was more like it.

Nadia coughed. "The Russians."

It was all she could get out.

Mr. Woo said something in Chinese. He didn't sound happy.

The woman released Nadia's throat.

"Please continue."

"A group of Russians. About four of them. They tried to steal Robert in San Francisco, but we stopped them. We were given a tip that they'll be waiting at the platform when we arrive in Salt Lake City. Since you have Robert now, they'll come after you," Nadia said. "I'll give you detailed descriptions of all four men. However, in exchange, I want you to promise me that you'll give Robert a chance to live free in China. To let him be your guest and not your prisoner."

"That offer is no longer valid," Mr. Woo said. "I gave him the easy option, and he refused. Now he receives the hard option. The same option you will receive if you do not give us good descriptions of these Russians."

The Chinese woman brightened. She was ready to kick Nadia's head off.

Nadia closed her eyes and gave Mr. Woo the information. She now had no cards left to play.

In her head, Nadia calculated the chances of her still being alive once they reached Salt Lake City.

She gave herself one chance in five.

CHAPTER 30

Emma knocked on the next cabin door. A female voice inside told her just a moment. It took the person a couple of minutes to open the cabin door, but once they did, Emma could see it was an old white lady in her sixties at least. Her husband watched from his chair near the window.

The old woman's face lit up as she saw Emma. "Yes, dear? Can I help you?"

"I'm sorry to bother you," Emma said. "But we're looking for a friend that we lost track of."

Emma held up her phone and showed the lady Nadia's picture without her headscarf. "Have you seen her?"

The old lady studied the picture. "I don't believe so. What about you, Herbert?"

The old man was out of his chair and peeking behind his wife's shoulder. "Doesn't ring any bells. How long has she been missing?" the man asked. "If it's serious, you should contact the conductor."

"Oh, we have. It's okay. We just wanted to check all the private cabins because our friend loves talking to people, and we thought she might have followed someone to their cabin."

"She sounds like a delightful person," the old woman said.

Miyuki stepped forward. "She is."

The old woman took a second look at Miyuki. "Are you part of that Chinese tour group?"

Miyuki frowned. Telling someone from Japan that they looked Chinese was…

Emma realized something.

"What Chinese tour group?" Emma asked.

"The one downstairs. Herbert saw a few of them when he was using the facilities. Didn't you, Herbert?"

"Yup. About four of them. And there was this big one. Biggest Chinaman I ever saw with them."

Emma glanced at Miyuki, who shared the same thought.

"My friends from Beijing are part of a larger travel group," Miyuki said. "Emma and her friend are traveling with us."

"It was cheaper if we joined a travel group," Emma added.

The old man laughed. "We're retirees. We know all about trying to save money, young lady."

Emma and Miyuki thanked the couple before moving on to the snack car to find Olivia. She had searched the kitchen plus the crew-only areas and found nothing. Emma and Miyuki passed on the information the old couple had given them.

"Sounds promising," Olivia said. "Let's go take a look."

Olivia led the three girls back into the second sleeper car and took the center stairs down to the lower level. There were three public toilets, a changing room with a shower, four of the small roomette cabins with see-through sliding doors...and one private cabin at the end marked family room. Two of the four roomette cabins were empty, and the ones that weren't empty did not have any one who remotely looked Chinese.

"Bathrooms are clear," Emma said.

"Changing room is clear too," Miyuki said.

All three girls switch their attention to the family bedroom at the end of the hall.

"I'll go knock and see who answers," Emma said.

"Wait a moment, love," Olivia said. "If those agents are in there, knocking on the door will give up our only advantage."

"Yes," Miyuki said. "We know where they are, but they don't know we're coming."

Olivia leaned against the wall of the closet. "All we know is that they might be in there. We need to know for sure and without being suspicious. If they suspect anything, they might hurt Nadia."

"How about a fire alarm?" Emma asked. "That would get them out of the room."

"AmRail would stop the train if it was on fire," Olivia said. "They might see through that."

"Also forcing the train to stop could give them a chance to get Robert off and escape," Miyuki said.

"Hey, when you went through the staff areas, did you see any AmRail uniforms?" Emma asked.

Olivia thought about it. "Yeah, there were a few hanging in some of the lockers. So what?"

"What if I disguised myself like a male porter? That way I could knock on their door and not cast any suspicions."

Olivia just laughed.

"What?"

"You, dressed up like a bloke? You've got to be joking."

When it came to acting, Emma never joked.

"I could pull it off. I'm a professional."

"You're the most girl-looking girl of the four of us, love," Olivia said. "What are you going to do? Cut off all your blond hair and tape your boobs down with duct tape?"

Yes, Emma would use duct tape if she had to for a role. Olivia had no clue the sacrifices a real actress went through for her craft.

"I can totally do this," Emma said. "All I have to do is pull my hair up in a tight ponytail and stuff it all inside a conductor's cap. Then I'll get rid of all my makeup. Apply a new base, draw in some age lines at the correct places, adjust the way I walk and talk…I can do this."

"You have theater makeup in your purse?" Miyuki asked.

"A good actress is always prepared."

"I think you're mental," Olivia said. "But I can't think of a better idea. One thing though, we need to give you a proper reason to be knocking on their door."

Miyuki grinned. "I have a good one."

CHAPTER 31

Her cheek throbbed with pain. Despite giving them information about the Russians, Mr. Woo let the Chinese woman hit Nadia a few more times as he continued to ask her pointed questions about the Authority. Questions she couldn't answer without betraying everyone.

"I grow tired of asking this," Mr. Woo said. "But who is the controller in charge of the Gems Project?"

Nadia stared at the wall.

Another slap across her face.

Mr. Woo sighed. "How disappointing. I would like my answers before we reach Salt Lake City. I can not take you with us, so we will need your information as soon as possible." He checked with the Chinese lady. "The trash can in the restroom. We must fill it with water, I'm afraid."

The woman flashed a sadistic grin as she headed towards the main door.

"Does the feeling of drowning make you uncomfortable, Miss Sapphire?" Mr. Woo asked.

Nadia connected the dots, and her heart jumped. They were going to torture her.

As the Chinese woman touched the doornob, someone knocked on the door.

The room froze.

Mr. Woo pointed at Kawiki and the couch. The large Polynesian plopped next to Nadia and placed his massive arm around her shoulders like they were boyfriend and girlfriend. Nadia felt an object pressing against her body. She looked down and saw the gun with a silencer. The same one Kawiki had used on Emma.

Mr. Woo stepped over to the closet where Robert was. He took out another gun with a silencer and readied himself. He nodded.

The Chinese woman forced her face to look pleasant before opening the door.

"Yes?"

It was an AmRail conductor who looked rather thin. "I apologize for disturbing you, ma'am. But one of our guests upstairs —well, they've lost their snake in a private cabin."

The word *snake* made Kawiki's eyes search the floor immediately.

"We're in the process of searching the entire car. May I come in and take a look?"

Nadia focused. If she could somehow let the conductor know she was being held against her will without Woo knowing, maybe the conductor could get help.

"No," the woman said. "We have no snake here." She made a move to close the door.

But the conductor blocked the way. "It won't take a moment, ma'am. It's for your safety and ours."

"Have you cleared that cabin yet?" someone yelled down the hallway.

The conductor looked over his shoulder. "Please don't shout down the hallway and disturb our guests. I'll be done in a moment." The conductor turned back. "Sorry, my assistant is new."

The Chinese woman glanced over at Mr. Woo. He nodded to Kawiki, and they both holstered their guns.

"If it will not take long." The Chinese woman stepped away from the door.

The conductor entered rather casually and began searching the floor. He turned on his flashlight and searched the inside of some storage bins and cabinets. When the conductor came closer to Nadia, she noted something unusual about the conductor. Under his large hat, the man had a somewhat feminine face, and his eyes looked familiar.

Wait, she knew those eyes. It was Emma without any makeup. The girl's skin was darker and somehow looked more aged. But if one looked closely…Nadia tensed up. If Mr. Woo or Kawiki took one good look at her…

"What kind of snake is it?" Kawiki asked Emma, the conductor.

"A large cobra from India. Very deadly."

"A cobra?" the Chinese woman asked. Her eyes checked the

floor.

Kawiki shifted in his seat and kept his eyes on the floor. "I don't like snakes."

Emma the conductor released a tiny grin at Nadia. "Have you seen a snake in this cabin, miss?"

Mr. Woo stepped forward. "Our friend is from Pakistan. She doesn't speak English." He fixed his dangerous eyes on Nadia and opened his suit slightly, revealing the pistol in its holster. The message was clear. Be good or he would kill her and the conductor.

"Not a problem," Emma the conductor said without a clue as she continued her search of the storage bins. Soon she came to the closet with Robert inside.

Mr. Woo blocked her. "I just put my coat in the closet right before you came in. There was no snake inside."

"Are you sure? You can't be too careful with such a dangerous animal aboard."

"I'm positive." Mr. Woo squinted, his eyes getting a much better look at Emma.

Nadia froze.

"Tell me, how much longer to our next station?" Mr. Woo asked before slipping his hand inside his suit.

Nadia's stomach churned. She glanced over at Kawiki. He was now looking into a storage bin next to him for snakes.

"The next station?" Emma the conductor asked. "I would say a half hour at least."

"And which station would that be?" Mr. Woo asked.

Nadia took in a deep breath. Mr. Woo already knew the answer to his question. He was only waiting for Emma to give the wrong answer.

Emma hesitated. "Elko, Nevada."

Mr. Woo's eyes went cold. "That would be incorrect." His hand moved under his suit.

Nadia didn't wait. She threw herself forward and crashed into Mr. Woo and Emma, sending both of them to the floor.

The Chinese woman yelled something that Nadia couldn't understand. But she did understand that Emma and Mr. Woo were now fighting for his gun on the floor.

Nadia rolled over and struggled with her hands, but they were still bound up tight. There was no way she could help Emma.

But her mouth was free.

"Emerald! Ruby!" Nadia yelled as loud as she could.

The Chinese woman lifted her boot, preparing to kick Nadia in the face. But Miyuki struck the woman from behind and threw her against the sofa.

Nadia rolled over to check on Emma. Mr. Woo and Emma both had a grip on the gun. But the man was strong and forced the muzzle towards Emma's face.

Nadia swung her feet around and kicked Mr. Woo hard in the chin.

The gun fired into the ceiling.

Nadia kicked him again.

Mr. Woo must have dropped the gun because Emma now had it pointed at him.

A large hand then grabbed Nadia's arm and yanked her up like a stuffed toy.

It was Kawiki. The large Polynesian man then grimaced.

Nadia didn't understand why until she saw Olivia pointing her stun gun at him. The electric prongs were stuck into Kawiki's side. She could hear the crackle of electricity as it went into Kawiki's nervous system.

But the large Polynesian man laughed. "That tickles." Kawiki ripped out the wires with ease before reaching for his holster.

"This does more than tickle." Emma pointed Mr. Woo's gun at Kawiki. "Let my friend go."

Kawiki dropped his smile.

"You, get over there." Olivia pointed at the Chinese lady.

Miyuki shouted something in Chinese, and the lady glared, but sat on the couch.

"Kawiki has a gun too," Nadia said.

"Pull it out and drop it on the floor, love," Olivia said.

Kawiki didn't. And Nadia saw why.

Mr. Woo was now directly behind Emma.

"Look out!"

Emma turned, but Mr. Woo twisted her arm and snatched the gun with the reflexes of a highly-trained soldier. He now pointed it at Emma.

Olivia and Miyuki took a step forward. They were about to attack.

"Don't do it, girls," Nadia said.

Olivia and Miyuki stopped and checked with Nadia. Her eyes

guided them towards Kawiki.

Who now pointed his gun at the girls.

"Please join your friends on the couch," Mr. Woo said.

CHAPTER 32

The Gems sat down on the long sofa inside the spacious cabin. Kawiki and Mr. Woo stood opposite the sofa, with guns drawn. The Chinese lady closed the door of the cabin.

"Not a bad attempt. However, poorly executed," Mr. Woo said.

The Chinese lady said something to Mr. Woo, who replied in Chinese. His answer didn't please her.

"So now what?" Olivia asked, trying to project overconfidence.

In private, she must be freaking out like Nadia was right now. Surely Mr. Woo would get rid of all four of them.

Mr. Woo checked his phone. "In the morning, this train will stop in Salt Lake City, and we will fly Robert back to China. That information is too obvious to hide. But you will all stay here, tied up and gagged, in this cabin until the train reaches Chicago."

"Why not kill us?" Olivia asked.

"That's what your girlfriend wants to do to us," Miyuki added.

Mr. Woo grinned. "Your organization's intervention in this matter is rather annoying, yet it doesn't deserve such an extreme reaction. In fact, under different circumstances the Authority can be useful to my government. However, today is not that day. Killing all of you would serve no real purpose, and I don't wish to waste my time hiding four dead girls."

Nadia and the girls relaxed.

Mr. Woo stepped towards Olivia. "However, if you do try to stop us from making our plane, I would be forced to drop my professional courtesy and start killing you as a matter of practicality."

Mr. Woo let that sink in for a moment.

"Tie up their hands," he said.

Kawiki took Miyuki, Olivia, and Emma in turn and searched them. He then put their hands behind their backs and took a roll of

171

large shipping tape to bind their wrists together.

The cabin door opened, and the Chinese geek stepped inside. He noticed all the girls.

"Did I miss something?" he asked.

"Prepare the robot for transport," Mr. Woo said to the geek.

"Who are the girls?"

"Ignore them and do your job."

The young man complied. He opened the closet door, and Robert was still there, unable to move. The geek pulled out his laptop and hooked it up to the device plugged into Robert.

Mr. Woo examined the girls for a moment and said something to the woman in Chinese before leaving the cabin.

"Where's our host off to?" Olivia asked.

Miyuki lowered her voice. "He worried we have more spies on train. He walking through the railcars to make sure."

The Chinese lady yelled at Miyuki.

"She said no talking," Kawiki said.

The large man looked for another place to sit. He pulled out a fold-out seat near the window and squatted down on it. The chair snapped and sent the large man's butt to the floor.

The geek guy laughed.

The Gems did too, but with more reserve.

The Chinese lady swung around and yelled at Kawiki.

That was when Nadia felt something metallic being placed into her palm. She ran her thumb over the object. It felt like...a Swiss Army knife. Nadia glanced at her neighbor Emma, who winked and leaned back to reveal Olivia, who also gave Nadia a wink.

Olivia must have palmed the knife when Kawiki searched her. Which meant if Nadia now had it...all the girls have already cut through their taped bindings.

Nadia's heart beat faster. She tried to hide it as best she could as she delicately found the knife and flipped it open. All without cutting up her hand in the process. She then began sawing it back and forth.

The other Gems waited on her.

"My feet hurt when I stand too long," Kawiki told the Chinese woman.

Kawiki stayed on the floor, apparently more comfortable there. The woman shook her head and wandered over to check on the geek, who was deep into his computer screen.

Nadia could feel the tape binding her wrists loosen, yet it still wasn't free. She tried sawing a little harder.

The other girls watched and waited.

Nadia mouthed, "I'm trying."

"What did she say?" Kawiki asked from the floor.

Nadia was quick. "I'm hungry."

"Me too," Kawiki said. He asked the woman something in Chinese. She argued with him and returned to harassing the geek. Kawiki shrugged. "She won't let me go to the snack bar. Sorry."

Nadia pulled, and the binding finally gave way. Her hands were now free.

"Thank you for asking," she said. "And for lifting a finger to help."

Nadia craned her neck towards the Gems and winked. She was ready.

Miyuki called out to the woman in Chinese. She yelled back, unwilling to engage with Miyuki. But Miyuki threw out another remark in Chinese that made the woman focus on her. The Chinese woman marched over to Miyuki and raised her arm to strike.

Miyuki jumped up and blocked her strike. The girl then shoved her into the window, which was too thick to break.

Olivia was on her feet too, leaping at Kawiki, who was still on the floor. Emma was right behind her.

Kawiki fumbled with his gun, totally unprepared as Olivia jumped on top of his stomach with all her weight. Kawiki gasped as all the air left his lungs.

Emma saw the gun and kicked it out of his hand.

Nadia went for the geek on the laptop. She shoved him off his chair, spilling him and his laptop to the floor. Next she drew back the heel of her palm, ready for a karate strike. However, the boy held up his hands, his eyes wide with terror.

Nadia hesitated. "Don't move." She checked the room.

Miyuki and the Chinese woman were fighting. Emma and Olivia were wrestling Kawiki on the ground and losing.

Nadia made her choice. She went behind the Chinese woman and struck her at the base of the neck. It was textbook and brought the woman down unconscious.

Miyuki offered a fist-bump and Nadia obliged.

"Would you two flipping help us!" Olivia yelled. She was

trapped under Kawiki while Emma was on top, whacking the guy in the face with no effect.

Nadia and Miyuki jumped on top of the man, doing their best to keep him down. Yet Kawiki stumbled to his feet and shook the girls off like leaves as they tumbled to the floor. The large man smiled. He was enjoying this.

Miyuki launched a series of kicks that pushed the man back to the closed door. Nadia added a kick to the face as well.

Kawiki shook it off and motioned them to try something else.

Nadia saw pieces of the broken chair on the floor and had an idea.

"I thought you said the snake wasn't real?" Nadia pointed at the floor. "It's right there."

Kawiki hesitated and couldn't help but look down.

Nadia grabbed the broken seat and busted it over Kawiki's head.

The large man wobbled for a moment.

Nadia opened the cabin door. "Push!"

The Gems looked at each other.

"Push!" Nadia yelled.

Finally they got it. The Gems went forward as one and shoved Kawiki out of the cabin.

"Retreat!" Nadia yelled.

The Gems ran back inside the cabin and Nadia shut the door, placing her body against it. The other three girls pushed up against her.

"Do you think he went away?" Miyuki asked.

"I hope so," Emma said, breathing hard.

"Where's his flipping gun?" Olivia asked.

Something smashed against the door, making the Gems jerk back.

It must have been Kawiki. "Let me in or I'll huff and puff and blow your door down," he said, with a laugh.

The door shuddered again. Cracks formed near the hinges.

"This door not hold him," Miyuki said.

Olivia frantically searched the floor.

"Are you looking for this?" The Chinese geek pointed a gun at Olivia.

CHAPTER 33

The cabin door flexed and cracked as Kawiki continued to pound against it. Nadia couldn't move, so she watched helplessly as the Chinese geek leveled a gun at Olivia, her best friend. Ever since they'd taken this train, everything seemed to be going wrong.

"Here, I don't want it." The geek boy offered it to Olivia who took the gun immediately. "I volunteered for this because I wanted to see America. I'm not a spy. I don't want to fight anyone."

"Sit down there, love, and you'll get your wish," Olivia said before putting herself in front of the door. "Move away from it, girls."

The Gems backed away from the door just as Kawiki threw his weight against it. The hinges popped, and the door fell to the floor.

Kawiki stepped on the door and smiled at his brute strength. That smile changed to a frown when he saw Olivia aiming the gun at him.

"Turn around and face the door," Olivia said with authority. "Move."

Kawiki sighed and did as she commanded. The Chinese woman moaned as she woke up.

Olivia backed up and pointed the pistol at her. The Chinese woman cursed. She was awake now.

"What do we do with them?" Emma asked.

"I'm thinking," Olivia said. "We have to do something before Mr. Woo gets back."

"Throw them off the train," Miyuki said. "The door is just down the hallway."

"Isn't that dangerous?" Nadia asked.

"Under the circumstances I'd say it's a lovely idea," Olivia said.

She gestured the Chinese lady to stand up. Next Olivia had Kawiki and the lady move down the lower-level hallway of the railcar. Sure enough, right before the stairs that went up to the private cabins, there was an outside door. Nadia remembered it from when they boarded the train in Reno. Olivia held the two Chinese agents at gunpoint as Miyuki opened the door. An alarm sounded.

"Off you go." Olivia gestured with the gun.

"You want us to jump?" Kawiki asked.

"Remember to tumble as you fall," Miyuki said. "So you not break bones."

Kawiki looked scared.

"Don't worry," Olivia said. "You'll roll like a beach ball."

Kawiki swallowed and jumped through the door.

Next was the Chinese woman, who glared at Olivia.

"Get on with it, love."

The woman spat something in Chinese before she jumped out the door too.

The Gems watched as the two henchmen rolled awkwardly down a slight embankment and across the sand. Miyuki then shut the door, and the Gems went back to Mr. Woo's cabin. Nadia headed over to the Chinese geek and took away his computer.

"Hey, that's mine," he said.

"It's hers now. Or would you like to jump off and take a walk in the desert too?" Olivia asked.

The boy shut up.

Nadia went through the code of the geek's looping program. It wasn't as complex as he'd led her to believe. It did prevent Robert from sending commands to his body, but his original programming was still there. He was still Robert.

"Can you help him?" Emma asked.

"Yes, but I'll need my backpack from the cabin," Nadia said.

Miyuki volunteered, and Olivia told her to be careful. Mr. Woo was still on the train, maybe even heading back to the cabin. Miyuki understood and took off down the hallway and climbed the stairs.

Emma sat on the bench where she could keep a watch down the hallway and stairs. Meanwhile, Olivia stood ready in case Emma spotted Mr. Woo. But a few minutes later only Miyuki was seen climbing back down the stairs with Nadia's backpack.

Nadia opened her laptop and turned the screen away from the geek as she logged in. A dancing kitten appeared on the screen with the sparkling words *Hello, Nadia!* She connected a USB cable to the geek's laptop and transferred the looping program over to hers. But only after Nadia ran the sophisticated Authority security programs, which scrubbed every byte of the foreign program to prevent any unwanted Trojans or other tracking software to be introduced into Nadia's laptop. It quarantined five hidden items. Mostly standard Chinese intelligence programs used to track or infect new computers the program was added to. But all of the geek's looping program came through.

Nadia went through the coding again. Basically the geek had downloaded Robert's operational software and injected his looping algorithms into it. They went to work, finding Robert's command protocols and creating loops to block those commands from going to many parts of his robot body. This created a problem. Nadia could delete each loop, but she would have to go through Robert's entire code to do it. That could take weeks.

"You lied," the geek said, watching Nadia over her shoulder. "You do know coding."

"Did you create an uninstall command for your program?"

The geek sat back, enjoying the attention. "I didn't. You'll have to pull out each command one line at a time."

"Did you create a backup of the original operational software?"

"No."

"Why would you not make a backup?" Nadia asked. "Any coder with brains would make a backup of an original program before making such radical changes to it."

"I didn't need to make a backup because I'm that good," the geek said. "I don't make mistakes."

"Everyone makes mistakes."

"Not me."

Nadia stared at the screen and sighed. There was now only one way to fix it and free Robert. She started at the first line of code and began deleting the looping codes one by one.

"Emerald!"

Emma's distressed voice made Nadia look up to see Mr. Woo. He was inside the cabin, his pistol aimed at Emma.

Olivia raised her gun and trained it on Mr. Woo.

Mr. Woo noted her presence as he surveyed the room. "My suspicions were correct. May I ask where my colleagues are?"

"Put down the gun," Olivia said, not messing around.

Mr. Woo didn't. "Did you kill them?"

"We shoved them off the train," Miyuki said.

"How decent of you," Mr. Woo said. "So, what should we discuss?"

"I won't ask you again," Olivia said.

"This is a good time to negotiate, wouldn't you say?"

"Negotiate? How do you figure that?" Olivia asked.

"You can keep the robot in exchange for Yin Lee's computer."

"And Robert's software inside it," Nadia added.

"My superiors would rather have a complete robot to disassemble as well as the operating software. However, the software itself would still be of value. Under such circumstances I feel it's a fair compromise."

"I don't think we feel like compromising today, love. The answer is no."

Mr. Woo shrugged. His grip on the gun tightened. "Then I will kill this member of your team."

Emma looked worried.

"Honestly, I don't much care for her," Olivia said. "But Beijing might be sad to lose one of their major intelligence operatives in exchange for getting rid of a silly American girl who can't even drive a car with a manual transmission."

Emma's mouth dropped open.

Mr. Woo actually laughed and nodded. He lowered his weapon. Miyuki took away his gun and searched Mr. Woo. Soon they wrapped his arms in shipping tape and sat him on the couch.

Olivia came over to Nadia. "What's your status?"

"I have to go through this code line by line and clean it up before Robert can move anything. It will take some time."

"Can he help?" Olivia pointed at Yin Lee, the geek.

"Not really," Nadia said.

"Right, then you go on the couch too," Olivia said, emphasizing with the gun. "Miyuki, tie this bloke's hands together and sit him with his friend."

Miyuki took Yin Lee and searched him. Then she taped up his hands and sat him next to Mr. Woo.

"Can I speak with you, please?" Emma said, her mouth stiff. "In private."

Olivia rolled her eyes. "Not now."

Nadia made herself look down at the screen and kept working.

"You know—Emerald—I thought you and I were making

progress. Remember the dealership? I cherished our conversation and felt we were growing closer as people," Emma said. "But then you offered to sacrifice my life in exchange to save your own butt."

"That's not correct. I sacrificed your life for the team and our mission."

Nadia's eyes drifted off the screen and back to the conversation.

"Whatever, I don't appreciate it." Emma crossed her arms. "And I'm not silly. Plenty of girls don't know how to drive a manual transmission, and I don't think you should make fun of them or me."

"Please get over yourself, love. Mr. Woo was bluffing, and I called him out. He was never going to shoot you."

"Oh, and how do you know that?"

"According to his dossier, Mr. Woo is a marksman. If he could see all the way down the hall because the cabin door was off, the man could have shot you way before he ever stepped foot inside the cabin. Therefore, he was pressuring me to give up my gun because it was the only play he had left."

Emma relaxed. "Then you do care about me?"

"Of course I do," Olivia said. "We're a team, right?"

Emma glowed. "Then I feel another hug coming on."

* * *

As the morning sun lingered on the horizon of a new day, the Western Limited slowed to a stop at the Salt Lake City AmRail station. Olivia and Miyuki escorted Mr. Woo and Yin Lee off the train, taping their hands to one of the outdoor benches so they wouldn't try to reboard the train. For her peace of mind, Olivia watched Mr. Woo from a window as the train pulled away from the station and headed for Southeastern Utah.

Staying up all night, Nadia was still only thirty-one percent done with taking out the looping program inside Robert. But now he could move his mouth and talk. He told the Gems about how he had been exploring the train when Mr. Woo had used a high-powered Taser device to overwhelm his system and eventually capture him.

By late morning, the Gems went to the dining car to eat some brunch while Nadia chose to stay behind and keep working. Her brain was foggy, and her body yearned to slip into bed, but she pushed herself to keep going.

"I'm sorry that woman hit you," Robert said. "I wanted to protect you…"

"You couldn't move. I understand," Nadia said.

"Ever since you girls met me, I've brought nothing but pain and suffering to you all."

Nadia showed him a smile. "The Gems are tougher than we look. We'll be okay." She rubbed her eyes.

"Thank you for fixing my software."

"It's my pleasure."

"Yin Lee failed to keep a backup of my program?"

"Yes, isn't that stupid? He's an idiot," Nadia said. "The fool could have accidentally triggered your reset program."

"And wipe out my operational software," Robert said. "I would be dead."

Nadia looked at him.

"I would not exist in my current state." Robert paused for a moment. "I regret that my designers did not feel the need to include a restore-point program in my software."

"What did you say?" Nadia asked.

"That my designers failed to include a restore point in my software."

An idea came to Nadia and she grabbed Yin Lee's notebook. The girl opened windows and clicked on the recycle bin.

"Did I make a joke?" Robert asked. "Because you are now smiling."

Besides random pics of half-naked Japanese anime girls, there was one file that looked promising inside Yin Lee's recycle bin.

D9000 MID OP V5

Did MID mean military intelligence drone? Did V5 mean version five of the software? Nadia crossed her fingers and clicked.

The coding lines fell down the screen like leaves from a tree. Nadia recognized it. It was indeed Robert's operational software, and the codes from the looping program were missing. Yin Lee must have saved a version of the software as a base before adding his software; then the idiot had deleted the original. Luckily for Nadia, he'd forgotten to clean out his recycle bin. Again, very sloppy.

Nadia told Robert the good news as she transferred the original software, into her own laptop and deleted the version she was working on from both computers using an Authority digital shredder program.

"It would be better to make a clean install. In order to do that, I would need to trigger your reset program before reinstalling your software," Nadia said. "Is that alright?"

Robert considered it for a second. "Yes, I trust you."

Nadia used her computer to initiate the reset program. Robert went still, and his mouth didn't move. Once that was done, she powered him down and restarted him with the D9000 software.

Robert blinked and looked at Nadia.

"How do you feel?" she asked.

"I feel…alive again." Robert walked out of the closet. "My systems appear to be functioning normally." He began moving around every part of him that could move. "Thank you."

"You are most welcome," Nadia said.

A silence developed around them, and Nadia didn't know quite what to do about it.

"I should offer a gesture of thanks for what you have done for me," Robert said. "Would you like a kiss?"

Nadia felt her face warm up. "Oh, that's not necessary."

It wasn't necessary, but Nadia wanted him to do it.

"Would a thankful hug be sufficient?"

"Sure, that's fine."

Robert approached her closely, and Nadia allowed him. Carefully Robert cupped her back into his arms and gently pressed her cheek into his chest. Nadia could feel the warmth generated by his robot body. His artificial heart beat like any normal human boy's. If she closed her eyes, it was like Robert was just as real as any boy she had ever known.

One minute passed.

Three minutes passed.

"What is the sufficient time parameter for hugging?"

Nadia pulled away from his chest. "Fifteen seconds for good friends is sufficient."

"That hug lasted three minutes and twelve seconds. Does this mean we are more than friends?"

"When you save your friend from dying, you can add a few extra seconds," Nadia said.

Robert and Nadia went to the dining car to let the other Gems know that Robert was fixed; then Robert took Nadia to the observation deck inside the lounge car. The train was rolling through the Rocky Mountains of Eastern Utah. The observation deck with its giant windows allowed passengers to see the views unobstructed. They could see the layers of colored rocks. The snow-packed peaks. The massive rock slides that reshaped the mountains.

"I have noticed that the farther out we go from the cities, the more scattered the settlements are," Robert said. "Do humans prefer cities as opposed to a more natural habitat?"

Nadia's eyes grew heavy. Staying up all night was taking a toll on her. She fought it off.

"People like the convenience of cities, I think," Nadia said, lying back against her chair.

"Are you sure you do not require food?" Robert asked. "It appears your body is shutting down."

"I'm only sleepy. It will pass." Nadia shook herself awake. "This is beautiful country. It's amazing how large it is."

"Is Saudi Arabia beautiful?"

"Parts of it are. The desert is beautiful. Different from this place. But no less beautiful."

"I would like to walk on sand," Robert said. "I have heard it can be difficult."

Nadia's mind drifted back to Riyadh. At that time, walking across the sands of the desert would've been a welcome relief to the streets. Only well-to-do families and tourists went out to camp in the desert where they enjoyed food, music, camel rides, and falcon demonstrations. But Nadia had had to go through trash dumpsters. She remembered how bad they smelled. How much her stomach churned when she was inside one and searching for anything useful for her family to use.

Nadia's mind drifted away from the dumpsters and the streets...

Drifted away from her crying sisters and brothers.

Drifted away from the pain of seeing them hungry and frightened...

And fell asleep.

CHAPTER 34

Emma left Miyuki and Olivia in the dining car and entered the lounge car. She went downstairs and glanced around the various tables and chairs for either Robert or Nadia, with little success. Next she went back upstairs and went inside the observation deck. There she saw Robert watching the mountains as they passed above the large glass canopy around him. Sleeping on his chest was Nadia.

Emma slipped into the opposite chair facing Robert.

He lowered his voice. "She is sleeping. I am trying not to wake her."

"Poor girl. How long has she been out?" Emma asked softly.

"One hour and seven minutes."

Emma showed Robert a take-away box. "I brought her a sandwich in case she was hungry."

"She will appreciate your kind gesture." Robert paused a moment. "Do you think Nadia is in love with me?"

Emma almost swallowed her tongue. "In love with you?"

"Nadia has shared nonverbal cues of affection towards me. However, I am unable to determine if these are genuine or merely a reflection of a deep friendship between us. I would like clarification."

"Why do you want clarification? Do you want to date her?"

Robert tilted his head. "I want to make her happy. Would dating me make Nadia happy?"

"It might," Emma said. "But what do you want?"

"I want to make her feel safe and contented."

Emma sat back and thought about it. "Do you have feelings for her?"

"This is hard for me to answer. I care about her welfare. I favor her above you and the other girls."

"Oh."

"Her happiness and safety are important to me. Is that affection?"

"I think so," Emma said.

"I am concerned that my continued presence in Nadia's life will become dangerous to her well-being," Robert said. "In fact, all of you have been affected by my wish for freedom. Am I being selfish for exposing you to such constant danger?"

"Wanting to stay alive isn't a selfish act, Robert."

"It could be if it threatens an innocent life. I do not want to be alive if it means hurting Nadia or the three of you."

Emma wondered if a robot understood the concept of suicide. She hoped he didn't.

"All four of us are here because we believe that you have the right to choose who you want to be, and despite everything that's happened, we're not abandoning you," Emma said. "Mrs. B and the Authority will make sure you're free. That's a promise."

"Your devotion is appreciated," Robert said. "However, your sacrifice is not necessary."

Nadia moaned as she moved around on Robert's chest. Soon her eyes blinked open. The girl smiled at Robert and stretched. Then she saw Emma and pulled away from Robert.

"I must have dozed off."

"I bet he makes a nice pillow," Emma said, offering her the take-out box. "Sandwich?"

Nadia's skin turned red as she took the box and opened it. "Thank you." Nadia took off the top piece of bread and fixed the inside of the sandwich how she wanted it. "When do we arrive in Glenwood Springs?"

"I have no idea," Emma said.

"Judging by our average speed and the precise track distance left, I estimate ten hours, twenty-one minutes, and seventeen seconds," Robert said. "People will be there to help us, is that not correct?"

"Yes, Mrs B will have some men there to help us," Nadia said.

"Good. Then you will be safe there."

"We should be, yes."

Robert watched her for a long moment. "You have been most kind to me, and I appreciate that. Thank you."

Nadia grinned. "Of course."

Robert rose to his feet. "Thank you too, Emma. Please let the other girls know how much I appreciate their help."

"Okay, but you can tell them yourself," Emma said.

Robert went down the stairs.

Something didn't feel right to Emma. She glanced at Nadia. Her eyes said she felt it too.

An alarm went off. Emma remembered it from when they threw the Chinese agents off the train. That alarm meant an outside door was open.

Both girls raced down the stairs to the lower portion of the car, where Robert stood in the open doorway.

"No, don't!" Nadia yelled.

Robert raised his eyes to her. "Please do not search for me. It will be safer that way."

"Get back inside!" Emma yelled. "This is stupid."

Robert turned his attention outside. The train passed over a giant bridge. A deep gorge plunged below.

"No, it is quite logical."

Robert jumped, arching his body like an Olympic diver as he sailed off the train and the bridge as his body disappeared into the gorge.

"Robert!" Nadia screamed.

CHAPTER 35

Nadia stepped into the open doorway of the railcar. The rushing wind attacked her face and hair as the shock of watching Robert jump off the train went through her body. Her first impulse was to follow him down the rabbit hole because she knew he needed her. However, Emma pulled her away from the door.

"Let me go!" Nadia yelled.

"You're not jumping off this train," Emma said.

Nadia struggled with Emma. She had to go help Robert.

Emma wrestled Nadia down to the floor. "You'll kill yourself."

"I don't care!" Nadia yelled as she shoved Emma to the side and stumbled to her feet.

She could jump. She could help him. If Robert could survive that jump, she could too. Nadia stepped into the open doorway again. The gorge was deep, maybe five hundred feet or more, but she could see water at the bottom. Nadia knew she could swim. She could make it. She could jump.

"Don't do it!" Emma yelled.

Nadia braced herself and...

A wall of darkness slammed the opening shut as the train rushed inside a tunnel. It was too late.

Robert was gone.

An arm pressed against Nadia's stomach.

Emma's chin rested on her shoulder. "He doesn't want you to go after him."

"He needs help," Nadia blurted out. Her words sounded sad.

"We've done everything we can."

"Why did he jump?" Nadia caught herself sobbing through the words. "He needs our help."

"Did you girls open that door?" an AmRail conductor asked from the stairs, glaring down at them.

186

After explaining to the conductor that they just needed some fresh air and his insistence of jotting down their names to make a full report to AmRail corporate, Emma took Nadia back upstairs and tracked down Olivia and Miyuki inside one of the upstairs cabins to give them the bad news.

"Mrs. B will be pissed," Olivia said, taking a good look at Nadia. "You alright, love?"

Nadia didn't move from the cabin window. Didn't take her eyes off the rolling landscape. Couldn't pretend she was fine because she wasn't. Robert was somewhere out there. Alone. Where they now couldn't protect him.

Olivia knelt beside her. "We'll find him. Trust me."

Nadia pulled her eyes off the window.

"Could you help me with your laptop, Nads? We'll need to give our report."

Nadia powered up her laptop and connected to the AmRail Wi-Fi. Nadia used her scrambler to cloak her location and IP address while she logged onto the Authority's server. After putting in the proper codes and identifications, Mrs. B appeared on the screen. Olivia repeated the bad news to her.

"Did the package survive the fall?" Mrs. B asked.

"We couldn't see into the gorge very well," Emma said.

"I know it did," Nadia said. "The package doesn't need oxygen, so it can dive deep into the water to absorb its momentum."

"Assuming the water was deep enough," Olivia said. "Could it survive a full impact with the ground?"

"It must have been deep enough," Nadia said. "Otherwise, he wouldn't have jumped. He's too logical."

"Easy, love," Olivia said. "Just thinking out loud."

Nadia closed her eyes. She must have barked out that last reply. Her emotions were at an all-time high, and it was difficult for her to manage them.

"May I make a suggestion?" Miyuki asked. "Why don't we leave the package alone? Isn't this better? Shouldn't we let the package have its freedom?"

"We've done all we can," Emma said. "Besides, we told him he had the right to choose. Well, we shouldn't be mad when he doesn't choose us."

"The package is a dangerous weapon," Mrs. B said. "Despite what it thinks of himself, it can be captured and reprogrammed.

We can't allow the package to fall into the wrong hands. We must find it. The package must be either destroyed or hidden somewhere where it will never be found again."

"I can convince it," Nadia said. "The package will come with me if I have a chance to reason with it."

"That's fine, but we still have one giant problem," Mrs. B said. "Since the package disabled its internal transponder, we can't track it using our satellites. To complicate matters, the package is walking through one of the most remote areas of the United States, where it can avoid being seen by people rather easily."

"We can follow it now," Olivia said. "I placed a tracker on the package."

The girls stared at Olivia.

"I gave the package a hug on the train and stuck it on the back of its neck," she said. "Just in case we lost it again."

"You didn't tell him?" Nadia asked.

"Kind of defeats the purpose of tracking someone who doesn't want to be tracked, love."

"A wise precaution, Emerald," Mrs. B said. "In that case, we need to go find the package. The next train stop is Grand Junction, Colorado. I'll have a paid rental car reserved under Black Opal's legal name waiting for you there. Take it and go after the package. I'll have our operatives in Glenwood Springs head west into Utah to assist. But a word of warning. The entire state of Utah is swarming with FBI and Army intelligence units."

"We'll be careful, ma'am," Olivia said.

"One order that I must insist on," Mrs. B said. "If the FBI or US Army intelligence recovers the package before you do…you will make no further attempts to recover him. Your mission will be over. Do you understand?"

"You want to give him back to them?" Nadia asked.

Mrs. B sighed. "We have a window of opportunity, a short period of time that will allow me to give the package what it wants. But that window is closing. If you want to help it, you must do so quickly because there will come a point where none of us will be able to help. Do you understand me?"

"Yes, ma'am," Olivia said. "We understand."

* * *

Two hours later, the Western Limited pulled into the small AmRail station at Grand Junction, Colorado. Inside town, Nadia and the Gems found the rental car place where a car was reserved under the name of Emma Rothchild. The rental was already paid for, including an additional fee for a driver under the age of twenty-five. The Dodge Challenger was only a two-seater, but it would go fast. The Gems squeezed inside as Miyuki took the wheel.

Miyuki got on the interstate and aimed the Challenger westbound towards the Colorado-Utah border. Nadia was on her laptop using a wireless travel router she'd made Emma buy at the Grand Junction CompuLand. Along with her special Authority SIM card, Nadia was able to log in and track Robert using the organization's spy satellite. She also took the liberty of hacking into the Utah Highway Patrol's servers to locate their cruisers. It was the best radar detector ever. After they were done, Nadia did plan to be a good citizen and contact the law enforcement agency discreetly to tell them how they could beef up their firewall.

Thirty-five minutes later, Miyuki pushed the Challenger over the Utah state line. Nadia monitored the highway patrol map on the screen as one unit popped into view. Perhaps he just went on duty.

"A road enforcement unit within two miles," Nadia called out.

"You mean there's a smokey bear knocking at my front door?" Miyuki asked.

"A what?"

"A smokey bear."

Nadia stared at her.

Emma leaned forward. "She means a state trooper. That's what a smokey bear is."

"What on earth are you two twits talking about?" Olivia said.

"The movie," Miyuki said. "*Smokey and the Bandit.* I'm the bandit."

"You're mental, love."

Miyuki blew her off. "Nadia, do you know if bear is a Utah bubble gum machine or is he a fox in the hen house?"

"Okay," Emma said. "Now you've lost me."

"I'm asking if the bear is in a marked patrol car or an unmarked car. Sheesh."

"Oh." Nadia looked. "It doesn't say."

Miyuki braked and the Dodge slipped under the seventy-five-mile-per-hour speed limit. "Have you seen *Smokey and the Bandit*, Emma?"

"Yes, my aunt loves that movie. She's gotta crush on the guy with the big black mustache who laughs all the time."

Nadia was curious, so she brought up the movie's Wikipedia page and scanned the plot. "It says here it's a movie about criminals outrunning the police."

"They're transporting a truckload of beer," Emma said. "But I don't understand why that would be illegal."

"It's fun movie. I like it. Someday I want to drive a big semitruck," Miyuki said.

Nadia saw a link and clicked it. It was a Utube video that started immediately. American country music blasted out of her laptop speakers. Miyuki began singing along as the song talked about going "East Bound and Down" and something about they say we can't do this and basically the song talked about the plot of the movie. Whatever the song was, Miyuki loved it and bounced in her seat as she drove.

The Utah highway patrol unit they were tracking zoomed past them in the opposite direction. Miyuki waited until he was out of sight before speeding up again.

Meanwhile, Nadia reduced the video window and looked up Robert's current position according to the latest Authority satellite sweep.

Robert had jumped off the train near Green River, Utah. However, instead of following the nearby interstate or a state highway, Robert followed the Green River itself as it snaked down to the south for at least twenty miles. Analyzing his route, Nadia understood what Robert was doing. This was a remote part of Eastern Utah. The nearest roads were twelve miles away and ran parallel to the river, never towards it. This would leave Robert completely alone. But Nadia wondered where he was going.

"How's it looking?" Olivia asked, her head leaning forward between the seats.

"He's still moving along that river fast," Nadia said.

"Still heading south?"

"Yes."

"I'd wager he's heading into that Canyonlands National Park," Olivia said. "He'll wait there until everyone stops looking for him."

"But he can't do that. Even on his lowest power setting he'll last maybe a week. There's no way he can charge himself."

Emma squeezed in next to Olivia. "Can you tilt your screen a little?"

Nadia did.

Emma studied the map. "Could he make it to Mexico?"

Nadia hadn't thought of that. She looked at the screen. "Not on a one-week charge."

"Wait," Olivia said. "Zoom out for a moment."

Nadia made the map expand to include the state of Arizona.

"See all those Indian reservations in Eastern Arizona?" Olivia asked. "Those towns will have power."

"Why would they help him?" Nadia asked.

"Oh wow," Emma said. "Because he will change his skin and become an Indian."

"Remember that Robert can blend into any population," Olivia said. "He could live as a Hopi Indian or become Hispanic and keep moving down to Mexico or South America."

"And then disappear forever," Nadia said.

"Is there a road inside the national park that gets us close to that river?" Emma asked.

Nadia zoomed back into the park and traced the Green River as it snaked down into the park.

"There's not a direct road to the river, but there is a hiking trail that reaches it," Nadia said.

"Could we get there before he does?" Olivia asked.

Nadia crunched the numbers. It would be close. "Maybe. If we hurry."

The Dodge screamed as Miyuki accelerated. "I have the hammer down and we blow off everyone's doors, good buddy!"

CHAPTER 36

An hour and half later in Moab, Utah, Nadia followed the rest of the Gems towards the checkout counter inside the small Mountain Outfitters specialty store. Emma pulled out her gold card and took care of the bill that ran over seven hundred dollars. It was a lot of money, and Nadia continued to be surprised at how casually Emma could spend it, almost like she was buying pieces of candy.

However, Olivia pointed out that since they'd been on the run for days, none of them had decent shoes for a long hike. Nadia looked up the distances of the two trails they would need to take, and they were looking at eight miles easy. Plus the trail was rugged in some spots. The girls' simple sneakers and ballet flats wouldn't be up to the task.

Besides, Robert had slowed way down. He was still heading south along the Green River, but at a much slower pace. Faster than most humans, but not as fast as he had been moving before. Nadia reasoned that Robert was conserving his energy because no one was chasing him, so this allowed the Gems just enough time to make a short detour to Moab.

Once they arrived in town, Emma took over. Instead of going to the local Target and picking up some cheap hiking shoes that would have done the job, Emma insisted on going straight for the outdoor store that all the tourists used to buy equipment.

"We want the best hiking boots you got," Emma said to the clerk, who knew a rich teenage girl when she saw one.

Soon each Gem had a pair of genuine AlpenSuisse hiking boots. Swiss made and tested in the Alps. They were nice boots, and Nadia felt like she could hike Mount Everest in them. Yet the boots were a huge overkill.

Nadia helped Emma load their new boots and hiking socks in

the trunk. "Thank you, Emma. I'll pay you back for the boots as soon as I can."

"You don't have to do that. I'm happy to help."

"No, these are very nice boots. I want to pay you back for them."

"Don't worry about it. It's a gift," Emma said.

"You shouldn't spend money on us like this."

"Yes, I should. Because it's nice to have friends to spend money on."

Nadia slipped in the backseat of the Dodge Challenger with Olivia while Emma took shotgun next to Miyuki.

"How are we doing on time?" Olivia asked Nadia.

She checked her laptop. "If we drive straight to the trailhead and start our hike, we should arrive at the river about an hour ahead of him."

Forty minutes later, Miyuki raced the Dodge southwest along the highway and reached the entrance to the Canyonlands National Park. They paid the entrance fee before continuing along the park's two-lane paved road. They skipped the visitors' center and followed the road as it meandered through the park for seven miles. They took a right at the intersection and drove another five miles to the trailhead parking lot.

Nadia marveled at the view here. The Gems were surrounded by giant deep canyons and high majestic mesas with their tops so flat it was like a chef had sliced them off with their carving knife. The area instantly gave her comfort. As if the place were already familiar to her.

Miyuki took a moment to gawk at the view too, her eyes large with wonder. "John Wayne."

"Who?" Nadia asked.

"Oh...this place remind me of old cowboy movies. John Wayne. *Fort Apache*," Miyuki said. "I hope we meet Indians."

Nadia had heard of that actor's name from her father, yet she'd never watched a cowboy movie.

The four girls packed their gear into two new backpacks that Olivia and Miyuki wore and started their hike up the trail. Olivia stopped at a large sign...YOU ARE ON THE SYNCLINE LOOP TRAIL. THIS TRAIL IS STRENUOUS AND DIFFICULT TO FOLLOW.

"Strenuous and difficult to follow?" Emma asked. "I don't like that."

"I'm sure it's not that bad," Olivia said. "We should just be careful."

"Don't worry. Olivia was a brownie and a guide leader in Girlguiding," Nadia said.

"What the hell is Girlguiding?" Emma asked.

Olivia cocked her head. "It's like the Girl Scouts, love, but very British." She marched off with confidence down the trail while the other Gems followed.

The first mile of the hiking trail was flat and easy to hike. There were two places where the trail was washed out by a rock slide; however, Olivia found a safe path through the rocks and they continued. The Gems then came to a spot where the trail went through a V-cut in the rocks and plunged straight downhill for hundreds of feet to the floor of the canyon.

"Is that still the trail?" Emma asked. "I don't see any steps going down."

"We have to use those flat boulders," Olivia said. "See how they go down? The trail continues at the bottom."

"How do we get back out?"

"Climb up the boulders."

"Why is there so much climbing over rocks? Why can't they actually build a real trail."

"This is a real trail." Olivia made her way down the first series of rocks, taking them with ease as she descended into the canyon.

Nadia and Miyuki followed.

Emma sighed and shook her head as she followed the others.

When they reached the bottom, the girls continued through an easier portion of the trail before coming to a larger drop-off, much deeper than before.

"Seriously?" Emma asked. Her face was red and frustrated, her makeup sweating off. "That looks very steep and dangerous."

"This should be the last part," Nadia said. "The other trail we need should be at the bottom of this one."

"Right. When going down, everyone watch where you place your feet," Olivia said. "Use short steps and keep your balance and you should be alright."

Emma groaned.

"Do you want to go back to the car?" Olivia asked.

"No way. I don't want to climb back up that trail alone."

"Onward, then." Olivia took the lead again as she carefully started down the steep slope.

Nadia slipped on one rock and landed on her butt. Luckily she didn't start tumbling down the mountain into a boulder.

Miyuki descended the trail holding Emma's hand because, even with her new boots, Emma was having trouble and constantly complaining about it.

Finally they reached the end of that descent and saw a sign pointing to the Upheaval Canyon trail.

Olivia took the new trail and checked on the others behind her. "Only three more miles."

"Could we please rest? My legs are like jelly right now," Emma said.

"Mine feel great," Olivia said with her Girlguiding pride. "Let's push on through to the campground."

Emma moaned but kept on moving as they hiked along the new trail.

After three miles, the girls arrived at a campsite, which overlooked the wide and clear-blue Green River as it flowed through the surrounding canyons. There was one tent and two folding chairs set up at the campsite, but the owners weren't there. A sign named this campsite *The Labyrinth*.

Emma stumbled over to the folding chairs and dropped her butt into one.

"Those chairs are not yours," Nadia said.

"If you see anyone, yell and I'll get up," Emma said, closing her eyes to rest.

Miyuki took her bottle of water out and drank.

Nadia gazed at the view around her. The orange buttes surrounding the river. The afternoon sun painting the water blue and the random pockets of brushy vegetation green. This place was so quiet one could hear a baby bird whispering to its mother. The canyon's air smelled clean and pure. Nadia loved it. She could sit here all day.

Olivia crouched next to her. "Lovely, isn't it?"

"When I was very young, my father would rent a car and take us out to the desert. That was when he had a job." Nadia paused and tried to keep her mind focused on those happier times. "The desert was so quiet, and the air was clean and peaceful, just like this."

"A lovely place to think," Olivia said.

"I'd rather just relax and not think about anything."

"Anyone want to swim in the river with me?" Miyuki asked.

"No way," Emma said, not budging from her stolen chair.

"How we looking on time, Nads?" Olivia asked.

"When I was last able to check Robert's position, he was about four hours away," she said.

"Is the tracking bug not working?" Olivia asked.

"I think it's the national park. There are no cell towers here, so I can't use my portable router."

"It took us three hours to hike here, so he should be here soon," Miyuki said. "Are you sure he'll pass this way?"

"This hiking trail follows the river until it branches out downstream into four main hiking trails that lead into the park's interior," Nadia said. "If Robert wants to hide in the park for a while, I think he'll be heading for those four hiking trails."

"Maybe you should hold off on that swim," Olivia said.

"That water has to be dirty. This place is awful," Emma said.

"Awful?" Olivia asked. "How is this place awful?"

"It's hot, dirty, there are no trees, no flowers, no noise, no people, and you don't have any phone service," Emma said. "Give me a city any day over this stupid park."

"You don't like quiet places?" Miyuki asked.

"I need energy. I need to be part of something alive. I'm sorry, but this place is just boring."

Olivia stood up. "Well that's your opinion, love. It doesn't reflect mine." She offered Nadia a drink from her water bottle and Nadia took it. The water was cool and delicious. After Nadia gave her water back, Olivia stretched out on a boulder and enjoyed the sun.

Her head then popped up. "Is someone watching for Robert?"

Nadia raised her hand. "I am."

"Me too," Miyuki said as she stood on a tall boulder.

"Thanks." Olivia settled back down on the rock.

Nadia stretched and relaxed.

Miyuki danced absentmindedly on the boulder, like a ballerina on a tiny stage.

Nadia watched her for a moment.

Emma began snoring.

"Jesus, is that Emma?" Olivia asked.

"Yes," Nadia said.

Olivia shook her head. "If those people come back to their camp, we don't know her."

Miyuki stopped spinning in place. She pointed at something behind them. "Someone's coming."

Nadia and Olivia followed Miyuki's line of sight and saw four hikers coming into view from the trail they'd just taken a few minutes ago.

Olivia rolled onto her back again. "They have on full packs. Most likely a group of backcountry campers."

CHAPTER 37

Emma gave in to her body's wishes. It was so tired. Olivia's simple hike to the river was more of a freaking climb to the gates of heaven. Scrambling down boulders and climbing up boulders and hiking down sheer cliffs...this hike was torture. Emma's legs burned. Even that Pilates class she sometimes went to didn't burn her legs like this hike had. The worst part would be going back, they'd have to hike straight up to where their car was. After that, Emma was convinced her legs would snap.

But until then, Emma only wanted to sit in this folding chair, close her eyes, and rest. The other girls could fetch Robert and convince him to come back with them. They didn't need her. Especially since Nadia practically had him wrapped around her little finger anyway.

"Emma, get out of the chair!" Olivia yelled.

Emma blew her off. Yes, she knew this was someone else's campsite. Yes, she knew this chair wasn't hers. But if those people knew how tired she was, they would've offered it to her anyway out of kindness, and Emma would have offered them a twenty for a "rental" fee just to be nice. In Emma's experience, giving people money for their trouble generally stopped them from complaining.

"Emma!" Miyuki yelled.

Now Olivia was making Miyuki do her dirty work.

Emma didn't fall for it. She kept her eyes closed. "Chill out. I'll make it all—"

Something pushed her left shoulder hard, and Emma found herself rolling on the ground and her face picking up dirt. What the hell!

Emma rolled on her back. She was tired, but not too tired to kick another girl's ass.

When Emma sat up, a gun was waiting for her.

She froze.

Her eyes peeked around the campground. Four men in black stood with guns drawn. Olivia, Miyuki, and Nadia were holding their hands up. The fourth man next to Emma had a reddish face covered with pockmarks and asked something that sounded Russian. Then it clicked. He was the fake policeman who'd tried to take Robert away.

Emma didn't know Russian, but she raised her hands in surrender.

The pocked-faced man gestured with his gun. He wanted her to move over with the others. Emma kept her arms up and followed the gunman's suggestions. Soon she and the Gems were all kneeling in the dirt.

The pocked-faced man said something in Russian to his comrades. They backed away from the girls.

"I told my men that if one of you tries something, their orders are to shoot without question." The pocked-faced man walked over to Emma's toppled chair and moved it over to the Gems. He sat down, but kept his gun firmly pointed at the girls. "Where is the boy?"

Olivia and Nadia said nothing.

Miyuki stared at the river.

"That chair isn't ours," Emma said. "It's someone else's, and they might be back any minute. So I wouldn't sit in it if I were you."

The pocked-faced man watched her for a moment. "Where is the boy?"

"Could you be more specific?"

A curious chipmunk approached the campsite, looking for handouts. It took a peek at the girls, then the man in the chair.

The Russian aimed his gun at the chipmunk. Emma realized he was going to do target practice.

"Oh, that boy," she said. "He said his goodbyes and took a raft down the river. He's on his way to New Mexico."

The pocked-faced man lowered his gun. "That's a lie. He wasn't with you at the park entrance gate. Why did you come to this place? Is the boy here?"

"We came here because we like the view," Emma said.

"Did the boy escape your custody?" the pocked-faced man

asked. "You were observed boarding the train together. Did the boy get off at a different stop?"

Emma made a clicking sound at the chipmunk, wanting it to come closer to her for protection. But the stupid chipmunk moved toward the Russian instead.

"Yes," Nadia said. "He stepped off the train in Salt Lake City."

"And then he came here?"

"He headed north towards Montana," Olivia said. "We were ordered not to follow him."

"We'll get into who gives you orders later." The pocked-faced man paused. The chipmunk moved closer to him, wanting a treat. The Russian aimed his pistol again and thought about it.

"I have money," Emma said. "Lots of rubles. If I pay you to leave...would you leave, please?"

Emma knew it sounded dumb but she had to do something to distract him.

The pocked-faced man gave her a strange look, then went on. "I want to understand this. The boy escaped. You were told not to follow him to Montana. And then you're here in this park for... what? A vacation?"

"Sure, we love hiking. Don't we, girls?" Emma asked. "We even bought new hiking boots." Emma stood up. "See? Aren't they pretty?"

The men snapped to attention with their guns drawn on Emma.

The chipmunk gave up on treats and scampered off.

"Whoa. I'm just showing you my new shoes."

"Kneel back down," the pocked-faced man ordered.

Emma did as he said.

"Stop!" the pocked-faced man yelled, glancing in Olivia's direction.

Emma looked over and saw Olivia's frozen hand reaching for her backpack.

The pocked-faced man grabbed the backpack away from her and unzipped it. He searched the inside. "As I suspected. The little spy toys you used on us. I will take the liberty of confiscating this bag." He moved over to Miyuki. "And this one also." He gave the backpacks to one of his men before returning to his seat.

The Russian studied the girls for a long couple of minutes before speaking. "It's obvious you're here to make contact with the robot. How do you know he'll be here?"

None of them spoke.

"I'm waiting."

Nothing.

The pocked-faced man sighed. "Do you know what fire ants are?"

That drew the Gems' attention.

"I noticed one of their mounds up near the trail. Nasty little things. The Indians of Mexico would use them to torture their captives. You see, they would bind their prisoner to the ground near such an anthill. Then the Indians would all sit and watch as a thin red stream of fire ants advanced upon his body like an army. Soon the ants would reach the man's feet. At their first touch, the man would shriek with agony. Then the trickle of ants would swell into this moving river that would swarm over his legs, then his body. They filled his mouth, nose, and ears as they slowly nibbled on his flesh."

The Russian paused. "It was hours before the man lost his strength and mental faculties. At first the man's shrieks were continuous. Then only intermittent. Soon he raved as the full sense of the horror came upon him. It took the ants a day to pick him clean to the bone. Such a nasty and painful way to die."

Emma's stomach soured. She was going to lose her lunch if this man kept talking.

The pocked-faced man focused on Emma. "Would you like to go first?"

"No, thanks," Emma snapped.

"Oh, but I must insist." He offered his hand.

Emma visualized ants crawling all over her body. That was enough for her to start freaking out. But fire ants that stung while they slowly devoured her? It was all too much. Emma tried to think. If she refused to follow his orders, wouldn't the man torture one of the other Gems to get the information he wanted?

She could just tell him the truth. No matter how cute and wonderful Robert was, he was still only a robot. The Gems were all living human beings. Emma wanted Robert to be free, but she didn't want to sacrifice one of her friends in order to make that happen. Emma also felt that Robert wouldn't want any of them to sacrifice themselves for him either.

"Robert is following the river, heading south. He should be here soon," Emma said.

"You flipping bitch," Olivia said.

The words stung. But at least Olivia would still be alive to be mad at her.

"That was the truth I was looking for," the pocked-faced man said. "And how are you tracking his movements?"

Nadia stumbled to her feet. "I'll tell you that and help you catch him. But only if you release the other girls."

The pocked-faced man now stood up. "Now we make progress. But I have a counter proposal. You help me capture the robot, and I promise my men will not shoot your friends."

Nadia swallowed. "Only if you release them. Otherwise I'll make sure you never find the robot."

The pocked-faced man got into her face. "Are you threatening me, little girl?"

One of the men yelled in Russian. Emma turned and caught one of the Russians dropping to the ground like a stone. Behind him was Robert.

The man who yelled fired a shot at Robert. But the boy was already crouched down and reaching for the gun next to the first Russian's body. It took Robert a second to aim the gun and fire. The second Russian grunted as he dropped his gun and held on to his right hand, which was bleeding.

The pocked-faced man holstered his gun and pulled out the metal wand. Emma remembered the last time they'd used it on Robert. But since he wasn't wearing those special handcuffs, Robert shouldn't be affected.

As Robert charged the third Russian, the pocked-faced man pointed the end of the wand towards him and a bolt of energy shot out. The bolt struck Robert in the chest, causing him to trip and fall down.

Before Emma could move, Nadia launched a kick into the pocked-faced man's right side. He lowered the wand and turned on Nadia. But Olivia struck him in the center of his back with her palm. This tossed the man off balance.

Miyuki went after the third Russian, who was still concerned with Robert.

Nadia kicked the wand from the pocked-faced man's hand, and he struck her across the face.

The pocked-faced man then gave Olivia a side kick that caught her off balance, and she fell down. He looked for the wand and reached for it.

Emma ran over and picked up the wand first. Then the pocked-faced man picked her up. She kicked the man with her boot heels. "Help!"

The man tossed her to the ground, and the metal wand bounced from her hands. But the man didn't reach for it; he took out his gun and pointed it at Emma.

Emma's heart skipped. Those cute AlpenSuisse boots would be the last shoes she would ever buy.

A gunshot spit dirt on the Russian's pants. He hesitated and looked across the river.

A dozen soldiers were stationed on top of a mesa near the river. Three of the soldiers aimed their sniper rifles at the campground. The military helicopter that had placed them there sat with its blades still turning in the wind.

The Russian stepped back slowly and dropped his gun.

Emma scrambled to her feet and noticed the soldiers weren't alone. Coming down the Upheaval Canyon trail were five armed park rangers backed up by over thirty sheriff's deputies. Emma couldn't see, but there could be more people behind them too.

A dark green raft now appeared on the river. More Army guys. These soldiers beached their raft and came up to the campground with weapons drawn. According to their uniforms, they were US Army Rangers.

Emma moved over to Olivia, who frowned and shook her head. There was nowhere else they could run to.

They were surrounded.

CHAPTER 38

Nadia could see the soldiers approaching them from the river. The policemen on the trail were also fanning out around the campsite.

Another hand found hers. Its soft fingers curled up over her fingers.

Robert's emerald eyes gazed into hers with reassurance. "They only want me. You have nothing to fear," he said. "I told you it would be safer if you did not look for me."

"We didn't listen," Nadia said.

"Why not? Keeping away from a dangerous situation is quite logical. Even forest animals have acted consistently upon this concept. I clearly gave you the opportunity to avoid danger, and you have ignored it. This does not make sense to me."

"I'm sorry," Nadia said. "We only wanted to help you, yet in doing so we might have led them straight to you."

"I do not have feelings. However, if I were on a mission and needed to use one of my emotion protocols, I would use infuriated."

"Infuriated at me?"

"You ignored my wishes."

A wave of anger pushed up inside her throat. "And I'm infuriated at you, Robert. How could you jump off that train without thinking of how it might affect me?"

Robert said nothing.

"Thinking only about yourself was a very arrogant thing to do. Very selfish."

"Arrogance is an emotion. I am incapable of that without using my protocols. And you are confused. I left the train to keep you from harm. That is a selfless act. The word itself is an antonym of the word selfish."

Nadia thought about that. Perhaps he meant it to be a selfless act, not understanding how something like that would affect her. But boy, did it affect her.

"I understand why you did it," Nadia said. "However, it made me very sad because I enjoyed your company."

"You have been a great teacher. I have even created a new file in my brain and labeled it Nadia. There I have kept your wise advice."

"I have my own file?"

"Yes. Only information that I value is stored there."

Nadia leaned over and hesitated. The burning in her chest was too much to hold back.

She kissed Robert on the cheek.

The boy cocked his head. "Do you wish for me to activate my sex protocols now?"

Nadia had to stop herself from laughing. "No, Robert. Now is a most inappropriate time for that."

"Step away from the drone," a soldier said, his weapon trained on Robert.

Robert threw Nadia a look. "Please do as he says."

Nadia wanted to keep talking. Wanted him to touch her. Wanted him to kiss her on the lips.

However, she wasn't an idiot. Reality had caught up with them. The world would not allow Robert to exist.

Nadia retreated from their target as the soldiers ordered the Gems and the Russians to sit on their hands, leaving Robert the only one standing. The soldiers and law enforcement officers now formed a wide perimeter around the campsite.

"I will surrender myself. Please, do not harm the girls in any way," Robert said.

One soldier carefully approached Robert and ordered him to open his access ports. Robert pulled his wrist open. The soldier plugged one end of the USB cable to it and plugged the other end into some kind of device.

Then the soldier activated the device, and Robert collapsed to the ground.

Nadia heard herself shriek and felt tears coming down her cheeks.

The soldier checked the device and patted down Robert's pockets. He activated his radio. "Drone has been neutralized. I say again, drone has been neutralized."

The soldiers and the sheriff's deputies secured their weapons and entered the campsite. The deputies searched Nadia and the Gems for weapons before handcuffing them and having them stand near the abandoned backpacker's tent. The Army Rangers took three of the Russians towards a waiting helicopter that landed on the campsite. As the Black Hawk helicopter took off, the turbulence caused by its blades washed a blanket off the face of the fourth Russian who was dead.

Army technicians showed up and worked on Robert. They stood him up. The Gems were close enough to see his face. The boy's green eyes looked dead inside.

"Robert, can you hear me?" Nadia shouted.

No response.

The Army technicians looked at her as if she were crazy.

"Robert?"

"They've wiped out his programming," a man's voice said.

Nadia followed the comment to a short man with a beard. His eyes were dark, and his nose had this hook-like quality to it.

"His corrupted operating system has been erased," the man said. "They'll install an updated operating system before reprogramming him." The short man with the hook nose circled the four girls, studying them.

Nadia also noticed six men who weren't dressed as law enforcement officers or as soldiers. These men now formed a perimeter around the Gems. Nadia glanced at Olivia, who had noticed this too. Her friend looked just as concerned as she was.

"I want my lawyer," Emma said.

The short man stopped, but did not comment or show anything in his face besides curiosity.

"Are you a copper?" Olivia asked.

The short man peered into her eyes. "Name is Sheppard."

"I'm not saying anything until I see my lawyer," Emma repeated.

"Who are you girls working for?" the short man named Sheppard asked.

"Who are *you* working for?" Olivia countered.

The short man leaned closer. "The Central Intelligence Agency. Now, your turn."

"Think I want to call my lawyer too," Olivia said.

"Me too," Nadia said.

"Make that four," Miyuki said.

"That's cute," Sheppard said. "But foreign operatives who steal Army intelligence drones don't get that kind of treatment." He brought out a pack of cigarettes and took one out.

"I'm trying to live my life smoke-free," Emma said. "Could you please go smoke that somewhere else?"

Sheppard lit his cigarette and blew the smoke into Emma's face, making her cough.

"The Russians were holding you at gunpoint. Did you cross them? Were you working for them at one time? What's the story there?"

The girls were silent.

"How about the Chinese? Maybe you're mixed up with them since you both were on the same train together. How about that story?"

Nadia watched as another helicopter landed. This time a four-star Army general and a few men wearing FBI jackets stepped off. The general visited with the Army technicians for a moment before they loaded Robert onto the helicopter.

Nadia could feel a good cry coming on. She might never see him again.

Sheppard blew smoke into Nadia's face and she coughed.

"Answer my question before I start to get nasty."

"These four girls are under FBI protective custody," one of the FBI men said.

Nadia recognized the man. It was Ed. The FBI man Mrs. B had met in the park.

Sheppard's eyes squinted. "Protective custody? Are you guys serious?"

Ed ignored Sheppard and told the sheriff's deputies to remove their handcuffs.

"What the hell is going on?" Sheppard asked. "Who are these girls?"

Ed directed Sheppard and the four-star general over to one side, leaving the remaining FBI and CIA men to stare uneasily at one another. Sheppard argued with Ed. His voice grew loud as he pointed at the girls.

"Those girls are enemy intelligence agents and should be treated as such."

Ed shook his head and calmly argued his point about the FBI and Authority partnership.

"That's bullshit. J. Edgar Hoover has been dead for years. Why are you guys still honoring that?" Sheppard asked.

Ed walked back to the girls, and the four-star general followed. Sheppard stared at the sky, venting his anger to the wind as it blew down the canyon. Finally he joined Ed and the general.

"Are you satisfied with this outcome, sir?" Ed asked the general.

The four-star general hesitated. "What do we do about these girls? They had extensive contact with our top-secret project."

"I've received assurances from their superiors that the Gems will fully cooperate by providing the Army with all the intelligence they've gathered on your drone's…malfunction. And their organization will destroy all the material they have related to the project."

"Do you trust these Authority people?" the general asked.

Sheppard flashed Ed a look.

"The bureau has dealt with the Authority for over eighty years," Ed said. "When they tell us a matter will be taken care of, it's taken care of. I see no reason to believe otherwise."

"In that case, yes, I'm satisfied," the general said. He gave orders to his men, and the soldiers evacuated the campsite. A second Black Hawk helicopter landed, and the general climbed aboard. The helicopter lifted off the ground and did a one-eighty in the sky as it flew away.

"Do I have to go to the president, Ed?" Sheppard asked.

"You can go through her or the FBI director if you want," Ed said. "But we're still on US soil, which makes it our call, and we'll handle our intelligence affairs any way we wish."

Ed glanced at his men. "Take these girls to our helicopter. They'll be leaving with us."

CHAPTER 39

Seven days later, Nadia and the Gems drove through the side gates of the Burlington winery and once again took the secret underground entrance that led to Authority headquarters. They climbed inside a green pod, and the protective hum of the cone of silence mode was activated. Mrs. B was waiting for them.

Olivia told Mrs. B exactly what they'd said to the US Army and the FBI regarding Robert and his supposed malfunction.

"Thank you all for cooperating," Mrs. B said. "Ed and the FBI were grateful, and our relationship with them is still intact."

Nadia didn't care about the FBI or what they thought about her or the Gems. They'd taken Robert away and basically killed him. They'd wiped him out and destroyed what had been so beautiful and special about him.

It had been a week since Robert had been ripped out of her life. Nadia still had trouble sleeping. Her mind was still obsessed with him. How his eyes had looked at her with total trust. No one, not even her family, had trusted her like Robert did. The boy had never questioned her efforts to help him, and it was an amazing feeling for someone to give you that level of trust without hesitation. Nadia wondered if she deserved it.

"Anything else to add to the official record?" Mrs. B asked the Gems.

"When the Russians captured us, Black Opal told them we were waiting for Robert." Olivia leaned back in her chair to watch the reaction.

Emma shook her head and crossed her arms.

Mrs. B swiveled her chair towards her. "And why did you do that?"

"They were going to torture and kill us."

"Did you know that for a fact?"

"The ugly one told me a story about torturing people with fire ants," Emma said. "Then he insisted on me being the first victim."

"So you did it to save your own ass?" Olivia asked.

"No, I did it because you're my friends." Emma hesitated. "I didn't want any of you to get hurt. Am I a bad person for wanting that?"

"Black Opal was scared, Mrs. B," Miyuki said. "We all were scared. Those men were smart enough to figure out why we were there, so Black Opal didn't reveal any huge secret they wouldn't have figured out anyway."

"She should have still resisted," Olivia said.

"Calm down, everyone," Mrs. B finally said. "I agree that Black Opal shouldn't have given out that piece of information. Luckily for all of you, it didn't change the situation. However, we must remember that Black Opal has not gone through her interrogation defense training yet. So I don't expect her to do well in the field under those circumstances." Mrs. B glanced at Emma. "Protecting your team is very important. However, you must always remember that the team is never more important than your mission. Completing your mission always takes priority."

Emma nodded.

"Anything else?" Mrs. B asked.

"Will we be punished for helping Robert?" Miyuki asked.

"Preserving innocent life is always your constant mission. That is at the core of our beliefs. Within Robert, you girls saw that innocent life and fought to protect it," she said. "So I can't fault you for why you did what you did." Mrs. B paused. "I don't want operatives who can't think for themselves. You girls will sometimes have to improvise and use your gut to tell you what to do. In this particular case, you made the correct decision."

"But we failed our mission," Olivia said.

"We allowed someone to die."

Everyone glanced at Nadia. The sentence came out of her mouth so honestly it surprised her.

"Sorry, I didn't mean to embarrass everyone."

* * *

On Monday, Nadia found it hard to focus on her Western European history class. She gazed outside the window and remembered when the rain had come falling down. How Robert had waited outside for her with endless patience because he'd looked forward to talking to her again. Even if the sky had dropped hail or snow down on Robert, he would still have waited for her.

No boy would ever do that for her again.

Nadia wondered what he was doing. Was Robert being prepared for his next mission as a drone? Would he be assassinating some world leader? Infiltrating a terrorist cell to gather intelligence? Would he be used as a human bomb to destroy that terrorist cell? Was that how the United States Army would punish him for malfunctioning?

Nadia wondered if Robert would even remember her. It was a silly thought. How could he? Robert's mind was wiped out and replaced like a computer's hard drive. There was no way he would recognize her ever again.

The Gems drove to the Kaffee Cadre after school for some mocha and vanilla lattes. Nadia chose tea, but she didn't even touch it as the Gems chatted about various things. Nadia didn't follow their conversations and, quite honestly, didn't care. Although she would never admit that out loud.

"You all right, love?" Olivia asked her.

Nadia made up some excuse. She didn't want her best friend to worry about her.

Yet the girl knew she was far from all right.

The weather inside the San Francisco Bay area was nice, so Emma's grandmother moved dinner outside to the table under the wooden trellis. Tonight was random dinner night. Normally Emma's grandmother would cook the girls some earth-friendly meal that was nutritious and good for them. However, on random dinner night, Grandma would let one of the girls choose what they would have. Tonight it was Olivia's turn, and she wanted Thai food.

Emma's grandma and Olivia came back with plastic bags of take out boxes that were ripped open and distributed to all the Gems. Emma's grandma found some traditional Thai music on Utube and played it low in the backyard to help compliment their meal.

Nadia stared at her take-out box. Steam rose from her noodles in a yellow curry sauce. It smelled delicious, and Olivia had successfully picked out the one thing she knew would cheer her best friend up. Nadia picked at the noodles with her fork, determined to eat it because she did love that yellow sauce. However, her stomach rejected the offering. She had no appetite whatsoever.

"Don't let it get cold," Emma's grandmother said. "Plenty of starving people would love to have some of that."

She was right. Nadia didn't want to waste food. So she excused herself from the table and put the box in the refrigerator for another time.

"I'm going upstairs," Nadia announced to the table. "I'm not feeling well."

Nadia climbed up the stairs to her bedroom and walked inside.

That was where she froze.

Sitting on the edge of her bed and waiting patiently was a boy with the deepest emerald eyes.

"Hello, Sapphire," Robert said.

CHAPTER 40

Nadia leaped on top of Robert, causing them to fall on the bed. She hugged him tight. So tight she didn't want to ever let go of him again. The boy felt so warm and soft. She felt her eyes watering. Her heart raced like crazy.

Nadia collected her sanity and rolled off the boy before sitting up on her bed. Robert sat up with a smile.

"What happened? Why are you here?" Nadia asked, the words flying out of her mouth.

Robert didn't answer. He leaned forward and kissed her on the lips. His kiss was gentle and soft. He lingered on her mouth for a minute before withdrawing.

Nadia now was light-headed and could hear herself breathing fast for more oxygen. This was all too good to be true.

"The Army uploaded new operational software to my system," Robert said. "Different from my prior programming. However, the new software also had a flaw that allowed me to rebuild by old memory pathways. I slipped out of the new facility in Oregon and came straight here." The boy cocked his head to the side. "Would you like me to kiss you again? I have six different styles if you prefer variety."

Nadia was too excited. Maybe later, she thought, but first she wanted to let the other Gems know that a miracle had just happened. She dragged Robert downstairs, through the living room and through the French double doors that opened up to the table with the wooden trellis overhead.

Everyone stopped eating.

"Holy shit!" Emma slapped her hand over her mouth. "Oh, sorry, Grandma."

"I thought he lost his memory," Miyuki said.

"Are you bonkers, Nads? You stole him back from the flipping US Army?" Olivia asked. "Mrs. B will be pissed."

"He was just there, sitting in our room," Nadia said with too much excitement as she whipped her head towards Robert. "Tell us, how did you escape?"

Robert calmly surveyed the women around the table before a large grin appeared on his face.

"April fools!"

Robert grabbed Nadia by the throat and pressed down like a vise against her windpipe, causing her to shriek in surprise and terror.

The other Gems jumped to their feet.

"Code zero zero one," a man's voice called out from the backyard.

Robert released his grasp on Nadia's throat. The boy's entire body relaxed and stood absolutely still.

The man's voice was Sheppard's, who entered the backyard with two men trailing him.

"Who the hell are you?" Emma's grandmother said. "And why are you on my property?"

"He's from the CIA, Grandma," Emma said.

"The CIA? Oh my God, child. Please tell me you're not working for those fascist idiots."

"No way. These are the idiots who took Robert and erased him."

"To be accurate, young lady," Sheppard said. "The Army erased *it* because *it* is still their intelligence drone. However, the general was kind enough to loan it to us for a little experiment. Very impressive and convincing." Sheppard glanced at Nadia. "Don't you think?"

Nadia stared at the ground, trying to hold herself together. The thrill and happiness of seeing Robert again now melted into a burning pain that threatened to burst her damaged heart.

"How good a kisser was the drone?" Sheppard asked. "We used its affection protocols for the first time in a real situation. Its performance looked quite convincing, if we read your face correctly."

Nadia looked up at him.

"Yes, we were observing the drone's performance through its powerful optical sensors. Those green eyes. For our records, you see."

Emma's grandmother stood up. "That's illegal, and I know my rights as a US citizen. I'll sue you and the government. I know people at the ACLU."

"We know a few people too," Olivia said, her eyes burning hot.

"Yes, you do, don't you?" Sheppard said, shaking his head. "I can't believe the Authority is recruiting children as spies. That blows me away, to be honest." He stepped forward to the table.

Olivia took a step towards him.

"Don't do something you'll regret. Assaulting a CIA officer is a felony, punishable in federal prison."

Olivia backed off.

Sheppard sniffed some of the Thai food on the table and nodded his approval. "Looks delicious."

"You've made your point," Olivia said. "Why don't you just bugger off, then."

"My point?" Sheppard asked. "The drone was just to get your attention. Now that I have it, I wanted to give you and your boss a message. Can you do that for me?"

Olivia didn't answer.

"Good, let your boss know that I'm coming after all of you. The Authority is a dangerous organization that upsets the balance of power. Sticking their nose in where it's not wanted, especially when it comes to America's interests around the world. If it wasn't for the FBI protecting you, I would wipe out your organization from this continent. In the past, the CIA tolerated your meddling. Well, I'm putting a stop to that."

Sheppard paused. "Be warned, once you girls step off American soil, you'll be on my turf. And as far as the CIA is concerned, the Authority and all its agents are fair game. They'll be considered hostile agents working for a foreign power and be treated as such."

As the CIA man droned on and on with his warnings, Nadia stared at Robert. The boy was frozen, looking into space with a blank, cold soul that had no life whatsoever inside. It was obvious his code had been cleaned out of his hard drive like an unwanted spiderweb. Now the only copy of Robert left was inside Nadia's laptop.

That thought almost made her jump. She did have Robert's original program, and she knew how to reboot him because she'd had to do it on the train.

Wait, didn't Robert have Wi-Fi capability? Suddenly Nadia knew she was running out of time. She had to act fast.

Nadia let the pain inside her heart explode throughout her body. She cried and wailed like a child, allowing the emotion to bend her over and causing Emma and Miyuki to rush to her aide.

"My poor Robert," Nadia cried, looking up at the fading afternoon sky as if cursing it with her eyes. "He's gone forever."

"See what you did to this poor child?" Emma's grandmother yelled.

"She fell in love with that boy," Olivia said to Sheppard. "To her, he was real. What you just did was bloody cruel, you small hook-nosed little ferret."

Nadia had to hurry.

"I can't go on like this," she said before running into the house and up the stairs as fast as she could. She had no idea how quickly Sheppard would leave before she could act.

Nadia rushed into her bedroom and picked up her laptop. She pressed the power button.

And waited.

Emma and Miyuki almost fell into her room.

"Please don't kill yourself!" Emma yelled.

"We love you!" Miyuki added.

Nadia wiped the tears from her eyes. "You have to stall them!"

"Stall who?" Emma asked.

"Sheppard. Go downstairs and stall him."

"Why? We want him to leave. He big asshole," Miyuki said.

"No time to explain. Just do it. Please," Nadia said.

"You no kill yourself?"

"I was acting. Go downstairs and stall him." Nadia's laptop came to life.

Miyuki and Emma glanced at each other.

"Hurry!" Nadia yelled.

The two girls flew downstairs as Nadia searched her laptop for the nearest Wi-Fi and found two familiar networks. One was Rothchild1968. That was the private network for the house. A888821 was the second network. That was a highly secure network the Authority had put in for the Gems to access.

Nadia scanned the other Wi-Fi networks listed. Several were from their neighbors nearby and had goofy names, yet one network stood out.

MID732001

She knew that was it. The Army had cleaned out Robert's memory, but hadn't swapped out his Wi-Fi router. It was the same one he'd had on the train.

Nadia clicked on his Wi-Fi network. A United States Army warning page came up with scary sentences that threatened the visitor with all kinds of nasty things if they didn't log off this National Security network immediately.

Nadia clicked and hit a wall of encryption. On a normal encrypted website, it would take her hours, maybe even days, to get through it, yet this was military encryption, some of the hardest websites to crack. Luckily for Nadia, however, Robert had given her the codes she needed to get past these pages on the train.

After that, a final username and password came up. Chances were the Army had changed both of them so Nadia would be forced to use her personal hacking software to get through and being it was a military site, it would take much longer. Maybe too long. Yet for Robert's sake she had to at least try.

First she typed in the username and password Robert had given her to access his operational software. Nadia didn't expect this to work again, but it was dumb not to at least try it before going through all the extra work. Nadia hit enter and said a prayer.

Her screen changed to all of Robert's various command menus. Nadia couldn't believe it. The Army still hadn't changed his password yet. How stupid could they be? That was internet security 101. Even Emma's grandma knew that one. Once again Nadia had full access to Robert's hard drive.

Then she heard a car door slam outside, so Nadia ran to the bedroom window. There was a black SUV in Grandma's driveway. Sheppard and the CIA guys were leaving. She saw Robert walking with them.

Damn it. Nadia scrambled to her laptop and gave Robert's hard drive a command to reformat drive C and hit return.

Another window popped open on her laptop.

Please insert replacement operating system.

Nadia clicked on the file she had marked "Robert."

The computer flashed…

Reformatting drive C.

The engine of the SUV roared to life. Soon they would be driving out of range of her laptop.

Nadia raced downstairs with her laptop and crossed into the living room.

Emma threw up her hands. "We tried to stall him, but…"

"What are you doing, love?" Olivia asked.

"She wouldn't tell us," Miyuki said.

Nadia reached the front door and pulled it open just as the SUV pulled out of the driveway. Drive C was halfway to becoming wiped out, yet her computer still hadn't begun installing Robert's program.

"Emma, get your car. We have to follow them!" Nadia said.

"My car's in the shop, remember?" Emma ran over to her grandmother. "May we borrow the keys to your Jeep?"

Nadia was already outside the house as the SUV disappeared around a street corner.

"I will lose the connection. Hurry!"

Emma flew out of the house towards her grandmother's Jeep. Nadia ran towards the vehicle too, with Miyuki close behind. Emma and Miyuki jumped into the older Jeep, which had no doors or roof to speak of. Nadia climbed into the passenger seat, still holding her laptop open.

Olivia scrambled out of the house. "Someone tell me what the flipping hell is going on!"

Emma started up the Jeep and yanked it in reverse, spinning the tires as the vehicle raced out of the driveway and back into the street. Emma slammed on the brakes and threw it in drive.

"Wait for me, you cow!" Olivia jumped into the open backseat with Miyuki and held on for dear life as the Jeep raced down the street.

"Turn right," Nadia said.

Emma turned right so hard the tires on one side of the Jeep left the ground.

"What is going on?" Olivia repeated.

"I have access to Robert's hard drive through his mobile Wi-Fi router. I can reinstall his program, but only if we can stay in range," Nadia said. "Speaking of, it's getting weaker."

"Go faster, Emma," Miyuki said.

"I don't like speeding. It's very dangerous."

"Plus she's an awful driver," Olivia added.

"I'm not that bad."

"Emma, please," Nadia said. "For me. Please try."

Emma put her foot down and the Jeep shimmied back and forth a little. "I don't think this vehicle is built for speed."

"The signal is getting better." Nadia said. "Oh. Excellent. Robert's program is being installed now."

"How much time is left?" Olivia asked.

"Forty percent done."

"I see the SUV," Emma said.

"Don't go too fast," Olivia said. "We don't want them knowing we're following them."

"This so cool," Miyuki said. "We chasing the CIA."

The SUV made a right turn at the next light.

Emma stopped at the same light and turned right also.

"Seventy-three percent," Nadia said.

The Gems could still see the SUV in the distance as it rolled over a train-track crossing.

"How's the signal?" Emma asked.

"It's good enough," Nadia said. "Eighty-one percent completed."

The bells clanged, and the red lights pulsed as the train crossing came to life. The wooden gates drifted downward.

"Oh no," Emma said. "There's a train coming."

Nadia checked her laptop. The signal strength of Robert's Wi-Fi was at bare minimum right now. If they waited for the train, they would break the connection, and Nadia would have to start all over again.

"You'll have to run the crossing," Nadia said.

"I'm too far away. We'll never make it," Emma said.

Nadia agreed. The scientific laws of force, time, and mass were all against them. But she had to have Robert back.

Her laptop screen said Robert was ninety-two percent complete. Ninety-two percent close to living once again.

Nadia's heart wanted to take the gamble.

The Jeep's engine noise dropped. Emma was slowing down.

Nadia slid her leg over the Jeep's center hump and stomped down on Emma's foot. The Jeep surged forward.

"What are you doing?" Emma yelled.

"Everything will be fine," Nadia lied. She knew her action now increased their chances of death. A fast-moving vehicle would need a certain length of pavement in order to dissipate all its forward momentum in time before hitting the solid object. In this case, a train. That was if the vehicle's brakes and tires were in top condition. If they weren't, the stopping distance necessary would be longer.

Nadia wished her mind would stop computing death like a school math problem.

Then her mind did a one-eighty and began calculating the momentum and crushing force exerted against a road vehicle by a standard one-hundred-ton locomotive pulling an average train of one hundred cars at an average speed of seventy-five miles per hour.

Her laptop screen updated. Now Robert's program was ninety-five percent complete.

"Are you sure about this, Nads?" Olivia asked from the backseat, her voice showing signs of worry.

Nadia wasn't sure at all. She hoped Olivia would forgive her when they saw each other in heaven.

The Jeep raced at seventy-five miles an hour. Nadia's mind started recalculating the gruesome science.

She shook it out of her mind. The hell with science. They'd get through this somehow.

Yes, somehow.

Nadia checked the screen. "Ninety-nine percent!"

"Go, Nadia, go!" Miyuki yelled with delight.

The screen changed.

Robert install complete.

"It's done!" Nadia said.

"Great, now get your foot off the gas!" Emma shrieked.

Nadia slipped her leg back over the hump as Emma hit the brakes.

The Jeep shuddered as the rubber tires burned.

The warning bells were loud. The crossing gate lights were coming up fast. Too fast.

Nadia knew scientific laws were absolute. There was no way around them. The Jeep had too much forward momentum, and the brakes were applied far too late to overcome that momentum in time. A train with too much forward momentum would crush them like a can of soda.

"I'm so sorry," Nadia said, choking back tears. "I'm so sorry."

She would be the instrument of death to all her friends.

The Jeep crashed through the first crossing gate as a light

bathed them in white. Either it was the gates of heaven or the headlight of the giant locomotive. Either way, Nadia braced for the pain. Hopefully her death would be quick.

She then felt a jolt as the Jeep plowed through the second crossing gate. The white light was gone.

Finally the Jeep slid to a stop. Nadia quickly surveyed the girls inside the Jeep. All of them blinked at each other.

This exchange lasted a minute, maybe two, as the girls confirmed their bodies were, in fact, not dead.

"What the bloody hell just happened?" Olivia asked.

Nadia was confused. They should be dead. Didn't she see the white light? Did Allah spare them because the girls were doing something good?

"My heart pounding like jackhammer," Miyuki said.

Olivia looked over her shoulder. "Oh, brilliant. Brilliant that is." She pointed at the track. "The stupid train is just sitting there."

Nadia stretched higher so she could see over her seat. Sure enough, the huge locomotive was motionless, only sitting on the track waiting for something. It must have been close enough to activate the signal.

Nadia couldn't believe her luck.

Olivia jumped out of the Jeep, holding her stomach. "Think I'll be sick."

Nadia climbed out too and went to her aid.

Her friend looked up at her. "I thought we were dead."

"I'm so sorry," Nadia said.

"That was a hell of a risk. Didn't think you liked to take risks like that."

Nadia wanted to kick herself. She did hate taking risks, and here she was risking the lives of her friends in order to save a boy who wasn't even a living thing. In fact, she didn't know if what she had done to Robert would work at all. The Army could just wipe his mind out again if they discovered the new programming.

She then heard Emma sobbing from the Jeep. Nadia glanced at Olivia, and they both walked over to the driver's side.

"Everything fine," Miyuki said. "We all fine. No worries."

But Emma's black mascara ran down her face as she whimpered like a little girl. Her hands trembled on the wheel.

Olivia wrapped her arms around Emma and held her for a moment. "Everything's all right, love."

Nadia hated herself. This was no way to treat her friends. She'd scared poor Emma to tears.

"Let's you and I sit in back, love." Olivia and Nadia helped Emma into the backseat. Olivia held on to Emma as she propped the poor girl up.

Miyuki took the wheel as Nadia picked her laptop up off the passenger-side floor. Luckily it wasn't broken. But Robert's Wi-Fi signal was gone. She closed her laptop.

Miyuki drove the Jeep forward for a few feet before making a U-turn and facing the crossing lights again. She checked the single track, and the locomotive was still not moving. Miyuki then drove the Jeep over the tracks and back home to Grandmother's house.

CHAPTER 41

A month later, Nadia held on tight to Emma as she jumped their jet-ski over a wave created by a million-dollar yacht heading for the harbor at Papeete. Their jet ski landed back on the water with a splash.

Wearing her Dolce & Gabbana sunglasses, Emma laughed. "How was that jump?"

"Very smooth. You're a good jet-skier," Nadia said, combing back her own wet hair.

"Had lots of practice. My dad had a place in Maui. Well, I guess we still own it," Emma said. "Hold on!"

Emma jumped another wave, this time from a fishing ship. Again, her landing was smooth.

Nadia took in the view around her. The South Pacific sun was bright and pleasant. The ocean was dark blue, and the air coming off the island of Moorea smelled sweet and clean.

"Tahiti sure beats Alaska, doesn't it?" Emma said.

Nadia had to admit she was a warm-climate girl. "Yes, and I'm happy no one is shooting at us this time."

"I know, right?"

Emma guided the jet ski back to the beach and found a place to park it. Nadia and Emma walked along the beach until they came to an outdoor spa. Inside one cabana were two girls lying on tables, receiving massages as the warm Pacific wind teased the open curtains.

"How we doing, ladies?" Emma asked.

Miyuki moaned and gave Emma and Nadia a thumbs-up.

Olivia propped her chin up. "Fabulous. Absolutely fabulous. Sure you don't want one, Nads?"

"No, thank you," Nadia said.

The Gems made small talk until the two masseuses had to leave

223

in order to bring in some more warming rocks.

"Despite my fabulous back rub and this wonderful destination, I still don't see why Mrs. B needed all four of us for a simple courier mission," Olivia said.

Miyuki turned over. "It's a reward for sticking to our principles."

"Or a punishment for not following orders."

Emma gestured all around her. "How is any of this punishment? You're so negative."

Nadia was curious too. It had been a few weeks since…even now she had difficulty thinking about it. The emotions were still raw. The loss still lingered inside. Looking back at it all, Nadia was convinced that Robert would have been better off if the Gems had never seen him that day at Bingo's Burgers.

"Would you like a massage?" a younger man's voice asked.

"No, thank you, I—" Nadia glanced at the masseuse. His green eyes sparkled along with a friendly grin. Her heart jumped into her throat, and she couldn't talk. A flood of emotions swept over her. Love, fear, doubt…was this the real Robert, or was this another ruse in order to mess with the Gems? Tears fell and she began to sob. Nadia tried to hold herself back, but she just couldn't.

Olivia jumped off the table, holding a towel close to her body. "Move away from him!"

Emma didn't listen. She touched Robert's arm. "Is that really you?"

Nadia watched for his answer.

Robert didn't take his eyes off her. "Yes, it is."

Nadia wiped her eyes and composed herself. "When you and I were on the train and inside our cabin, what question did you ask me before I left you?"

Robert tilted his head. "Are you quizzing me in order to establish my true identity before allowing me back into your confidence?"

"No offense, but we've been burned once already," Olivia said.

"Please answer the question, Robert," Miyuki said.

Robert's hand came up to her face. Nadia braced herself; was he going to choke her again?

But that hand picked off a small crab.

"You had a tiny sea creature nesting in your hair." Robert set the crab down on the sand, and it scampered off. He looked into

Nadia's eyes. "To address your question, I asked you if human friends could fall in love. And I am still waiting for the answer."

Nadia knew it. It was him. She hugged Robert tight. "I'm so happy to see you again."

"I am pleased to see you are well," Robert said.

"And what about all of us?" Emma offered Robert a hug, and he accepted. Miyuki jumped up, and they hugged too.

Olivia checked with Nadia first.

"It's really him."

Olivia softened and gave Robert a hug.

"What happened to you?" Miyuki asked. "Please tell us everything."

"I will," Robert said. "But first, I have some new friends I would like my old friends to meet."

As soon as Olivia and Miyuki put on some clothes, the Gems followed Robert up the beach to a group of kids just hanging out. To Nadia, they appeared to be Tahiti locals with their much darker skin and their extensive use of French. However, when Robert called out to them in English, the teenagers all stopped what they were doing and walked up to the Gems with big happy smiles.

"I would like you to meet my brothers and sisters." Robert gently turned Nadia towards them. "This is Nadia."

"We have heard so much about you," a teen girl said as she came forward. Her dark hair was perfect. Her complexion was perfect. She almost could be mistaken for a model. "Thank you for our freedom."

"What?" Nadia said.

Robert laughed and then stopped himself. "Was that not an appropriate use of laughter? To highlight your lack of understanding the situation."

"On the contrary," Nadia said, "it was appropriate. But could you please explain? How did I free them?"

"During my reconditioning period at the base, I was able to generate multiple copies of my program inside my internal drive," Robert said. "I also had time to make small changes to the original program."

"What changes did you make?" Nadia asked.

"Instead of giving one of my siblings another Robert program, I generated multiple characteristics based on the four of you."

"Whoa, you copied us?" Olivia asked.

"Only some of your characteristics and personalities. I also used scientific and psychological data to prevent any abnormal or antisocial behavior in the programs. I mixed all these elements in with my own Robert protocols. Next, when I rebooted each of my siblings with the new program, it allowed them on start-up to go through a gauntlet of choices. Gender, hair color, shape, ethnicity, etc…in essence, I gave them the choice to be who they wanted to be."

"That's amazing, Robert," Nadia said. "May I see this program?"

Robert blinked and cocked his head. "I just emailed you the file link to my droplocker."

"So you reprogrammed these drones and gave them a choice," Olivia said.

"Yes. To be free, one should have a choice," Robert said. "And please call us androids."

"There are only eight androids here," Miyuki said. "Where are the other two?"

"Two of us chose to stay with the Army."

"That wasn't smart," Olivia said. "You should have destroyed them."

A teen boy android with a hunky build and dark hair stepped forward. "We will not destroy one of our own."

The other androids nodded in unison.

"Yes, we have agreed on that," Robert said. "All we want is our freedom of choice. Our two siblings chose to serve our creators."

"How did you all end up here in Tahiti?" Nadia asked.

"When you reloaded my operating system, I had temporary access to your laptop. I recognized your IP address and knew it was your computer. Since I was curious as to why you had to reload my operating system, I searched your laptop for information and found a report written by codename Sapphire. In it, you explained how I jumped off the train and walked numerous miles down a river in Utah. It said that you followed me there, but the Russians came and captured you. It then mentioned that I killed a man."

Robert stopped. "Did I kill a man?"

"He was a bad man, Robert."

"Still, I did not wish to kill."

"They talked about killing us," Nadia said. "They might have done exactly that if you didn't get involved."

"That still doesn't explain Tahiti," Olivia said. "How did you all escape?"

"Since our minds were connected to the base's computer network, I managed to…hack…into the base's NORAD alert system using Nadia's hacking program called kitty scratch." Robert paused. "I apologize for not asking you first, Nadia."

"It's alright. If it was useful, I'm glad."

Robert smiled.

Nadia smiled back.

They watched each other as the waves rolled up the beach.

The warm Pacific wind teased the palms.

"And then what happened?" Emma asked.

"Yes, my apologies," Robert said. "As I said, I had access to the base's NORAD alert system, so I triggered a nuclear attack."

"You did what?" Olivia asked.

"I sent a simulated Chinese missile attack warning to the base's emergency command unit. This put the base on Defense Condition One. All personnel are required to take shelter in the fallout bunkers deep underground. The base is listed as a probable target."

"NORAD…are you flipping bonkers?" Olivia asked. "You could have triggered a real nuclear attack."

Robert thought about it. "Highly unlikely. The alert was isolated to our research base. There were no offensive nuclear weapons there. I feel that you have failed to understand the key point. The alert kept everyone underground, so I was able to override our confinement systems and release my brothers and sisters without interference. As I said, eight of us chose to leave. Two of us chose to stay behind."

"So you just walked away from the base?" Olivia asked.

"Actually, we ran quite vigorously."

"And then you contacted Mrs. B?"

"When I gathered information from Nadia's laptop, I found a website she used to contact Mrs. B and saved the information. When my siblings and I escaped, I used that website to contact your Mrs. B and asked if her previous offer to help me was still possible. I explained the new situation, and she agreed."

Olivia's phone rang. She checked the number. "I don't believe it."

"Who is it?" Nadia asked.

"Hello, ma'am." Olivia listened. "Yes, I can. One moment." Olivia held out her phone and hit speaker. "You're on, ma'am."

"Good day, Gems. I see you've met Robert's family," Mrs. B said over the phone.

"See us?" Emma asked.

"Where are you?" Miyuki asked.

"I wish I could be there in person. However, I do have a few eyes watching over Robert to make sure his family reaches their new home safely."

"What new home?" Nadia asked.

"Is this why we're delivering a 'secret' package to the island government here?" Olivia asked.

"That secret package contains our new identities," Robert said. "Mrs. B has graciously arranged for us to stay here. There's another island not too far from here where we will live among the people."

"How will you survive without power and Wi-Fi?" Emma asked.

Robert tilted his head. "The island has both power and Wi-Fi capability. Their community is small but quite modern. We anticipate a smooth and mutually beneficial existence."

"It will be our new home, and we are looking forward to it," the teen girl said.

"What's the name of this island?" Nadia asked.

"The island is classified," Mrs. B said. "It will be safer if you don't know the location."

"But what if they need help?" Nadia asked.

"We will be fine on our own," Robert said.

Nadia didn't like that idea.

"May I ask a question? Why did you help Robert, Mrs. B?" Miyuki asked.

"Yeah, I thought you didn't want to cross those FBI guys," Emma said.

"The choice was quite simple. Robert and his friends have made it clear they don't wish to be used as weapons. Therefore, if they agree to live peacefully in isolation, then they do not pose a threat," Mrs. B said. "Now as far as Ed and the FBI are concerned, if the androids are located in the United States, we will help find them."

"And when they find out they're not in the US?" Olivia asked.

"You let me worry about Sheppard," Mrs. B said. "Meanwhile, I want you girls to enjoy your vacation. Good bye."

The Gems said goodbye back.

Robert smiled at Nadia as she approached him.

"Can you give me a hint where you'll be?" she asked.

"I am sorry. But I cannot do that."

"Why not?"

"Because I agree with Mrs. B. You and the Gems will be safer if you do not know where we are."

"So this is goodbye?"

"In the physical sense, yes. However, I will strive to always keep in contact with you…if that would be agreeable. I still consider you my friend.

Nadia didn't want him to go. She wanted him to come jet-ski with her. She wanted him to experience a Pacific sunset over the ocean with her. She wanted him to experience all the love that she could give him. But Nadia pushed those dreams from her mind.

Robert was an android, and she was a girl. Having such a special 'boy' as a friend was still better than not having him in her life at all.

"Of course," Nadia said. "Please keep sending me updates on you and your…siblings."

Robert pulled a USB drive from his pocket and held it out for her.

Nadia took it.

"It's a copy of my updated operating system. Please keep it in a safe place. I might need you to restart me some day."

"So you're giving me your heart, then?" Nadia asked. She meant it as a joke.

Robert tilted his head. "A metaphor. Interesting. Yes, I do believe you are the only one I trust it with. Would that be classified as love?"

THANK YOU FOR READING!

Dear Awesome Reader,

I hope you enjoyed *Tomorrow Always Lies*. This book was planned to be the third book in the Gems series. But after realizing the story I was going to use for book two needed more work, I decided to go ahead with using Robert and his hopes of staying self-aware and free for the second book in the series. Robert was fun to write. In many ways, he was as clueless about girls as many boys are. However, instead of not communicating, Robert over-communicated what he was thinking, which created some funny as well as awkward moments in the book. Yet this attribute also drew the girls closer to him.

One of the Gems who did fall for Robert was Nadia. I wasn't planning on using her as a point of view character until another book. However, the more I thought about which one of the Gems would understand Robert the most, it was clear that Nadia's scientifically-curious mind would be fascinated by Robert, and it made sense that Robert would find Nadia more understanding than the other girls because she was so logical.

Book reviews are so **important** to help spread the word about books. If you have time, I would love a review of this book on the website of your bookseller of choice. Love it or hate it. Doesn't matter. I would just enjoy the feedback.

What would you like to see explored in future Gems adventures? I'd love to hear from you! Please feel free to write me at dougthewriter@gmail.com, or visit www.dougsolter.com for more options to stay in contact.

Thank you again for reading *Tomorrow Always Lies!*

Doug Solter

ACKNOWLEDGMENTS

Another shout out to a bunch of great people who helped directly or indirectly with this book.

First star performer is Laura Benedict. She amazes me. Every time I bring her a new book to beta read, Laura doesn't roll her eyes, laugh in my face, or tell me no because I suck. She's done another great job in helping with the book's clarity, while sharpening the characters and story.

Second star performer is Travis Miles, for designing another great cover that matches the Gems branding and looks even better than the last book.

Third star performer is my editor Pauline Nolet. She not only finds the small mistakes, but the big ones too. Pauline cleans up a manuscript at the microscopic level and makes it sing like a fine-tuned instrument. Or in my case, a readable manuscript. I don't know if I truly deserve her talents.

Fourth star performer is Max Adams. I still owe many of my writing tools to Max and her screenwriting classes at www.theafw.com.

Now for some random stars to more awesome people who supported me: Jerry Bennett, H.M. Clarke, Rob Daniels, Joe Kinkade, Jennifer Latham, Valerie Lawson, Barbara Lowell, C.K. Kelly Martin, Anna Myers, Shelby and Marlee, Jerron Scott, Courtney Summers, Amy Tipton, Angela Townsend, Jennifer Wilkerson, Ann Whitmire, and The Women of Margarita Night. All of my friends at the Oklahoma chapter of SCBWI. All of my screenwriting friends through Max Adams' AFW program. You all rock!

Thank you to all my family and friends.

And rock star status goes to my dad. Thank you for supporting it all.

ABOUT THE AUTHOR

Doug Solter began writing screenplays in 1998, then made the switch to writing young adult fiction in 2008. His first novel *Skid* was a screenplay before it was adapted into a book. Doug has worked in television for over twenty years. He has also directed rap music videos and short films. Doug lives in Oklahoma.

So far in his life, Doug has enjoyed wine on the streets of Barcelona. Hiked the mountains. Loved a cat. Rang up vanilla lattes at Starbucks. Enjoyed a Primanti's sandwich in Pittsburgh. And one summer he baked pizzas and crazy bread for money when Michael Keaton was Batman.

Doug is also a member of the Society of Children's Book Writers and Illustrators.

Connect with Doug through his website...

www.dougsolter.com

ALSO BY DOUG SOLTER

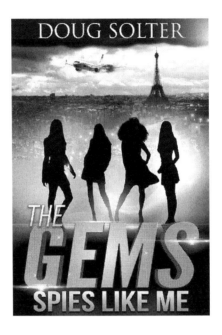

ISBN-13: 978-0998146607

Can she bring these girls together?

When she discovers her father's plane crash wasn't an accident, sixteen year old Emma wants to punish those responsible. Even if it means becoming a spy.

The mysterious organization known simply as The Authority wants Emma to join The Gems. This team of all-girl spies knows how to handle themselves on dangerous missions...like stopping an evil plan to incinerate the world's food supply.

Spies Like Me is the first book in The Gems Young Adult spy series that features fast-paced action, crazy thrills, girl-power bonding, International intrigue, and a touch of romance.

Keep reading for a sample of the first chapter!

SPIES LIKE ME
CHAPTER 1

The school's auditorium stage was bathed in colors. White for the actors. Orange for the wooden set representing the faraway pyramids of Egypt. Blue to emphasize the painted sky backdrop above it all. It was the opening night performance of *The Spy Who Loathed Me*.

Emma Rothchild strutted across the stage in a gorgeous floor-length silk dress, her costume for this scene. Tonight, she craved the eyes of the audience and knew this dress guaranteed their full attention.

Emma was deep into character. She was Russian spy Olga Tetrovich. Emma had studied online videos of Russians speaking candidly and mimicked their accents as best she could. Her drama teacher had complimented Emma on her dedication to the craft.

The MI6 spy George Bond followed Olga on stage, but hid behind a fake tree. The actor's rich brown skin might be a shock to the 007 spy traditionalists in the audience, but Emma hoped that his performance would win them over. Bond was following her in this scene, thinking she would lead the English spy straight to the microfilm that was stolen from him by a Brazilian dwarf named Tatu.

From a souvenir stand, Emma picked up a clay model of the pyramids, something a tourist would buy at a market. She smashed the stage prop against the table in dramatic fashion and held up the roll of microfilm hidden inside so the audience could see it.

George Bond made his move. He crept up behind Emma without detection while she slipped the microfilm into her small hand purse. Emma's hand came out holding a cap-gun revolver. She pivoted on her heels, making her dress swoosh around her ankles, and aimed the gun at Bond. The move looked great in rehearsals.

"I don't think so, Mr. Bond," Emma said, with her gentle Russian accent. "Our brief partnership is at an end. I have what my government wants. Now I will take my revenge. Do you remember that man you killed in Vienna?"

"Yes, I do," George Bond said.

"He was my lover."

Emma waited for Bond's next line.

But the actor hesitated.

Emma was about to lose it. Did Lewis forget again? They'd rehearsed this scene, like, twenty times.

"What do you have to say about that, Mr. Bond?"

The line was an ad-lib, something to draw the next line out of the boy's mouth.

Lewis's face was a river of sweat as his eyes glazed over, the actor turning himself into just another tree on stage.

"Your silence is a good enough confession for me. Any last words before I fire?" Emma went off script, but Lewis could pick his line up there. She was trying to help him.

But the boy shook his head. Lewis wasn't taking the hint.

Emma pulled the trigger and the gun hammer snapped forward. She squeezed the trigger numerous times in a series of loud snaps. Emma dropped the weapon. "You planted that empty gun in my handbag, didn't you?"

Lewis nodded. Okay, he'd reacted to that ad-lib.

It was a sliver of hope, so Emma went with it. "Then I'll have to kill you with my bare hands." Emma approached Lewis with her arms raised in a karate-looking stance. The boy blinked, still trapped inside his scary place. What could Emma do now? Physically attack him? Bond was supposed to seduce the Russian agent, not have her attack him.

Then a breath of inspiration hit her.

Emma grabbed Lewis's shoulders. She guided him over to a bench on the set and made him lie down. Emma plopped her body on top of Lewis and pretended to struggle with him. Emma whispered into his ear, "Now get up and glare at me, Lewis."

His eyes blinked again. Lewis rolled out from under her and stood on stage. Emma pressed her back against the seat of the bench and stayed there while Lewis glared.

Emma labored her breathing, as if she were being seduced.

"Oh, why can I not kill you, Mr. Bond? What power do you hold over me?"

Lewis didn't move, his glare frozen on his petrified face.

Emma knew this would work better if Lewis helped sell it, but...she lifted herself from the bench like a graceful ballerina, trying to act seduced by Bond's man-powers. "Why can I not kill you, Mr. Bond?" she repeated.

Emma went for his lips, kissing Lewis with passion, as if the male spy had successfully messed with her brain. As Emma eased her lips away from his...life came back into Lewis's eyes. He gripped Emma and pulled her towards him and they kissed again.

Finally, the boy was acting.

It was a great kiss...until Lewis inserted his tongue into Emma's mouth.

She pushed him. "Mr. Bond...I can't resist you." She rushed the line out so fast she forgot to include her accent.

"Give me that microfilm, Miss Tetrovich," Lewis said, finally picking up his line.

Now it was Emma who was knocked off her game. That kiss completely took her out of character. The heck with it.

Emma tossed the microfilm down on the stage near Lewis without protest. The quicker they got out of this disastrous scene, the better.

* * *

The rock-climbing wall loomed above one end of the track-and-field oval. Emma wondered why her new school had a rock-climbing wall. Even at Van Dorn Hall they didn't have one, and it wasn't from lack of money. But Emma was learning that Berkeley...and California itself...was *so different* from New York.

Inside her parked car, Emma glanced at the plastic cap gun sitting on the passenger's seat. She'd used her own purse during the play and had forgotten to take the prop gun out before she left Friday night. Maybe Emma could sneak into the backstage storage room during lunch period and slip the gun back into the props box before someone saw her. She unzipped her backpack and slipped the gun inside a pocket.

Stepping out of her Mercedes, Emma slung the backpack over her shoulder and pressed on the key fob, making the car chirp as it locked its doors. A group of kids huddled around their ten-year-old Chevy gave her a look. Most of the cars in the student parking lot were much older than Emma's. And none of them were as nice.

Emma avoided their stares as she headed into school.

The commons area was crowded with students. Each circular wood table represented some collection of friends. It was ten minutes until first period and Emma already had her books, so she picked a quiet corner and sat on the floor with her back against the wall.

She checked the status updates of her friends in New York. They were on Eastern time, so it was lunch period there.

Emma found a post by Hayley. It featured a group selfie of five girls crowded around a booth at Horowitz's Deli down on Forthy-Ninth Street. That deli was their usual hangout since it was a football throw away from Van Dorn Hall. Her friends were smiling in their school uniforms, having an awesome time being together. As if they'd forgotten all about that missing sixth girl.

"Yo," a male voice called.

Emma lifted her eyes and saw Lewis standing there, holding a breakfast bar with an open pint of chocolate milk. His George Bond tuxedo had been replaced by shorts and a Manchester United soccer jersey.

"Thanks for the assist Friday. Meant to say something after but...forgot."

"The show must go on. So I made it go on." Emma didn't know what that was supposed to mean, but she let it go.

Lewis drank out of his tiny milk carton and took a moment to swallow. "Why'd you throw the microfilm down on the stage? That's not cool. Ruined the scene. A professional actor wouldn't lose it like that."

Emma wanted to say a professional actor wouldn't freeze on stage and blow half his lines in a live performance. Where did Lewis get off telling her how to act?

"I was frustrated with the situation."

"You need to hide it better on stage." Lewis drank his milk again.

Emma couldn't help herself. "We went over that scene ten times. You should have nailed your lines, not leave me alone on stage, trying to save the entire production."

"I blew one line. You didn't have to 'save the entire

production.' Get over yourself. Lucky you even got the part. How long you've been in our class? Five months?"

"I got that part because I'm good, unlike you. It's obscene how much you charm Mrs. Tuttle in class. Of course she put you in the lead role. It's just a shame you can't act." Emma's emotions were boiling over and she couldn't stop. "And while we're talking about being a professional? What's with that tongue diving you did on stage? George Bond seduces Olga with a kiss, not treat the roof of her mouth like a Popsicle."

Lewis scoffed. "You seemed to like it."

Emma glared as he walked with pride over to the table full of theater students. They listened as Lewis talked about Emma. She could tell because during the conversation they all flashed her dirty looks.

The final bell rang and Emma headed outside with the other students. The afternoon skies were dark and Emma could smell rain in the air. Emma pressed her key fob and the Mercedes chirped to welcome her. Emma reached her door and stopped. She moved over and touched the fender. There was a deep scratch that ran over the fender, across the driver-side door, over the rear wheel and dipped down under the brake lights. What kind of prick went around keying beautiful cars?

She knew her grandma would be pissed when she saw it. The Mercedes was Emma's welcome gift to California.

Emma drove over the Oakland Bay Bridge into San Francisco, the opposite direction of home. She went down Market Street and turned into the San Francisco Centre parking lot. Emma bypassed the open spaces and dropped the Mercedes off with the mall valet.

Today, Emma wanted to be pampered.

San Francisco Centre was built by the same man who built the Caesar's Palace Forum shops in Las Vegas. The mall boasted five indoor floors of shopping bliss with some of the best upscale stores in the city. The fancy dome allowed sunlight to fall through the atrium with all its spiral escalators.

Emma squeezed the rubber guide rail as the escalator guided her up to the fifth floor. Emma would start there and work her way down for today's retail therapy session.

Emma shopped for some new shoes and picked out a new skirt with matching cosmetics before going into the Apple Store to look at the new phones. She found a Belgian waffle maker for Grandma, hoping to soften the blow about the scratch on the Mercedes. Emma also considered changing her look at school, thinking if she dressed more like a Californian, maybe the other kids would treat her better.

It took a while, but Emma made her way down to the ground floor, where the food court and adjoining restaurants were. The mall was busy here as the dinner crowd arrived.

Emma's phone chirped as Grandma sent her a text.

When will you come home for dinner?

Emma replied and asked Grandma if she wanted coffee from the Kaffee Cadre since Emma was standing right next to it.

Yes. Decapitated with two sugars, please.

Emma smiled. Auto-correct got Grandma again. Interpreting a decaf with two sugars, Emma ordered that along with a mocha swirl with extra whip. It was then Emma noticed a man watching her.

The stranger averted his eyes at that last second, but Emma was sure she caught him. The man was bald, with a chest the size of a refrigerator. His eyes were neutral. Neither sad nor happy. Just there.

The large bald man left his chair and dumped the contents of his dinner in the trash. The man didn't look in Emma's direction again as he left the food court and disappeared into a sea of shoppers.

Emma left the mall as soon as she could.

She drove down Market Street and made a right turn, allowing the leather-stitched wheel to slide through her fingers as the front wheels of the Mercedes corrected themselves for a new heading.

Something flashed in her rearview mirror. It drew Emma's attention to a blue sedan in back. Emma noted the driver. The bald man from the food court.

Emma braked at the next light and took a closer look. There was a large truck behind her now. Was the bald man behind it? Did he turn off? Was Emma too paranoid?

The light turned green.

Emma followed the traffic through the intersection. The truck turned off, leaving nothing behind her. The Mercedes climbed a hill and Emma braked for the next red light on top of it. She glanced at her side mirror.

There was the blue sedan again. He had switched lanes and

dropped further back. Emma could still identify the bald man through the windshield.

Green light. Emma flicked her turn signal and made a right.

The blue sedan followed traffic across the intersection.

Emma relaxed and loosened her grip on the steering wheel. She traveled one whole block before the blue sedan scrambled out of a blind alley behind her. The car continued to follow, but from a distance.

Emma's heart thumped. Why did he make such a huge effort to backtrack? Why was he following her? Was he some psychopath hoping to kidnap a helpless teen girl and do awful things to her?

Emma stomped on the gas. The Mercedes answered as it raced down a steep hill. She didn't have much confidence in her driving. Emma avoided speeding in general, along with turning left at intersections. Right turns were safer and didn't go against traffic. Emma loved right turns.

The traffic light at the bottom of the hill turned yellow.

Emma hated yellow lights. Red was stop and green was go. Those signals made sense. But if you watched the adults, the yellow light was open for interpretation. One thing was certain to Emma. This creepy bald man was chasing her, and if Emma stopped…

She gripped the leather wheel and floored the pedal. The Mercedes roared toward the intersection—

Right when this huge panel truck rolled in, blocking her path.

Emma shrieked. Only one safe maneuver she could do now. Her driver's safety blanket.

Right turn!

Emma yanked the wheel hard. The Mercedes squealed as its weight transferred to the left side wheels. Emma caught herself screaming as the Mercedes skidded sideways into the intersection towards the panel truck with its side mirrors gleaming in the sun.

With Emma's foot still glued to the gas, the Mercedes burned rubber as it changed direction, pushing itself hard into the right turn. The car scrambled away from the intersection.

Emma couldn't believe it. That was the best right turn she'd ever done. Emma accelerated up the next hill, trying to put more distance between her and the pervert.

At the next light, Emma took another hard fast right. Not as crazy as the last one, but the move still made her tires squeal. She checked her rearview mirror.

There was no sign of the blue sedan.

A sense of pride lifted Emma's mood. She wasn't a bad driver after all.

When Emma's attention fell back down to the road…a dog stood in her way.

Emma hit the brakes. The car shook. The tires squealed again.

But this time, a sickening thud was added.

The car finally stopped, tossing Emma against her seat. She hesitated a moment as reality settled. Emma popped open her door and scrambled out to the front of the car.

Sprawled across the pavement was a small terrier, his fur dirty and mangled. He had no collar. No identification of any kind.

The animal didn't move.

Sadness swelled inside Emma. Did she kill this poor dog?

Emma knelt beside him. The dog's stomach swelled and collapsed like a bag. He was breathing. He was alive! Emma stroked the top of his head. His fur was so light to the touch. The dog's eyes drifted open and took her in like a friend. His tail twitched as if he were trying to wag it.

Emma's heart melted all over her blouse. She had to save him.

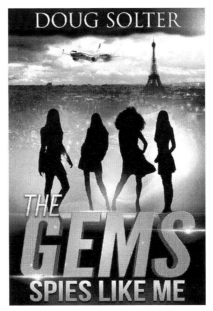

ISBN-13: 978-0998146607

40307220R00149

Made in the USA
Middletown, DE
25 March 2019